Praise for
COME FIND ME

★ "A smart, dark, and ultimately hopeful story of
the power of belief." —*Booklist,* starred review

"[A] riveting . . . exploration of how grief transforms us."
—*Kirkus Reviews*

"Multifaceted and utterly believable."—*SLJ*

———

Praise for the works of
MEGAN MIRANDA

"For thriller fans who can't get enough of the genre."
—*Kirkus Reviews* (for *Fragments of the Lost*)

"Intoxicating, well crafted, and suspenseful."
—*Booklist* (for *Fragments of the Lost*)

"Perfect read for thriller fans."
—*Bustle* (for *Fragments of the Lost*)

★ "A fast-paced, suspenseful treat."
—*PW,* starred review (for *The Safest Lies*)

"Positively movie ready."
—*Kirkus Reviews* (for *The Safest Lies*)

★ "A clever, stylish mystery that will seize readers like a riptide."
—*PW,* starred review (for *The Last House Guest*)

"Extremely interesting. . . . A novel that will
probably be called Hitchcockian."
—*The New York Times Book Review* (for *All the Missing Girls*)

"Are you paying attention? You'll need to be; this thriller
will test your brain . . . and it's a page-turner to boot."
—*Elle* (for *All the Missing Girls*)

ALSO BY MEGAN MIRANDA

Fragments of the Lost
The Safest Lies
The Last House Guest
The Perfect Stranger
All the Missing Girls
Soulprint
Vengeance
Hysteria
Fracture

COME
FIND
ME

MEGAN MIRANDA

EMBER

FOR MY FAMILY

Text copyright © 2019 by Megan Miranda
Cover art under license from Shutterstock.com

All rights reserved. Published in the United States by Ember, an imprint
of Random House Children's Books, a division of Penguin Random House LLC,
New York. Originally published in hardcover in the United States by Crown Books
for Young Readers, an imprint of Random House Children's Books,
a division of Penguin Random House LLC, New York, in 2019.

Ember and the E colophon are registered trademarks of Penguin Random House LLC.

Visit us on the Web! GetUnderlined.com

Educators and librarians, for a variety of teaching tools,
visit us at RHTeachersLibrarians.com

The Library of Congress has cataloged the hardcover edition of this work as follows:
Names: Miranda, Megan, author.
Title: Come Find Me / Megan Miranda.
Description: First Edition. | New York : Crown Books for Young Readers, [2019]
Summary: Told in two voices, sixteen-year-old Kennedy Jones and seventeen-year-old
Nolan Chandler are drawn together by strange signals related to family tragedies, and
find they are more connected than they could have imagined.
Identifiers: LCCN 2018049010 | ISBN 978-0-525-57829-1 (trade) |
ISBN 978-0-525-57830-7 (lib. bdg.) | ISBN 978-0-525-57831-4 (ebook)
Subjects: CYAC: Supernatural—Fiction. | Brothers and sisters—Fiction. |
Missing children—Fiction. | Death—Fiction. | Family problems—Fiction.
Classification: LCC PZ7.M67352 Com 2019 | DDC [Fic]—dc23

ISBN 978-0-525-57832-1 (pbk.)

Printed in the United States of America
10 9 8 7 6 5 4 3 2 1
First Ember Edition 2020

1

KENNEDY

They say the universe is constantly heading toward disorder, and I believe it. Walls go up, and walls come down. Buildings crumble, governments fall, civilizations collapse. Stars explode.

People live.

People die.

On and on it goes.

Everything falls apart.

Please don't think I'm a pessimist. These are just the facts.

I am, truth be told, an optimist. Otherwise I would not set my alarm for after midnight, when I'm sure Joe is sleeping, and I would not sneak out the side door behind the kitchen, and I would not bike six miles in the dark to the farmland behind my old home to pull the data from my brother's radio telescope.

But I do.

I do all of this, every few nights, because I am an optimist.

I leave my bike at the side of the house, hidden by the wide front porch, the swing creaking in the breeze. There's still a split-rail fence from when this place had horses, and a faint scent of hay remains—something I only really noticed once I was gone. There are lights in the distance, to my left, from the neighborhood jutting up against our property. But to my right, it's all darkness—untouchable forest.

There's no light on the footpath to the old stable, now makeshift observatory, behind the house, and I don't want to turn on the outside house lights in case someone sees. On the off chance one of the neighbors notices that *something's happening at the Jones House*—and calls Joe.

The night is hot and sticky, and I could really use the air conditioning, a drink of water from the faucet, and the bathroom, in that order. Joe may have cut the TV, the phone, and the Internet, but he can't shut down the electricity yet—hard to show a house in the middle of Virginia during June without the air on.

The Realtor must have had the locks changed last week, but she didn't know about Elliot's window around back. He'd reconfigured the mechanism when we first moved in so the window tilted in and out, instead of sliding up and down, and he'd sacrificed the locks for the design. So if I used the deck railing, I could reach up and push at the top, and then the bottom would swing open. He was always tinkering with things, down to the smallest detail. Bedroom windows, before he got to radio telescopes.

I feel my way through Elliot's room, none of the furniture where I remember it. Someone—the Realtor, I guess—thought to turn this room into an office. Really, no amount of staging can change what people already know about this house.

Our house has a quirky layout: it was probably designed as a sprawling ranch, with three bedrooms and the living areas on the main floor, but there's a newer second-story loft that must've been added on after the fact, which now holds a storage area and an entertainment room. It's where I used to bring my friends, to hang out. But I haven't touched the second floor since the day I moved.

Walking from Elliot's room, I wait until I'm out in the hall to turn on the flashlight I've brought, keeping the beam away from the windows.

The hall and the living room look much the same as when I last lived here, six months ago—except all the photos of us have been hidden away. There must've been a showing recently, because someone has finally closed the kitchen cabinets. But I smile, picturing a family standing at the edge of the kitchen, seeing all the empty cabinets swung open in an eerie formation, imagining the chill making its way up their backs.

I don't believe in ghosts. But it helps that other people do.

This time, I decide to mess with everything on the walls. I tip the paintings so they hang at odd angles, and I take a few off the walls, laying them haphazardly along the floor—so they look like they were knocked down in a rush. I stand back to assess the room. The whole effect is vaguely unsettling, which is kind of the point.

The air feels cool against the sweat on my legs, and I drink the water from the kitchen sink, and use the bathroom attached to my room—which is nearly empty, as everything of value to me, including the furniture, has been relocated to Joe's.

In the distance, standing near the window of Elliot's room, I hear a voice. Even some laughter. I quickly turn off the flashlight and crouch below the window. I already know who it is: Marco, Lydia, and Sutton, probably. I should be annoyed that they still use the land beyond our house to meet up. I should probably feel some sense of propriety, or betrayal. I should want to know *why* they're here, on a Friday night, without me. Mostly, though, I just want them to go.

But it's too late. I hear gravel kicking up as someone jogs toward the house.

I peek out between the curtains, see a shadow near the detached garage behind the house. I can tell it's Marco from the way he stands with his hands in his pockets, and the way his hair, which I used to love to run my fingers through, sticks up at odd angles.

"Kennedy?" he calls, his voice unsure. He takes a step closer. But not too close.

When I don't answer, he rocks back and forth on his heels and drags the side of his foot through the dirt. He takes a tentative step forward, and then back, before looking up at the sky as he turns around. He stops moving.

"Come on," he calls, turning back to the house. "I saw the light. I see your bike. I know you're in there." I watch as he shifts from foot to foot. "I'll just wait you out," he adds.

But he won't. He also won't try to come in. He hasn't even crossed into the yard.

Marco spends what feels like an eternity hovering around the garage. Standing beside it, sitting in the dirt, standing again. "Kennedy!" he finally shouts, drawing out each syllable and tilting his head back like he's a wolf and I am the moon, and I wonder if maybe he's drunk. The voices nearby stop. "I'm sorry," he adds, and that's how I know he *must* be drunk. The words come six months too late.

He eventually walks back toward the voices, shaking his head. I check my watch. Seven minutes. A Herculean effort, for sure.

I have to wait another hour for the voices to disappear. Unlike Marco, I'm practiced in the waiting. I've grown comfortable in it, though nothing quite like Elliot, who was patience personified. *Everything takes time*, Elliot told me, fidgeting with the tiny wires of the satellite dish, turning it into something that could listen to the vastness of space. *Anything worth something.*

After I'm sure I'm alone again, I slip out the window, heading back to the observatory. The dish sits in the middle of the abandoned farmland, a cable running to a shed that had once been a small stable, until Elliot converted it to *this*. Now it holds an old computer with several monitors set up—the base of his solo operation and his contribution to the search for extraterrestrial intelligence (SETI)—and it still works as long as the electricity is kept on, even if I can't access it through the Internet. I wouldn't let the Realtor touch it.

I take my flash drive and download the last few days' worth of data, searching for radio signals that could've been sent out by intelligent life beyond our world. I'll spend the weekend sorting through it, unspooling the data like a lie detector test, little blips in frequencies giving rise to more questions: Is it real or background noise? Is it the truth or something else, like a trick of light? I'll map the coordinates, check the amateur SETI message boards, and tag and file every one, like Elliot taught me.

Most searches have scanned just a fraction of the universe. They're guessing, grasping, listening for a very specific signal. It's no wonder they've come up empty so far. Elliot said there had to be something more. We're new, he told me. Humans, I mean. Earth is 4.5 billion years old; the universe, closer to 14 billion. Modern humans first came on the scene 300,000 years ago. That's a lot of unaccounted-for time in the universe for intelligent life to develop elsewhere. That's a lot of chance.

This is boring, I told him the first time I sat beside him in this very room. We were the new family in town last summer, and I hadn't met anyone yet. Hanging out with my older brother was better than nothing, but it didn't stop me from complaining, even then.

This is everything, he said, his face glowing, his fingers mapping the frequency readouts, as if he could commit them to memory. *Three hundred thousand. Fourteen billion. Do the math. Don't tell me there's nothing else.* All I saw were tiny peaks and tiny valleys on a screen, meaning nothing. Elliot was like that, though, seeing something where the rest of us couldn't. Excited by the possibilities of the things he imagined—the world he believed might exist one day.

I should start back for Joe's, but I'm tired, it's the weekend, Joe sleeps late. This is what I think as I climb back through Elliot's window, feel my way to my mother's room on the other side of the living room, sprawl out on top of her covers, and shut my eyes, listening to the sounds of the empty house.

Elliot was right, of course. I can see that now. There must be something more than this.

Marco in the night, the empty house, the endless sky.

This cannot be everything.

This cannot be all that exists.

2

NOLAN

I could tell you at least ten different stories about the woods of Freedom Battleground State Park—mostly ghost stories, a couple of legends thrown in for good measure—but there's only one that matters.

Here it is: Seventeen-year-old Liam Chandler takes his dog for a run into the woods during a family picnic held between the tire swings and the park-owned grills. His younger brother gets a premonition—one of those *all the hairs stand up on your arms* moments—when he suddenly remembers the dream he dreamt the night before, the one he hasn't remembered until *that very moment* when it's already too late. The dream was one of those running-in-molasses types, where no matter how fast you run, you never seem to get anywhere. And no matter how hard you try to scream, your voice won't come. So the word he'd been trying to yell—*Liam*—remained lodged in his throat until morning, when his mother woke him for the picnic, and the light from the window made him groan, and he promptly forgot the dream entirely.

Liam and the dog—this mutt of a thing they'd adopted years earlier that preferred Liam to all other life-forms, except maybe rabbits—had been gone for, what, ten minutes, maybe, by the time the dream came back to the brother? By the time the hairs on his arms all stood on end and the boredom turned to panic? Ten minutes, we'll say.

"Where's Liam? Liam!" The brother starts running. He starts searching, tearing through the twigs and underbrush, following the unpaved paths deep into the woods and back out again. Eventually his parents, hearing the desperation in his yells—this time, not stuck in his throat—ask him what's the matter. The brother tells them, with an air of inevitability, that Liam is gone. *No*, they say, *he's with Colby. He's out for a jog. He'll be back soon.*

The premonition tingles like static electricity.

The boy and the dog are never seen again.

That was two years ago. My brother is still gone. Missing. The police, the FBI, the volunteers who have devoted thousands of hours of labor, have found nothing. The newspaper headlines crackled for attention: *The Unsolved Mystery of Promising Student Athlete; All-State soccer goalie, National Merit Scholar, golden child of Battleground High, disappears without a trace.* Liam Chandler, stuff of legends.

Liam Chandler, reduced to nothing more.

Allow me to set today's scene: It's Saturday morning, barely dawn. I've got a loaded backpack, schoolwork dumped out on my floor. The phone rings. My dad paces downstairs while he talks. My mom works at the computer station in what was once our living room with earbuds in, her head nodding in agreement to some statistic or statement on one of her podcasts. Eventually, the doorbell will ring, and the hum of activity and the scent of coffee will overtake the house. It's the same every weekend. Worse, now, with the influx of kids back from college, partnering with my parents' foundation for volunteer credit. Even worse because I recognize a few of the names—kids who were at my high school a few years ago.

This is the best time to leave, before the phone lines become congested, before their voices start to carry up the steps, before they decide they could really use another set of eyes, or hands, or ears, and somebody inevitably calls, "Nolan?" I head down the back steps, out the back door, walking around the outside of the house to the driveway, partly to avoid my parents, who will ask why I'm heading to work *so early*, but mostly to avoid the pictures.

I should explain the pictures.

They started in the living room—just a few taped sporadically to the walls—but they've slowly and steadily seeped into the dining room, down the hall, and have recently begun encroaching on the kitchen. They're like wallpaper, their edges overlapping, eyes of the missing following as you pass. Their names and measurements, birth dates, and *last reported seen* statistics written in Sharpie underneath. A girl, age twelve, from Florida, over my seat in the dining room. Next to a boy, age fourteen, from West Virginia. Round and round they go.

It was a rapid progression from a seemingly normal house to *this:* First, the police, the FBI, the psychic my parents consulted—clinging to her every word even while looking embarrassed for themselves—failed to provide any answers. Next, the volunteer-run center migrated from the generosity of the coffee shop meeting space to our living room, and my parents redoubled their efforts. Then, getting nowhere, they tripled them, spinning faster and faster until they finally landed in some exponential realm so that instead of just finding Liam, they'd inadvertently taken on the case of every missing child on the East Coast. Or so it seemed to me.

Okay, the truth: They run a nonprofit foundation for missing children throughout the Southeast. They've channeled their grief into action (so said the local paper). But if you ask me, they just feel at home in it now. And so they've willingly inherited the cause of every grief-stricken parent.

Meanwhile, I've inherited Liam's old sedan, which was my father's before that. It's kind of a toss-up each day whether it will start, and beyond that, whether the air will kick in. *Please start,* I beg the car. Especially because Abby's apparently home from college now, currently in running gear, tying her sneakers in front of her parents' front door, doing her best to look like she hasn't noticed me—and I'd really prefer to do the same. Nothing's quite as awkward as casually waving to your brother's old girlfriend, who accidentally—and only once—in a moment of weakness, or grief, or whatever, ended up in the back of this car, with me. Not something either of us would really like to relive. Betting it's worse for her.

The engine stutters and then catches, and even the air kicks in, the scent of Freon bordering on intoxicating.

I don't look at Abby as I drive past. Today will be a good day.

The ranger at Freedom Battleground State Park thinks he's got me all figured out. *EMF meter?* he once asked when I pulled the gear from my backpack. *You got one of those infrared cameras, too?*

Apparently if there are enough ghost stories in your area, you're bound to get some amateur ghost hunters. I guess I wasn't the only one roaming the woods, looking for signs of the unexplained. I don't have one of those infrared camera things, though—or a temperature gauge—because I'm not looking for cold spots or orbs or anything. I'm not even looking for *ghosts*, exactly. But I let the ranger think that's what I'm up to, because he mostly leaves me alone. I must seem harmless enough.

But, like he assumes, I *am* measuring, and mapping, high-electromagnetic spots, and I also have a Geiger counter to detect radiation pockets, and an extra-low-frequency meter, all of which are typically associated with the *other side*. With signs of ghosts. Or spirits. Honestly, I'm not exactly clear on the proper terminology.

That psychic my parents hired came out here with us, and she said she could feel some *energy*, that *something happened here*—well, of course it had, we'd told her as much. And she gave us some hard sell about her colleague who was an expert and could help pinpoint spirits, or energies or something, and this was the point where she lost my parents. *She preys on the desperate,* my father said when we got back home, and my mother, with her silence, agreed.

But I looked it up after, which is how I stumbled onto all this stuff, but also how I stumbled onto the Quest for Proof: a group of people devoted to proving the existence of anything paranormal. Not just showing on some questionable video, or explaining with a persuasive paper, but *proving.*

I know there's something here. There's a reason for all the stories. There's a reason for the ghost hunters.

My brother and his dog disappeared with no earthly explanation. And if I can prove it, I'll have the backing of people who will admit, finally, *Yes, this is what happened to your brother.*

Because what the police kept stressing when Liam first disappeared was that the only way to find a missing person was to first understand what had happened to them.

So, step one.

I guess at the end, I do want the same thing as my parents: answers. A way to understand. It's just that I'm pretty sure they're looking in all the wrong places.

A dream. A premonition. An unexplained disappearance. A forest of ghost stories and legends, and my brother vanishing into thin air. There are things that have happened since that make it clear there is no rational explanation.

But I'm not here to chase ghosts. There are enough people who've taken that angle, coming up empty. I've got a different plan: drop a rock, and the same thing happens over and over again, predictable.

But what if it doesn't? What if there's something unexpected, some failure to predict?

The unpredictable, the unexplained—*that's* the proof. *That's* my plan. I know I'll find it here. I'm the one who felt it, after all.

What I don't like to admit to myself too frequently is this, the second half of what the police were implying. Step two, if you will: if we understand how my brother disappeared, then it follows that maybe we can get him back.

I'm in the northwest corner of the park, a section I've never scanned before, when it's finally time to call it quits.

I stop taking readings when the visitors begin arriving. Their cell phones might interfere. The walkie-talkies of the other rangers. I leave my own phone in the car, every time. I know I should really be doing this at night, when nobody's around, when it's just me and the stories, and the dark.

But then it's just me and the stories, and the dark.

So, I'm a coward.

I pull out the map to mark off my progress, jot down the readings, before heading back for my car. The park spans three townships, a four-mile area, drawing the line between counties and school districts. Where I stand, the woods stop abruptly, giving way to open field, a split-rail fence, a barn. A house.

The Jones House.

A shudder rolls through me. I know about the Jones House because everyone knows about the Jones House. Because Sutton went to school with the girl who survived it, because he made himself a part of the story, told pieces at a baseball clinic this winter to anyone who would listen. And because it was splashed across the headlines for weeks, just like Liam's disappearance two years ago. It was the train wreck from which people could not look away.

And apparently, I'm no different.

There's nothing paranormal about what happened in that house. But I remember what the psychic told my parents, about energies. I think about what could be left behind in a place like that. It could be useful for some sort of comparison or something. But mostly, I think—*What can it hurt?*

I'm across the field and over the fence before I can talk myself out of it. The house is abandoned, though there's a FOR SALE sign in the front yard. I take out the EMF device when I'm far from the house, just for some baseline readings. Then I step closer, walk up onto the front porch, and press my forehead to the closest window, peering inside.

The curtains are pulled open, and I can see the outline of a couch, a lamp, pictures. But something registers as off in my mind, and I look again. The pictures hang crooked, and some have been knocked to the floor. The house is *not right,* and goose bumps rise on the back of my neck.

I steel my nerve and hold the device up against the stone-covered front wall, and then I hear it—

Footsteps. Lightning fast, but barely there.

My heart's in my throat when a blur emerges from the

side of the house, and it takes me a second to realize this is not a ghost but a girl. Long, pale legs and a dark tangle of hair and her back hunched over the handlebars of a bike.

A girl, the articles said, Sutton said.

I watch her go. She doesn't even notice me standing there.

The pizza delivery car is pulling out just as I'm pulling in, and suddenly I'm faced with a weekly dilemma: have pizza and get sucked into the world of missing children, or sneak up the back steps to the comfort of my room and let the hunger eat away at my stomach lining. I'd love option three: go to the drive-through. But I've spent most of my savings on this equipment, and my job is a figment of my parents' imagination, after all.

As I walk to the house, I imagine I'm a gazelle in the savannah. The hunger wins out. The lion pounces.

"They let you out early?" my dad says as my hand reaches into the box of pizza.

"Uh-huh," I lie. I said I was tutoring. I said it was a job at the library. I said I needed the money for college, since I knew my parents were running on fumes by now. They'd sunk so much into the search for Liam, and then into this foundation.

How can I be thinking about who would pay for college when these children are missing? Priorities, Nolan.

"Well, I'm glad you're here," he says, handing me a plate. "We could use your help sorting through the tip line. . . ."

I make some excuse about studying for finals and pile

a few slices onto the plate. The finals part isn't a lie. The studying part, on the other hand, will have to wait. I need to get upstairs and transfer the data points. Plot it out on one of the park maps on my computer. See if there's any overlap, any pattern, any *failure to predict* within.

I grab a soda, and there's a new face taped to the wall, just beside the fridge in my peripheral vision. I don't look. Those pictures, man. They'll gut you, or they'll numb you, and either way, you die a little.

I have to get out of here. I'm surrounded by ghosts.

3

KENNEDY

When I finally make it back, Joe's up and in the shower. By the time he gets out, I've returned the bike to the garage and changed into pajamas.

I can't believe I slept so long at the house. I woke with a start, with a feeling that someone was there, like a presence. As if the stories the other kids told in the dark, whispered low to scare one another, were real. But then the light filtered in, everything clarified—and I remembered that I was alone.

Joe says he has to be on campus for most of Saturday, but *has to* is probably an overstatement.

He does work sporadic hours, I'll give him that. But occasionally I think he builds in some extra time, just to have an excuse to leave. I don't even blame him.

Truthfully, we get along just fine for roommates thrown into an unforeseen living arrangement. And in practice, everything's working out as far as the courts are concerned. But in theory, he hasn't taken too well to suddenly being responsible for his sixteen-year-old niece. Can't say I've taken too well to it, either. It's hard to take him seriously as a voice of authority—he was always just my mom's slightly irresponsible, much younger kid brother, who took a few years off before attending college to *see the world*, with a spotty attendance record when it came to family affairs—and my presence probably doesn't help with his bachelor lifestyle.

But on the plus side, he pretty much leaves me to my own devices. He's adopted a random assortment of ground rules, which he came up with on a whim one night, but I mostly try to stick by them so I can fight the good fight where it counts. No drinking (not a problem), no boys (also not a problem), and no skipping school (mostly not a problem). If he ever catches me sneaking out, I can tell him that technically I haven't broken any of his rules and hope that holds. I'm fighting him hard, though, on the house thing.

He wants to sell it. I don't. After a lifetime of moving around campus housing with my mom, this was the first time we'd had a house in our name, and land. According to my mom, it would be a place for us all to grow roots.

It's the only place I can feel them, still.

Technically, the house is now mine.

Technically, it's Joe's decision, since he's the one who'd have to send the checks.

All these technicalities.

• • •

We finally cross paths at breakfast. Lunch? I look at the clock: too close to tell. He's got two different kinds of cereal out on the kitchen table—we shop separately but buy vaguely similar things. The one time we went grocery shopping together, the woman at the checkout gave him some seriously judgmental looks and pulled me aside to ask if I was okay. Joe's too old to pass as my brother, too young to be my father, too unsure of how to act around me to look casual. Anyway, that store clerk's comment? I mock-gagged and laughed it off. But Joe was mortified. Now he drops me off with cash for my own stuff while he "runs errands." I think he just drives around for a while until I text him.

"What are you doing today?" he asks, drinking the remaining milk directly from the bowl.

"Nothing," I say.

He nods like I've somehow given a satisfactory response.

"The Albertsons wanted me to tell you that you're welcome to use their pool whenever you want—it's the yellow corner house, you know it? They have twin girls who are about your age."

"I'll keep that in mind," I say. I do know the Albertsons' house, and I also know the Albertson twins (for the record: two years younger, *not* my age), and not even the stifling heat could get me into their backyard pool.

He takes his bowl to the sink, rinses it out, and puts it in the dishwasher, then pulls open the freezer. "I'll bring back something for dinner," he says.

"Okay."

He's in jeans and a gray T-shirt, apparently acceptable attire for a postgrad at the university. I don't know what

20

he does exactly—some sort of anthropology research, along with a bit of teaching, I think. He used to travel a lot. Yet another thing I've disrupted. But his presence there was one of the main reasons my mom accepted that teaching position. He's why we're here, in West Arbordale, Virginia, after I spent most of my life in the suburbs of DC. Same state, very different reality.

Joe lives a little like a student, too, which is not nearly as glamorous as I'd imagined, in anticipation of college. Mostly it means ramen noodles and a lot of caffeine and a questionable laundry situation. I tried to get him to move to my house instead—more room for both of us—even suggesting we renovate, so we wouldn't have to be reminded of the things that happened there. But he, like most people, won't set foot in there any longer. "We can use the money from the sale to get a bigger place," he suggested after our first couple of weeks together, when the realities of sharing a bathroom with a teenage girl, and vice versa, bordered on cringe-worthy.

As if I intended to stick around any later than graduation. "Let's not make any long-term plans," I said.

He looked relieved.

But now we're still cramped in a two-bedroom, one-bathroom ranch, when there's a sprawling house with land and an observatory just a handful of miles down the road. He'll cave. I know it. The sting will pass. But in the meantime, that house can't sell.

"Okay, well, call if you need anything. Or if you go to the Albertsons' house."

"Will do," I say. We do that awkward dance where he

can't decide whether to pat my head or my shoulder and I hold up my hand to try to wave him off with a halfhearted goodbye before he gets started. Too late. He goes for the top of my head today, patting it twice, like I'm a puppy.

I'm trying to cut him some slack. He's doing me an enormous favor—yet another technicality, if we're keeping track. There was a brief discussion back in December about whether it would be in my best interest to live with my father.

It would not have been.

The things worth knowing about my father could be tallied on one hand: he gave up parental rights when I was just a baby; he currently lives in Germany with a new wife; I hadn't seen him in over seven years by the time he showed up in December.

Though Joe was listed as guardian in my mother's will, he still had to agree to the responsibility. There was another option, if it proved too much for Joe. My father and his new wife (Betty? Betsy? I'm still not sure) came to visit after Joe called, to offer their brief and awkward condolences, and to sit down with Joe and discuss what was to happen to me. I heard them talking it over at night, in the living room. A list of pros and cons, of which I was the subject.

It would only be another year and a half, I told Joe the next day, desperate to tip the scales. A year and a half until I was eighteen, off to college, out of his hair. We could make it work, I promised.

Joe pretended he hadn't been thinking it over. He said, *Of course, Kennedy, it's not even a question.* But come on. The walls here are not as thick as he would like to imagine.

He's twenty-nine. I've thrown his life into chaos. He's missed all the nuance of the first sixteen years of parenting. So. I'm trying.

I retreat to the cramped space that used to be Joe's TV room but now fits my bed, desk, dresser, and boxes. The only décor in here is a framed picture on the windowsill beside my bed, a photo from last fall: me and Elliot and my mom at the top of a lighthouse, my hair blowing in Elliot's face, Elliot trying to push me away, my mom laughing. The last photo I have of all of us together, when we went with her on a long-weekend work conference.

The photo was taken by my mom's colleague-slash-new-boyfriend, Will. The outing had been Will's idea—I don't think he was expecting us to be there. Honestly, at the time I would've preferred to spend the last day at the hotel pool, but my mom insisted, and so there we were.

Two hundred and twelve steps to the top, with my mom talking about the history of the place, and Elliot reciting facts about the construction, Will correcting them both, and me trying to tune them all out, my hands on the cold, spiraling concrete walls as I counted in my head, my mother's voice echoing through the stairwell.

I wish I could focus on her words, remember them. But all I have in my memory now is the tone of her voice, over the count I was keeping. Elliot was probably listening, and not just because he thought he was supposed to. He was probably actually interested, as he was in all things new to him. For two people who shared so many physical traits, we were so different at the core. My mother used to joke, *I swear I raised them the same.* Elliot used to joke, *I locked her in the closet whenever you were away.* Which is a lie. He would never. But that was just like Elliot, taking the blame for setting the bar a little too high for my life.

Other than this picture, my clothes, and my computer, I haven't really gotten around to unpacking or making myself comfortable. Like I said, I'm an optimist.

I've got the radio telescope data pulled up on the computer now, but right away I can see something's wrong. And not the *good* type of wrong, which would make it seem like the telescope was picking up something other than background noise. Instead, this is the type of wrong that makes me think something is broken.

Usually, the radio telescope is set to monitor frequencies where signals can be transmitted through space. The readout typically looks like one of those medical heart monitors, almost a flat line, but with little peaks and valleys.

Today, it's nonexistent. Not even background noise. It takes me a second to realize that the radio telescope didn't register the right frequency channel. It's set to something different, or else it's pulling in some interference, I think.

Elliot built the dish and made the program, so I have to drag the scale around for a bit before I finally find the data set where there's actual activity, and at first my heart jumps, seeing a section of the readout—it looks like a repeating pattern of pulses: a quick spike, then a longer pause, over and over again, like a signal, or a message.

I lean closer to the screen, until I can see my own reflection in the monitor: openmouthed, wide-eyed. But then I realize there's a serious mistake somewhere, either with the program, or with the radio telescope itself. Because this potential activity is registering where no frequency should exist. The program is displaying what would be a typical radio signal range, except it's negative.

Negative.

I let out a groan of frustration. I may have only taken a year of physics so far, but I do know there's no such thing as a negative frequency. Not in reality. And definitely not something that Elliot would have programmed to record, either. It makes no sense.

Just to double-check (because, again, only one year of physics so far), I type *negative frequency* into the search bar, but it only tells me what I had assumed: it only exists in mathematical theory, not reality.

I scan the data, looking for the time stamps, and see that it registered from just after 1:00 a.m. until I pulled all the data, a short time later.

Freaking Marco. I hope they didn't damage the satellite dish last night. I hope Lydia didn't perch on the edge of it, and Sutton didn't throw a beer bottle at the center. I hope Marco didn't stumble into it on his way back last night, knocking it off axis.

It's probably just the computer program, though in some ways, that would be worse—I wouldn't even know where to start with that.

God, it's hot. But another six-mile bike ride it is.

• • •

The dish looks fine, but Elliot built it, so I'm not really sure what could be happening on the inside. It's still angled at the right spot, and structurally, everything looks sound. The cable's buried underground, though, so that will have to wait. Best to track down the most likely culprit first.

I head in the opposite direction from my house, over the split-rail fence, to the other side of the fields. There's a development here, mostly modest two-story homes with landscaped backyards and two-car garages. Marco's house is the third on the right from the way I enter—from the field, not the road. His car, an old green sedan, is parked in the driveway, and I'm assuming one or both of his parents' cars are in the garage.

I ring the doorbell, hear footsteps before his mother opens the door in workout clothes. Her face is makeup-free, her hair brushed up into a messy bun. Like this—relaxed and casual—she reminds me so much of my mom that I instinctively look away at first.

"Hi," I say. "Is Marco here?"

His mom has that look of surprise and sympathy, which eventually merges into a painful smile. "Kennedy, how nice to see you! Did you call him? I think Marco's still sleeping." Then the sympathy and surprise swing in my favor, which I've grown used to with teachers and parents alike. She pulls the door open before clearing her throat. "Well, go on up."

"I'll just be a minute," I say, to reassure her.

I knock once, wait to the count of five, and then let myself into Marco's room. He pushes himself to sitting in his bed. From the noise that escapes his throat, he must be nursing a hangover, not that I'm surprised. But he doesn't even question what I'm doing here, just flops down on his back, lifting a hand at me in greeting. He's so disoriented by my presence I feel my stomach do that flip from the first time I was in his room last September, working on a school project, when I knew he liked me and he knew I liked him and the anticipation was so all-consuming I could only think of things in proximity to Marco.

Current calculation: five steps from Marco's feet.

"Marco," I say, and he flings an arm over his eyes. "Last night, did you guys mess with the telescope?"

"The . . . what?" He rubs his eyes, pushes himself to sitting again, folds his legs up under the sheets. "Hi, Kennedy," he says, like we're starting over.

I take a step closer. "The radio telescope. The satellite dish. Did you do anything to it?" Current calculation: four steps from Marco's bed.

"We didn't touch it," he says, now fully awake. He blinks his dark brown eyes twice, frowning. "How'd you get in here?"

"Your mom. What were you doing out there last night?" I ask.

Marco lifts one shoulder in half a shrug. "It was Lydia's idea."

And this is where my affection for Marco wanes. Nothing is ever his fault, or his idea. He's painfully indecisive, even more so in hindsight.

"And why did Lydia want to go there?" I ask. Lydia is Marco's best friend, and Sutton is usually kind of her boyfriend, not that they like the label. But that's the best way to describe them. They all live in the same sprawling neighborhood behind my house.

"I don't know, we were at Sutton's, and his parents came home, so Lydia said we should go *there*, and I don't know, I couldn't think of a reason *not* to, really."

And that, in a nutshell, is Marco. He runs his fingers through his messy hair, and no part of me wants to do the same. It's been six months since I touched him last, but I'd be lying if I said I hadn't thought about it since. Six months, it seems, is enough. "You swear you didn't touch it," I say.

"I swear," he says.

I turn around and leave. He calls my name. I don't look back.

Back at Joe's, I look over the data again. I'd ignore it, except there's definitely a pattern. A spike every three seconds or so. And it repeats. On and on it goes. I log on to the amateur SETI forums, and I compose a message:

```
Anyone ever register a signal at a
negative frequency? I'm picking up
a pattern of pulses. Interference
probable.—KJ
```

I post it.

I wish Elliot were here.

4

NOLAN

It's quiet now, which means it's finally safe to venture out of my room. Dad is cooking, which is marginally better than the days when Mom cooks, but unquestionably worse than takeout. He stares at the pictures of the missing while he stirs the pasta. "How's the studying, Nolan?"

"It's all right," I say.

"Listen, can you help out tomorrow afternoon until Mike shows up? Someone needs to supervise the new volunteers. I've got a meeting downtown, and you know how your mother is with the phone," he says, lowering his voice conspiratorially.

"How your mother is with what?" Mom says, pulling out the earbuds and winding up the wires.

"With cooking," I say. "No offense, Ma." *How my mom is with the phone* is actually like this: She takes it all too personally. She becomes too invested. And that's saying something, seeing as the baseline for normal here is the downstairs of my house covered in pictures of other people's missing children.

"Mmm," she says, ruffling my hair as she passes.

Dad raises his eyebrow at me in question. I nod, admitting defeat. And they wonder why I don't come out of my room more often.

The maps aren't really making any sense. Or maybe it's just that they're not coming together like I'd hoped—nothing registering outside the range of any normal household appliance, it seems. But then I think maybe I'm expecting too much, that I should be looking for the subtle. For tiny fluctuations; the unpredictable. I have a map with all the ghost stories and legends (and missing brother) pinpointed as much as possible. I've got another map with EMF, ELF, and Geiger readings, but they don't seem to overlap in any meaningful way. I need to dig into the details.

I couldn't spring for the top-of-the-line digital EMF meter, so I've got one with a dial that looks kind of like the speedometer in my old car. After I hear my parents' footsteps on the wooden staircase, I decide to take some baseline readings around the house, for comparison. I wait an extra hour, just to be sure everyone's asleep. They're not exactly aware of my extracurricular endeavor.

I leave the stairway dark but turn on the kitchen light and take readings of the refrigerator, microwave, and anything else that seems to be functional, jotting them all down in a notebook. Back in my room, I add the computer and my cell. As I get ready to compare all the readings, I toss the EMF meter onto my bed, but it ricochets off the wall beside it, and I cringe. *Please don't let it be broken.* For consistency's sake, I really should use the same device for all readings. Also, I can't exactly afford a new one.

It looks intact, but before I even touch it, I can see I've screwed something up. Surprise, surprise.

It's sitting on my bed, beside the wall, and the dial keeps jerking down past zero. I pick it up, turning away from the wall, and the dial settles to zero. Okay, maybe it's fine. I hold it to my computer again—same reading as before. Phone— same reading. Okay, everything's fine. No problem. I set it back on the bed, facing the wall, same position as before, and the dial starts diving below zero again.

There's nothing on the other side of that wall anymore. Nothing electronic, anyway. Just Liam's old bed, same comforter, same clothes in the closet, same notes from Abby.

His computer is mine now, along with anything else of perceived value. And I've been through his drawers enough to know there's nothing of interest anymore.

Still. I let myself into his room, flipping the light, shutting the door behind me. Even after two years, the silence and the emptiness catch me by surprise each time. The worn blue blanket at the foot of the bed is the spot where Colby used to lie, even when Liam wasn't home. It sits there now as another reminder of all the things that are still missing.

In my hand, the meter continually bounces back and forth from neutral to below zero. I check under the bed, in his drawers, in the closet—but find nothing.

Must be something in the walls. All the pipes and wires and ducts running through, creating an electric current. Maybe there's some faulty wiring. Well, one way to find out.

I head down to the basement and open the circuit breaker, and impulsively flip everything off.

Impulsively, because now I'm standing in the pitch black, in the basement, with nothing but an EMF reader, and I suddenly don't want to look at the readout.

Impulsively, because it's hard to research the paranormal without letting your imagination run wild. Because if it's possible for one thing to exist, it's therefore possible that other things do, too.

The display is backlit, and everything appears normal. I walk slowly, using the meter as a flashlight. Back upstairs, I return to Liam's room, and every hair on my arms and the back of my neck stands on end. The dial keeps moving, in a pattern—to negative, back to neutral, over and over again.

It's giving me the creeps.

And then it's just me and the stories, and the dark. And the dark whispers that there's something in this room, and the room whispers the stories it remembers, and my stomach aches for my brother, all at once.

I'm seventeen. My parents are down the hall. I shouldn't be afraid of the dark anymore.

I shouldn't be afraid of the ticking of the gauge, or the way the dial shoots down into the red for no apparent reason. A quick spike. A long pause. A quick spike. A long pause.

I shut it down, because it's giving me the chills, the way it keeps up the pattern. I back out into the hall, open my parents' bedroom door, hear my father's predictable snoring.

"Nolan?" The sheets rustle as my mom wakes up.

"Yeah," I say. "Sorry. The power's out. I'm gonna go reset the circuit breaker."

"Just a minute," she says, getting out of bed. I wait for my mother to grab a flashlight so I don't have to go down to the basement alone. God, I'm an embarrassment to the male teenage species.

It's 2 a.m. and I can't sleep. I feel something, like that premonition from two years ago. Like there's a dream I'm not remembering, and by the time I do, it will be too late.

Which is how I find myself at the computer, typing *Negative EMF signal?* into the search bar.

The results get me nowhere. I add the word *pattern*, but nothing seems relevant. The meter starts at zero, which leads me to believe there shouldn't even be a negative possibility here.

It must be the meter. Maybe I can pretend it came that way from the store. Maybe I can get a refund, or exchange, for the same model.

Except.

There, deep in the search results, is a link to a SETI message board. The acronym sounds familiar, but my mind isn't really placing it. I click on the link, and I see the initials spelled out—*search for extraterrestrial intelligence*—and I almost close it automatically.

But the message is titled *Signal at Negative Frequency?* by someone named *KJ*.

It talks about a pattern.

And it was posted within the day.

5

KENNEDY

I've got seven responses when I wake up, all telling me more of what I'd already assumed. That there's something wrong with the dish, or the wire, or—most likely—the program setup.

And something from a Visitor357.

Most visitors without account names are trolls, and I've heard enough stories about online message boards being the new Internet hookup site, which is why I use my initials and keep all my personal data off the site. Visitor357's message begins:

```
Hey, I was taking readings in my house
with my EMF meter and kept getting a
negative reading.
```

I do a quick search for *EMF meter* and let out a groan. Not only is this guy possibly a troll, but now it looks like I have a ghost-hunting troll.

My finger hovers on the delete key, but something makes me stop. It's the way he describes it.

```
A spike, then a pause, like a pattern.
```

And the way he signs off:

```
I turned off all the electricity.
Sounds like this interference you
speak of. Glad to know I'm not alone.
```

I tap my pointer finger on the desk a few times, debating. Then hit the button to send a private message:

```
Hey Visitor357,
    This is a site for signals we
are receiving FROM SPACE. Not our
houses. Probably a different type of
interference (say, your microwave),
but if you want to send me what you
got I can take a look at it for you.
    —KJ
```

In the meantime, the most likely reason for my own signal is either something mechanical or something computer-related, and there's only one person left I know who can help me. The phone rings four times, and I'm on the verge of hanging up when she finally answers, clearing her throat before speaking.

"Hello?" Her voice is quick, unsure.

"Hey, Lydia. It's Kennedy."

"Yeah, Kennedy. Hi. I know. Your name is on the display."

A pause.

"So," I say.

She clears her throat again.

So, it's going to be like this. Awkward, because we haven't really spoken in six months. More awkward, because the only reason we ever did was because she's Marco's best friend and I was his girlfriend. Most awkward because I once heard her refer to me as *Child of the Corn*, and no one called her on it, which led me to believe she probably used it more than once. I even Googled *Children of the Corn* later to see what she meant, but there was zero resemblance that I could tell, which made me wonder what she was really saying about me.

"I was wondering if you could help me with some computer thing today," I finally say.

"I don't have a car," she says.

"Right, no, at my house. By the satellite dish. You can walk. I mean, you were there Friday night, right?"

And with that, I know I have her. "Sure, okay," she says, like I haven't just accused her of trespassing at my house, a crime scene, a place she has no right to be anymore. "What kind of computer issue are we talking about, though?"

"I have no idea," I say. "That's why I called you. I'll be there in one hour."

When I arrive at the house and round the corner to the backyard, Lydia's already there, leaning against the split-rail fence. I walk the bike toward the shed and wave for her to come closer. She steps tentatively away from the fence, as if even this—being this close to the house, alone—is too much.

Though I did just accuse her of trespassing, so.

Even there, at the edge of the property, she's hard not to notice. Lydia's tall and thin and has these hazel eyes offset by her brown skin, which makes you look twice. When I first met her through Marco (*This is my friend Lydia*), I was on the edge of jealousy and insecurity, but it soon became obvious that Lydia was only interested in Sutton, and vice versa.

"Well," she says, peering at the house over my shoulder instead of at me, "what are we looking at?"

"Either the computer in the shed or the satellite dish," I say, walking toward the makeshift observatory.

"A dish issue is not the same thing as a computer issue, you know," she mumbles.

Her steps fall in sync with my own, crunching the dead grass underneath our feet, dry from lack of water and scorched by the sun. The antenna on top of the shed flashes with the reflecting sun before a cloud passes overhead.

Lydia wrinkles her nose when I open the shed door, because the first thing you notice is the dim light, the dust particles suspended in the air, the smell of earth and wood.

"Oh," she says. "Wow." Because the second thing you notice is Elliot's setup: three computer monitors, several humming towers under the desk, and a tangle of wires threading through a hole in the wall, and then underground—where they run in a path to the satellite dish. At least, I think. I never paid much attention to the logistics. There's also a drawer full of cables, headphones, and speakers, like Elliot truly believed he'd make direct contact with something out there one day. He was like that: sometimes more focused on the great possibilities out there than on what was staring him in the face.

Once, when he was working on his laptop at the kitchen table, my mom told him he absolutely needed a haircut, that he was looking particularly ridiculous, and that really, how could he even see what he was doing? Instead of brushing her off, like a normal person would, he paused for thirty seconds to take the scissors from the drawer beside the refrigerator. He ran the blade through the hair in front of his eyes, shaking out the dark strands as they fell into the trash can. Then he returned to his seat while my mom and I stared at each other, openmouthed. Until eventually her shoulders started shaking with silent laughter, and mine followed less silently, and Elliot shook himself from his world long enough to grin at us from under his uneven bangs.

Lydia doesn't wait for instructions from me; she makes herself comfortable in the chair in front of the terminal, and she begins by pressing a few keys. Her mouth scrunches up, but she leans closer to the screen, now illuminated with the green-on-black readout, with peaks and valleys and numbers below. "Is there a manual somewhere?" she asks. But she's still looking at the screen.

The rest of the shed is empty. Wooden planks, a small window with a view of the satellite dish, which is planted in the center of the ground, pointed up. There's just this computer desk and chair inside now.

"I can check," I say. Somewhere in the house is a box of

Elliot's personal items, where his journals or manuals would be. We've kept all his things, but the Realtor or the stager tucked those boxes out of sight—upstairs in the storage area, she said, like it was no big deal. I shift from foot to foot until Lydia turns around, focusing her eyes on mine. Waiting. "Okay. I'll be right back."

The heat and the sun beat down on the back of my neck. But there's something in the air when I walk toward the house, something that feels like static electricity, that makes my hair stand on end. I try to shake it off as I crawl through Elliot's bedroom window again, like I did Friday night.

The air conditioner is set to cooler than I was expecting, or maybe it's just the contrast with the outside heat, but a chill runs through me as I exit his room. Next: the hallway. To the right is my room, and then the living room, where the pictures still hang at odd angles. To the left are the steps at the back of the house, leading to the loft on the second floor.

When Joe and I were arguing about the house, I told him we could renovate this part. Cut out this section of the house, block it off, redesign it. With just the two of us, the downstairs is more than enough anyway.

But for now, here it is.

I place my hand on the wooden banister, my thumb on a groove of wood.

There's a new layer of paint here, on the walls. Fresh carpeting. The railing has been replaced with a beam made of reddish wood, smooth and polished. It's darker here than the rest of my house, tucked away from the windows. But I don't turn the light on.

It's my house and it's not my house. Close your eyes, and the shadow house is here. I keep my eyes down and step sideways on the first step. I skip the next one. I feel like a fool, as if I'm like Joe, who won't set foot here at all. As if where I place my feet now will make any difference.

It's just a step. Just a house. I try to picture a stranger's house instead. Wood and nails and carpet. But my imagination will not play.

Still, I keep moving, one foot in front of the other, until I'm on the second-floor landing.

To my right is the television room, and to my left, the storage area—a room halfway between the size of a closet and a bedroom. The inside smells of cardboard and ozone, like no one has opened the door in months. None of the boxes are labeled. There was no point. It wasn't like Elliot was going to need them anymore, asking us, *Which box has my clothes?* or *Where are the books?* So it's sort of a job now, piecing through them.

I hesitate with the first lid, imagining him watching, saying, *Out of my stuff, Kennedy.*

What I wouldn't give for that now.

Opening the first box, with his clothes inside, I can almost feel him here. Only, it's not even him. It's my mom's choice of laundry detergent, nothing more.

After unpacking half the storage area, I finally find the box that holds the contents of his desk drawers: notebooks, journals, the inner thoughts of Elliot's brain. It's stacked full, but nothing inside is labeled, so I take the whole box with me, walking back down the hall, eyes focused on the open lid as I approach the staircase.

Don't look, don't look.

I keep moving until I'm downstairs again, unlocking the front door, walking down the porch steps, circling around to the back shed, in hopes that Lydia can help me find what we're looking for.

6

NOLAN

I'm being catfished. Maybe as a joke, but maybe not.

Send me what you have, and I'll send you mine?

This is inevitably the start of every child abduction warning seminar my parents have been to, or have spoken at. KJ is some creepy dude trolling for some hapless kid, and the next thing you know I'll be sending him my picture and meeting him in some dark mall parking lot under a streetlight that doesn't work where he pulls up in an unmarked white van and I'm never heard from again.

Hard pass.

I already feel like a fool, now that it's daylight. The whole thing seems like a dream now, like I was in some fugue state where my imagination was getting the best of me, ignoring every rational explanation.

But it's still doing it. The dial. It keeps jumping around, like something's over there, in Liam's room. I set up my phone as a camera, and I hold it in one hand, and I take the reading against Liam's wall with the other. So I have proof, in case it amounts to anything.

There are several likely possibilities: some unaccounted-for magnetic field. A solar flare. Or something outside—the wires that run along the side of the road; the electrical box outside the neighbor's house. Last night, I took a bunch of readings in Liam's room with the other equipment, but there was nothing unusual. Just the pattern, the needle bouncing around, like something's messing with the readout.

Still, I stare at that wall connecting my room to Liam's, and then at the gear hidden under my desk. And I get this hunch, this *feeling*, as my mind keeps drifting back to that house. The Jones House.

It was the only thing I did differently yesterday, other than visiting the back corner of the park. I held up the device to the outside wall of the house before I heard the footsteps, before I saw the girl. I watched as she biked down the driveway, her dark hair flying behind her, pedaling fast like something was chasing her. And then I got the hell out of there myself, running across the field, back to the park, and making my way to my car.

But now I start to wonder: Maybe whatever I thought was happening in the park is actually happening *there* as well. Maybe I was onto something yesterday, checking it out.

I run a search for the articles about the crime last winter, and quickly get a few hits. *Double Homicide Rocks West Arbordale Community*. There's a picture of the house standing all alone in the middle of the field, taken from a distance, through the trees, so that it looks haunted and ominous. I read the summary again. This isn't paranormal. The case is solved. There's no mystery here. But I think of the feeling I got on their front porch, staring in the windows.

Liam disappeared after a feeling.

The phone rings downstairs, and I jump back from the screen. The house comes into focus again: I smell pancakes. I hear the squeak of the front door, the sound of my mom's car. It suddenly feels like the perfect plan: pancakes, and an exit.

I have my bag slung over my shoulder, and I eat at the counter as my dad flips a fresh pancake onto his plate. "Thanks, Dad," I say, still chewing as I head toward the door.

"You remember you're helping this afternoon, right? I'm leaving at one and Mike can't show up until three or so."

I did not remember. "Yes, no problem." Once again, I'm thankful for Mike, who is more reliable than me, and always willing to fill in when he can, which makes my lack of availability less questionable. But he has to split his time between here and the youth shelter, where he and Liam both volunteered. Still, it could be so much worse than just needing to fill in for two hours on a Sunday.

I hear the chatter of low conversation from the living room. "New volunteers?" I ask.

My dad peers around the wall. "Sophomores at the college," he says, then stops. Like we're both remembering—that's how old Liam should be right now. He clears his throat. "Dave and Clara." Then his brow furrows. "Maybe Sara." He shrugs, like it doesn't matter. Maybe it doesn't.

They'll be gone by the end of summer anyway. This is probably something for their résumés, not their lives.

I peek my head around the corner, and for a second, I can almost see Liam and Abby instead, sitting beside each other on the sofa, laughing in their own private world. Dave, I recognize. He's got distinctively red hair, and I remember him from school, in Liam's year. But I don't think I've seen the girl before.

My dad frowns at my bag, the line between his eyes deepening. "Library again?"

"Finals, Dad," I say, and he gives this noncommittal nod, like the idea of finals takes place in some other plane of existence. Or maybe he can see right through my lie.

My teachers say I'm not living up to my potential. But nobody here seems to care. You try holding up a report card, good or bad, in a room covered in faces of other people's missing children. It's like everything gets forced into perspective in an instant. Some things get wedged to the periphery.

For the record, one of those things is me.

This time, I don't stop at the entrance to Freedom Battleground State Park. The address puts the driveway for the Jones House here, about two miles beyond the turnoff. I'm on the right street, but I can't find the right house number. I end up driving past it twice before I spot it, a post in the road that looks like nothing more than a mile marker, the numbers engraved in the same color, barely visible. You can't see the house from the road, either. It's set back through the trees, and the driveway is long and unpaved, with no mail-box out front.

Once I pull into the drive, it angles to the left, and finally there's the mailbox. It's deceptively friendly, with a bright red flag and a decal of the sun. Then everything opens up behind the trees: the house, the field stretching in both directions, to the woods and the state park on the right, and another neighborhood past the fence, to the left.

I pull the car slowly up the drive until I'm parked in the roundabout directly in front of the porch. The dirt from the tires still hovers in the air when I step outside.

I listen for signs of life, but the day is quiet, and everything is still. There are birds in the distance, some sort of insect that hums in the grass to the side of the house. The sun is bright, and it reflects off the front windows, making me look away as my eyes start to tear.

"Right," I say to myself. I turn back to the car and sling my backpack onto my shoulder. Then, on second thought, I take a photo of the house with my phone. I turn on my map program, marking the GPS coordinates. This is, after all, for science.

I note the time of day. The sun in the sky. The heat. The location: *West Arbordale, Virginia. 323 Lance Road.*

Nothing is irrelevant.

Or maybe I'm procrastinating.

"Right," I say again. I leave my phone in the car so it won't interfere and carry my gear up the front steps, cup my hands around my eyes, and peer into the windows again. It's the same as yesterday: pictures off-kilter, that feeling of *wrong*.

My hand shakes as I take the EMF meter from my bag

and hold it to the window, but nothing happens. It registers the same baseline reading as it does around my house. A normal measure of electricity—the dial doesn't jump or do anything creepy, like diving back below zero. I make some notes, taking some more readings with the other devices.

The porch creaks under my steps as I walk the front perimeter, and the chain of the porch swing jangles as my arm accidentally brushes the wood. Just outside the front door, I can feel the tiniest gust of cold air seeping from underneath, and I freeze. I press my ear to the front door.

I think, I hope, it's the air conditioning clicking on. But just in case, I knock.

I *knock*. I have just knocked on the door of an empty house because I felt a gust of cold air. *Seriously, Nolan.*

On a whim, I take the knob in my hand and twist it gently. There's no resistance. My lungs are in my throat. My heart is in my stomach. What the hell am I doing?

Still, I twist it, and the door pushes open. A gust of air rushes out, and I was right—it's the air conditioner. I laugh to myself under my breath.

From where I'm standing in the entrance with the door swung open, the house looks like any other house. Older wood floors, a rustic coffee table, drapes that hang in front of the windows, pulled back. If it weren't for the fact that it looks like a windstorm went through the room, knocking the paintings askew, or off the walls, it would look like a normal house.

But there's also this smell, something too fresh, too new. Like carpet fabric and paint, like wood polish and those pine tree things people hang from their car mirrors. Like something else needs to be covered up here.

I think of the article I read, picture the headline, the photo, and I step across the threshold. I close the door behind me, and I wait for something to happen. But when nothing does—no alarm, no automatic lights, no phone ringing—I decide to take the risk.

I keep the EMF meter in my hand as I circle the downstairs. The doors are all open, but I don't step inside any of the rooms. I keep walking, staring at the device as I go. The kitchen. The living room. Three downstairs bedrooms. At the end of the hall near the back of the house, I round the corner, away from the open windows, and everything falls to shadow.

In front of me, there's a dark stairway, where the smell of things new and replaced is the strongest.

Here. It happened here.

I blink, trying to imagine the scene, but it's all hidden under shadow. There's only a dark hallway upstairs, and a dark hallway here. Running my hand against the nearest wall, I flip the switch, and the area lights up, too bright. The bulb must've been recently replaced, because it's too white. It buzzes all around me, like there's a charge. My temple throbs with the start of a headache.

The device shakes in my other hand, the needle rising. I drop my bag to the ground to find my notebook, to document this, but my hand is trembling. There are footsteps in the fresh carpeting—a trail up and down. I turn off the light, and the dial settles again.

Just the electricity. Just the normal background noise. Just the footprints of a Realtor, or prospective buyers.

In the dark, the hallway falls to shadows again. This was where they were found. No, that's not all of it. Sutton told us, whispered low the morning of the tri-county baseball clinic. This was where *she* found them. That girl he knew. On the staircase.

7

KENNEDY

Inside the shed again, Lydia looks at the box in my hands, and her eyes go large. "Please tell me you know what we're looking for," she says.

"I was hoping it would make more sense to you," I say, dropping the box between us.

She bites the side of her nail, lowers into a squat, doesn't move to touch anything. She sees the letters written in ink on the cover of the first journal. *Elliot Jones.* "This was all his?"

"Yes," I say, and I grab a handful of notebooks off the top, spreading them out before me, to break her trance. They're just *paper*.

Lydia takes a few, opening and closing the covers. "These are physics. Wrong subject." She keeps going until we're halfway down the box, and she opens a journal and says, "Oh, hold on." She hops back to the chair, pivots to the computer screen, starts moving her fingers in time to some music I don't hear at all.

"What are you—"

She holds up a finger. Her gold nail polish sparkles in the light from the window. She slides a pen between her teeth and starts typing. "I'm just," she says around the pen, "seeing how the script runs. Can't see if anything's wrong before I know what it's supposed to do."

The screen turns black, and commands scroll across it. I'm in over my head there.

I keep looking through the journals, in case he's left specific notes, or labeled things. I picture him sitting at his desk, reading some textbook, his hand off to the side scribbling notes at the same time, like he was split in two. When he was working on something in his bedroom, I could walk right up to his shoulder and he wouldn't even notice, especially when he had headphones on, which was often. I did it all the time, as a game. Seeing how close I could get before dropping a hand on his shoulder, or shouting *Boo*—how high I could make him jump. He'd drop his pen and yell, but once the shock passed, his laughter would echo mine.

The problem with Elliot's notes is that, however organized he was in person, his mind was not. Or it was, but in a way that only he could decipher. Nothing is labeled. Nothing is summarized. Still, I try.

My phone abruptly rings, cutting through the air. I fumble for it, sucking in a deep breath, like I've fallen asleep in the bathtub and am fighting my way to the surface. Lydia stops typing, too, peering at me over her shoulder.

The call is from Joe, and I answer before he can start to worry, calling the neighbors, asking if anyone's seen me. "Hello?"

"Where are you, Kennedy?" He sounds irritated. Impatient.

I frown. It's still Sunday morning; he's probably just getting up. I think of my options: risky to claim I'm at the Albertsons', if he's still home. Or anywhere farther than a quick bike ride would take me. "I'm with a friend," I say.

There's a pause before Joe repeats the question, lower this time. "Kennedy, where are you? We're supposed to be on the road soon."

"On the . . ."

"Road," he says, clearly exasperated. "Come on, Kennedy. You know this."

I press my lips together. "I forgot," I say.

Lydia spins around, and I hate that she's listening.

"You forgot?" Joe says, his voice rising. He repeats things I say a lot, I've noticed, as if he expects the phrase to suddenly bring extra meaning. Will used to do the same, sitting across from me at the dinner table, though in his case, I thought it was probably more to seem like he was interested in what I had to say, as his girlfriend's child, than a real question.

"Sorry."

He sighs. "You weren't here when I woke up." It sounds like he's trying to accuse me of something, but he's not sure what.

"I just forgot to tell you. I was meeting my friend."

"You were meeting a friend," he repeats. I mean, I don't blame him, the way he's questioning this. I haven't met up with a friend on the weekend in, oh, all the time I've been staying with him.

"Yes, here, Lydia, say hi to my uncle." I hold the phone up in her direction.

She looks at me like I'm out of my mind, but after a beat she calls, "Hi, Kennedy's uncle."

This must appease him, as he doesn't seem to know what to say. Finally, he relents. "Okay, we're leaving in an hour. Do you need me to pick you up?"

I cringe, imagining him driving by this house on the way to Lydia's address. I don't want to draw any attention to the fact that I bike over this way on a consistent basis. "No," I say. "I'm not far. I'll be back soon."

When I hang up, Lydia returns to typing. She doesn't ask any questions. "So . . . I have to go," I say.

She stops, spinning the chair around, with that pen in her mouth again. She takes the pen from between her teeth, twirling it in her fingers, and seems to choose her next words carefully. "I can stay here, see what I can find. As long as you don't mind."

"Yes," I say, so grateful that I can feel my face pulling into an almost-smile. "Thanks. Okay, call me if you find anything?"

She waves a hand, but she's already turned away, focusing on the screen again.

As I walk my bike back around the side of the house to the driveway, I freeze. There's a car in the drive. It's old, and blue. It must be a Realtor checking out the house before a showing. I mentally kick myself, knowing I didn't lock the front door on my way out. I imagine whoever's in there fixing the paintings, making a phone call. *The door was unlocked. It looks like someone's been in here again.*

Moving as silently as I can, I make my way to the car, whose back window is covered in a layer of dust. I think about dragging my finger through the dust, leaving a message. Maybe *Boo* or *Help* or *SOS*. No. Maybe *Get out. Run.*

I wrinkle my nose. It all feels too cheap. I worry I'm losing my edge.

8

NOLAN

Mission failure.

I don't know what exactly I'm doing in the house, what I expected to find. A connection, maybe. A sign. I'm looking for proof that the world is more than it seems. I'm looking for the reason my device freaks out near Liam's room, even when there's no electricity running through the house.

I need to turn off the electricity here in the Jones House, like I did at home. But after a quick search of the downstairs, peeking my head into each of the bedrooms, I can't find the electrical box, and there doesn't seem to be a basement.

Best guess, it's out in the garage. If there is a garage. There doesn't seem to be a door leading to one, though, so I decide to check outside.

From the back window, two structures are visible: the first, nearby, is a stand-alone double garage, with windows. Beyond that is some sort of horse stable or something. I take the side door through the kitchen, walking down the small wooden steps, which look like they were added on recently, or replaced. A cicada cries from the nearby trees, setting off a whole colony of them, until it sounds like they're screaming. My hands are shaking, and I keep thinking this is some sort of sign, some warning, and I should turn around and get the hell back to my car.

If it were nighttime, I probably would.

The garage has a double door that appears automated, with no handle on the outside, but there are several windows along the side. Peering in, I don't see any cars or boxes or anything. Just packed dirt, and beyond, a fuse box set into the wall. Bingo.

The windows don't open, but the door around back does—thankfully unlocked, as there's nothing of value inside. Inside smells like exhaust and gasoline, as if there was once a car in here. But now there's only the ghost of it left behind.

There's some sort of master switch below the fuse box, a red lever, and I pull it to the side. But as I do, the lights brighten for a second, as if there's a sudden surge of electricity instead of a cutoff. Like the light in the hallway, too bright, buzzing. And then everything goes dead.

I head back into the house to take a few quick readings, but it's all more of the same. Three bedrooms and a dark staircase. There's nothing here.

Nothing like in Liam's room. Nothing that makes me believe there's any sort of remainder here—some energy, or just *something* left behind.

I don't go upstairs, though. I don't set foot on that

staircase. It feels like a line I am not meant to cross. The back of my neck prickles, like someone's watching.

I quickly return to the garage and flip the master switch on again. Then I make sure to lock the side door and do my best to leave no trace of myself inside the house before exiting through the front door.

But when I'm halfway down the porch steps, the sun catches off the metal of my car, and I halt. Something's wrong. I walk closer, holding my breath.

The rear window of my car is covered in handprints. Like someone was trapped in the backseat, trying to escape. I imagine their face pressed up against the window.

A shiver runs through me, and I picture, for a moment, Liam.

I picture, in another moment, Abby.

I run my finger through the dust, streaking through the handprints, and see that they were left on the outside, by a real person. Still, it gives me the creeps.

I take the edge of my sleeve and run it across the window, erasing them.

Someone's been here. Or someone's *still* here. I'm not alone, and I'm the one who's not supposed to be here. I quickly slide into the front seat, locking the doors behind me. Then I check the time on my phone, to make sure I'm home in time to cover for my dad.

There's a missed call and a voice mail from an unknown number. I start the car, the air conditioner choking out gasps of cold air, and I keep peering in the rearview mirror to make sure no one is about to sneak up on me, telling me to get out of here.

I play the voice mail, but there's nothing there. No, that's not true—there's *something*, I just can't hear it well. Turning up the volume, I listen again. Just static. Nothing more.

I call home, just to check. My parents have already lost one child, and in case it was one of them trying to reach me, stuck with some bad connection, I'd hate to make them worry.

"Nolan?" My dad picks up so quickly I assume it was him.

"Hey, did you call me?"

"No." He drops his voice. "It must've been your mother. Abby's here, Nolan. With her parents."

I'm squinting out the windshield toward the woods, trying to figure out what Abby and her parents have to do with anything. If maybe he had to call them to cover for him on the phones because I got the time wrong.

"I thought I had until the afternoon," I say.

There's this pause, where I think I can hear something else. Almost like static, cutting in and out. Until he speaks again. "You need to come home, Nolan."

Nobody notices at first when I walk in the front door. Dave and Sara or Clara, the college kids who were here to volunteer, appear to be gone. Abby is wedged between her parents on our family room sofa, the three of them sinking together almost comically. My mom is in the chair across from her, and my father stands behind her, his hand on her shoulder. There's a stillness here that seems heavy. I've seen it before. After the chaos, after the search of the woods and the search of his room and the police interviews, after everyone left, and we were all alone, facing the facts.

Abby sees me first. "Nolan," she says, and my parents turn around. This may be the first time she's spoken to me since the *incident in the car.* Abby's always been thin, but college seems to have sharpened her edges. Or maybe it's just me that's changed. I can't look at her without feeling my stomach knot.

"Nolan," my dad says. "Come sit."

But I don't. I stay exactly where I am, one foot out the door. "What's going on?" I say.

My dad reaches an arm for me, like he's trying to compel me closer.

"Dad?"

He shakes his head. "We don't know," he says. "Abby got an email, and we've just called Agent Lowell—"

"What?" I say, because none of this is making sense.

It's Abby who speaks this time. "I got an email," she says. "Last week. It said, *I know what happened to your boyfriend,* and—"

"You've got to be kidding me." I swing the door shut behind me then, cutting her off. Making her jump. Firmly in this house now, I shake my head at her. Oh my God, the whole case is going to happen again, over a stupid email. "It's probably a joke," I say.

Her mother is holding her hand. They are mirror images, staring at me.

"Why would someone joke about that?" my dad says.

"Have you *met* the Internet?" I ask, walking closer. I know they understand. The number of tips that come in that are useless. More than that, that are careless.

I narrow my eyes at Abby. "Which email address?" I ask her.

Her wavy blond hair hangs partly over her face, and she peers up from behind it, her eyes watering. "My college one."

"Who would have your new college email, from something that happened two years ago?" And why would someone contact her, instead of me? Instead of my parents? The police?

"It wouldn't be hard to find it," she shoots back. "You can search for it on the campus website."

"Dad," I say, trying to appeal to him, but his eyes have this hyperfocused look I know too well. And my mom hasn't moved since I walked through the door. I feel sick. It's happening again, and I can't stop it.

"Abby, enough," I say, turning away from her and waving my arm at my parents. "Can't you both see this is for attention? She was the grieving widow and everyone felt bad for her here, only she's not here anymore, and now she's no one."

"*Nolan,*" my dad almost yells. My dad doesn't yell. But this comes close.

Abby sucks in a quick breath. "You are so cruel," she whispers.

Maybe that's true, but someone had to say it. I was doing them all a favor.

I storm up the steps to my room. There is no reasonable explanation for my brother's disappearance. That line has been exhausted. All she's doing is cracking everything open again. God, does she not even *notice* the downstairs of my house?

I'm full of adrenaline, pacing my room. I need to do

something. Emptying my bag, I hold the device up to Liam's wall, but nothing happens.

The signal is gone.

It's just . . . gone.

I walk into his room—still nothing. I hit the side of the device, jarring the needle, and try again. Nothing. I start to worry I imagined the whole thing. That I conjured it into existence, from my imagination.

Hands shaking, I pull up the video I took earlier in the day, just to make sure it exists, that it happened.

As it replays, I let out a breath of relief—it's exactly how I remembered it. The spike, the pause, over and over, in a pattern.

Then I hit Reply on KJ's message and upload the video.

I write: Something's happening here.

9

KENNEDY

The room we're sitting in could use a makeover. There's a table with plastic chairs like from a school, where Joe and I sit on one side and a man with brown-gray hair wearing wire-rim glasses and a brown suit jacket sits on the other. His tie is crooked, off-center and twisted, and I keep getting the urge to reach across the table and fix it for him. He introduced himself with a couple of letters, followed by what was obviously a last name, but I missed it.

There are no pictures on the walls. But the paint is fading in sections, like something must've hung there once.

"Thanks for coming in today," Crooked Tie says, drawing my focus from the lack of décor to the state of the tabletop (old, worn, in need of a polish). "Kennedy, you've probably heard that we've been preparing for the upcoming trial."

There's this crack running through the surface of the table in front of me, dips and valleys, and I trace my nail through it.

"Kennedy?" Joe says, and then he sighs. "Yes, she knows."

"Okay." Crooked Tie stacks a pile of papers on the table. For a moment, I think the crack in this table must come from him, from doing this day after day. He lays the papers in front of him so I can see a few notes in scribble, in his own handwriting.

"Today we're just going to walk through how the questions will go. It's nothing you're not expecting. It's basically everything you've already said."

I see the shadow house again for a moment, and then it's gone. Replaced by fresh paint, fresh carpet.

"Then why do you need me to repeat it?" I ask.

Joe sighs again, but the other man smiles.

"Kennedy, the timing is important," he explains. "*You* are important."

"The police have my statement," I say.

"Yes, they do," he says, nodding. He looks down at the papers, readjusting his glasses. "So let's go over the statement. Can you tell us, once more, where you were on the night of December third and the early morning of December fourth?"

I sigh. "I was at Marco's house."

"Marco Saliano," he says, as if correcting me, or asking.

Then I realize he's waiting for me. "Marco Saliano. Yeah," I say.

"Great," he says, making a check mark, like I've just given the correct answer on a pop quiz. "And would that be Marco Saliano at Fifteen Vail Road?"

"Yes." At least, I was pretty sure that was his address. Since I cut through the fields to meet up with him there, I never really noticed the street signs. I described his house to the police as *third on the right from the fields.*

Another check mark. "Okay, so, on the early morning of December fourth, you left your boyfriend Marco Saliano's house, located at Fifteen Vail Road, sometime after one a.m."

He pauses, looks up at me, raises his eyebrows.

Apparently, that was a question. "Oh, I guess. I don't know."

He frowns, then looks at the paper. "That's what you said."

"Exactly, that's what I'm trying to tell you. You have the statement. The person who made it remembers more than I do by now."

He blinks slowly, his eyes looking unnaturally large behind his glasses. The pen hovers over the paper. He doesn't make a mark. "You're the same person."

I mentally roll my eyes. "I know."

He's getting frustrated, and Joe is fidgeting beside me.

"We need you to confirm it, Kennedy. The timing. On the stand. It's important. You have to confirm it."

"I'm sure I meant it back when I said it—isn't that good enough? I can't exactly remember *now.* It was over six months ago." Just barely. Almost six months, to the day. "Do *you* remember what time you got home six months ago?"

He sighs and twists in his chair, leaning for his briefcase, and I'm momentarily hopeful that this interview is over. But it turns out he was only rummaging through his bag, because he pulls out a small recording device.

"What's this?" Joe asks, sitting straighter.

Joe seems to understand something I don't, and a sliver of panic works its way through me, from his body language.

Crooked Tie presses a small button with a thick finger. "Sometimes this helps, to listen. To remember," he says, not looking directly at either of us.

Joe holds out a hand as if to stop him, but it just hovers there, unsure.

A small, robotic voice speaks first, in stilted syllables: *December fourth. One-eighteen a.m.*

I sit straight, my shoulders rigid. And then Joe's hand comes down over the device, hitting the button. "Is this really necessary?"

I'm not breathing. There's not enough oxygen in the room.

Crooked Tie frowns at both of us. "If she can't remember, then yes, it is."

He presses the button again, and this time, Joe doesn't stop it. Suddenly it's a woman's voice and not a robot. "Nine-one-one, what's your emergency?"

The room is silent except for the sound of breathing on the tape. Until suddenly, it's my voice, filling the room. "Something happened. Something terrible."

And I'm there again, at the shadow house—

"Ma'am? Can you tell me your name and location?"

More breathing, until I speak again, ignoring her question. "Something happened in the hallway . . ."

"Miss? Are you in immediate danger?"

"He's gone. I saw him. He's gone."

"Stay on the line. We've got officers out to your location right now."

Suddenly, the sound of Joe's chair scratching against the floor cuts through the static of the recording as we wait for someone to speak. The wait is infinite, then and now.

Eventually, the doorbell will ring, and the woman on the line will instruct me to open the front door. I won't look as I follow her orders.

Joe hits the button again, and the room falls to silence.

"You know what," Joe says, "I don't think now's the best time after all. Why don't you wait for me in the hall while we finish up here, Kenny." Which is something he called me when I was much younger. Much, much younger.

Still, I take the gift I am presented with. He gives me a few dollars, tells me to get myself something from the vending machine we saw on the way in, and to get him a soda, too. *Something with caffeine, for the love of all that is holy,* is what he actually says.

The door shuts behind me, and the hall feels over-exposed, fluorescent-lit.

A man in uniform passes by and nods in my direction. I trail my fingers against the grooves in the wall as I make my way back to the vending machine at the entrance, near the double front doors.

I stare at the options. Paper and aluminum and chemicals. My reflection in the glass. The buzzing of the light inside. Another crack in the glass at the upper right-hand corner. I get two Cokes, and I wait outside.

• • •

"So," Joe begins, when we're in the car, on the highway. My soda is beside his in the cup holder, and at this point I've forgotten which one is mine.

"He's sort of obtuse," I say, peeling the visitor label from my shirt. It's got my name, a time stamp, a grainy black-and-white picture with only the top half of my face in the frame, taken at the front desk. I look like a ghost.

"Kennedy, he's on your side."

"I didn't know I had a side." I shove the crumpled label into my pocket. "If they have the nine-one-one recording, they don't really need me to remember."

He sighs, just faintly, and I assume that's the end of it. Until he adds, "You're the only witness, Kennedy."

I don't understand how that's possible, standing as I was underneath a dark sky, full of a thousand stars. But that's what they keep telling me. The night hid us from sight. The storm concealed the noise.

Joe reaches an arm across the console, but I look out the window and he picks up one of the Cokes instead. There's a white line zigzagging across the sky, the trail of an airplane.

But I'm starting to think there's a crack running through the whole universe and I'm the only one who sees it.

Lydia hasn't texted or called by the time we arrive back at Joe's, so I log on to the computer to see if I have any more messages about my question on the forum.

But the only thing in my inbox is a message from Visitor357. There's also a video attachment, which I immediately open.

The camera is trained on the dial of some device pressed

up against a blue wall, and I watch as the dial dives below zero, back to neutral, over and over. You can't see what's out of frame, and I know anything could be causing this. *This guy* could be causing this. *Faking* this. But I watch it again. And again and again. I pull up my own readout from the radio telescope on the computer screen, and I set it to run in real time. The two images are side by side; I've stopped breathing.

Spike. Pause. Spike. Pause.

They line up completely.

I was wrong. There's *not* something wrong with the computer program, or the satellite dish.

I lean closer to the screen, goose bumps rising across my arms.

I think: *The timing is important.*

10

NOLAN

Nobody remembers dinner. Nobody remembers that this investigation has *already happened* and an email isn't going to change the outcome of that, either. They move as if time is still on our side, two years after the last shred of evidence led us nowhere. As if there's still some piece of Liam left, and it's been hidden away inside an anonymous email all along, and it's going to slip from their grasp if they don't all migrate over to Abby's house at warp speed to inspect this new piece of evidence ASAP.

When Mike showed up, at three o'clock, as promised, he was quickly sent away.

"What's happening?" he asked me, surveying the scene.

"Nothing. They've lost their minds."

Mike patted my shoulder, and I knew he understood. The first months after Liam disappeared, the house was filled with Liam's teachers, his coaches, his friends. When they dropped off, one by one, Mike pulled on the volunteers from the shelter where Liam had previously worked with him.

The reason Mike joined the call for help was because his sister disappeared when he was a kid, never to be seen again. Not like the other volunteers who come and go, drawn to the unsolved mystery, or fueled by the guilt that it could've been one of their loved ones instead, or, like Dave and Clara/Sara and the rest of the college interns, needing the hours for school.

Mike has spent his whole life searching, too. Something that's painful to think about, considering the salt-and-pepper hair covering his head, and the gray scruff of his beard. Eventually his search for the lost led him to dedicate his time to the ones he can still help.

Now, suddenly, no one cares about the phones anymore. They keep ringing downstairs, and instead of turning the lines to silent, I leave them be. I keep hoping they'll jar my parents back to reality, pulling them back home.

I'm watching out the window when the police car shows up next door, and my mom gestures for them to follow her inside the house that is not hers. I'm watching as my father paces on the sidewalk, his voice carrying, as I imagine Agent Lowell on the other side.

I feel this urge to just *go*, and if I were any other kid, in any other family, I would. I would throw this gear into a bag, pack a change of clothes or two, take this car, and leave, and no one would even notice. Until much later. And that's what has me stuck.

I remember my mom's face as I shouted Liam's name into the trees. When I called for Colby, straining to hear the sound of his bark in the distance. When the humor turned to annoyance turned to panic. And then later, when the panic turned to something else, this look of hard resignation that's become her new permanent existence. I don't even notice it anymore, usually. I only notice now because it's gone. In its place is something else. Something worse.

Hope.

I don't know what will happen to her next, what sort of place she'll end up in, when that gets crushed, too.

The house is empty and silent, and for once, I'm alone here. This place is usually the hub of activity. It may seem odd, but it's still possible, maybe even more so, to feel invisible with so many people around.

It's only now, when it's empty, that I wonder if something has been in Liam's old room all along. If only I'd been listening for it.

I place my hands against the blue wall dividing our rooms, then feel ridiculous. Wondering what I expected to feel—some beat, some pattern, moving through the walls? Some surge of electricity? As if that pattern were some sign that there was a shift in the universe, in what we believed possible, and it was finally within reach.

My steps echo on the hardwood as I walk from my room out into the empty hall, extending in both directions, unlit. My parents' door is across the hall, closed. Liam's room is beside mine, door also closed. Usually, when I leave my room, I close mine out of solidarity. Like part of a set.

The knob on the door of Liam's room feels cold. Has it always been that way? I suddenly can't remember. I was never focused on the little, odd details that were here.

Only on what was missing. As I open the door wide, some things remain the same: the squeak of the hinges as the door swings open; the moss-green paint, the brown comforter, the blanket for Colby at the foot of the bed, the layout of Liam's furniture. But in other ways, the room has been stripped bare. The electronics are now mine. Even the scent is gone. Liam hasn't touched anything here in over two years.

And yet.

As I take a step inside the room, none of those facts matter. I hold the device in my hand once more, but still, nothing happens. I can feel the ghost of the movement in my palm, the way it felt the first time. The mechanism inside the device, the needle moving, like a pulse.

I close my eyes, breathe in, feel a chill. Something was here. It might be gone now, but I'm sure of it: something was *here.*

"Liam?" I say. The word lingers in the silence.

Something buzzes in my back pocket and I jump, my heart suddenly pounding in my head. I back out of the room, fish my phone from the pocket of my jeans. It's an email notification letting me know I've received a new message from the forum.

I drop my gear inside my room, slam my door, and scroll through the message.

There's a video attached, only this one isn't mine—it's not the one I sent, nothing like it at all. I don't know what I'm looking at. It looks like one of those hospital heart rate monitors you see on TV. Maybe in real life, too, but I wouldn't know.

The message from KJ explains that this is coming from a radio telescope, a satellite dish pointed at some sector in space, none of which means anything to me. The note ends:

```
Count the time. This is what the
pattern from my signal looks like
if you let it run. It lines up with
yours.
```

I do as the note says. I count the time. A spike. The pause. A spike. They move in synchrony, the same pattern, the same time.

The note continues:

```
Tell me everything about this event.
Where it originates, date and time,
location coordinates, etc, etc.
```

And the sign-off:

```
I think we have something here.
```

From this note I gather that KJ is bossy; KJ is overly excited; KJ and I are not going to be on the same page with this, with all these questions, *etc, etc.* Who says *etc?* Professors. Teachers. Random people on SETI message boards with satellite dishes pointed into space.

We're not looking for the same thing here. The answer to me is obvious, and simple. If (a) my brother disappeared with no earthly explanation; and (b) this signal was coming from my brother's room; then (c) whatever's happening here is related. If not exactly proof, it's definitely a sign. Even if I don't understand what it means yet.

KJ wants a list of facts and figures. This house is already full of facts. It's full of statistics, and documentation, height and weight, hair color, eye color, *etc, etc.* Everything about my life is Liam *etc.*

None of it brings anyone back.

```
Tell me everything about this event.
```

Well, okay. I hit Reply. Here's everything:

```
My brother disappeared. This was
coming from his room.
```

These are the only details that matter.

I hear a car door, the bustle of activity outside Abby's house, and I know they're looking in all the wrong places.

Screw it, I think, grabbing my bag, just like I planned. I'll leave a note. Tell them I'll be back. And I'll bring my phone.

Downstairs, a gust of air funnels through the open space. Someone left the front door ajar, and the photos ripple with the breeze. All those faces, smiling at me.

I back out the front door, giving them one long look— because I should, because I never do. Turning around, I collide with something hard and immobile. Hands reach out for my shoulders, and I face forward, looking straight into the familiar ice-blue eyes of Agent Lowell. I used to have to look up to see him. I used to find his downward gaze intimidating. I don't anymore.

Now I'm just pissed that he's here at all, catering to the whim of a girl looking for attention. He's still holding me by the shoulders. "Wow, you've really grown these last two years." Then he notices the bag on my shoulder. "Where are you going, Nolan?"

11

KENNEDY

I need to get back to the house, to the radio telescope, and pull the rest of the data. To figure out where the telescope is aiming, and to see if it's still happening, because now I realize *it's not a mistake.* Two incidents make a pattern. Make this an *event that is happening.*

Lydia still isn't picking up the phone. I send her a text, asking if she's still at my place. But the message just sits there on my phone, staring back at me. I wonder if maybe she's like Elliot, who would get lost in his work, the rest of the world falling away.

I hear Joe talking on his phone through the thin walls between our rooms. He's just there, on the other side, but it's still too far to hear clearly. But I can tell from the rise and fall of his voice that he's agitated, and I'm guessing he's agitated by me. Or the whole situation.

Well, join the club. I'm on edge, made claustrophobic by the generic walls of this room that isn't mine, and the half-unpacked boxes taking up floor space, and how every day we talk about these little trivial things to fill the silence (breakfast, what's on television, the rising temperature)— when there's a whole universe out there, waiting to be uncovered.

And now I believe there's something out there. Something reaching back.

By the time Joe comes out of his room, I've wracked my brain for excuses. But I don't need one, because it seems he's been trying to come up with his own. "I need to head to campus for a couple hours," he says, running his hand through his hair. He's not even looking at me.

"Okay," I say. I hope he's meeting up with friends. Or a girl. Maybe lunch, or a movie, where he doesn't have to think about being responsible for a sixteen-year-old who's supposed to testify at a trial next week.

I don't even wait for his car to turn the corner down the street before pulling my bike out of the garage.

I'm sort of a mess by the time I make it to my house, but at least I realize that. The heat is still strong, but the sun is hovering lower, turning the sky over the trees a glowing amber.

When I steer my bike into the dirt drive, the dust clings to the sweat on the back of my legs. My backpack clings to my T-shirt, which clings to my skin, and a cloud of dirt hovers in my wake.

I hop off the bike at the side of the house and leave it resting against the porch as I jog toward the shed around back. As I approach, I can see that the door is slightly ajar. I don't want to spook her, so I say, "It's me, I'm back," but no one answers from the darkness behind the door.

"Lydia?" I call as I push the shed door all the way open, the creak cutting through the silence. There's no one here. The box is still on the ground, half of Elliot's things strewn around the floor and covering the desk. The computer monitor is on, and the chair is just faintly crooked, like Lydia was here just a moment ago and took off midthought.

I poke my head out the door and call her name into the fields. Her name echoes through the open space, but I don't hear anyone call back.

Dinnertime, I think. But the way she's left everything, the way the door is still open, sends a chill up my spine. I shake it off, then insert the flash drive into the computer and pull the rest of the data, all of it, from the last time I was here.

There are open notebooks around the desk, with Elliot's instructions, or diagrams, or notes on the results. I wonder if maybe she's left me a note, so I scan the papers on the surface. There's a pad of paper to my right with nothing on it but a number. I pull it across the desk, closer to the computer, and look again.

12/4

No, I realize, it's not a number. It's a date. I can't tell whether Elliot once wrote it down, or if this is Lydia. If it was written *before* or *after*. Only that this is the date that divides the before and after, that divides my life; that splits the universe straight in half. 12/4. December fourth.

As if everything is connected. Before. After. Here. There. As if this was meant for me to find.

. . .

I've been pacing the short length of the shed with the phone pressed to my ear. She hasn't answered my calls, or my texts, and she's gone. My head fills, suddenly, with a thousand different possibilities. Lydia scatters in my mind, existing both nowhere and everywhere. Like I'm scanning the universe for her, and she's always there, at the edge of my vision, but fades from view each time I look head-on.

The possibilities are endless: *taken; disappeared; ran away.* I wonder if I should call someone, or whether I'm overreacting. I picture her simultaneously at home, at Sutton's, in the woods, fading into a void . . .

I step outside into the late-afternoon sun, ready to make my way to her house, to check on her, when I suddenly see her walking in the distance, on the other side of the fence with Marco.

My immediate relief is replaced by aggravation that now Marco will be involved.

They're deep in conversation, Lydia moving her hands, gesturing to the house. To me.

I wave, but no one seems to notice at first. Marco climbs over the fence, and Lydia ducks underneath, between rails. They slow when they're within earshot. "Oh, look," Lydia says, her voice dripping with sarcasm, "she's here." She places her hands on her hips.

Okay, then. "I've been calling you."

She shakes her head, her high ponytail swaying, and strides across the empty space between us, Marco lagging a few paces behind. "What, so you can spook me again? No thanks, Kennedy, I'll pass. I'm just here for my phone." She holds out her hand, palm up.

"Your what?"

"My *phone*." She wrinkles her nose, and it makes her look younger, more vulnerable. "I left it behind when . . ." She shakes her head. "Come on, I know it was you."

"*What* was me?"

Lydia widens her eyes at Marco, clearly exasperated, as if this is his part, his line, which he's forgotten.

Marco clears his throat. "Kennedy," he says, but he's not even looking at me. Marco's expression is far-off, like he'd give anything to be somewhere else, not having to pick sides, navigate the complexities between his best friend and his ex-girlfriend. "Look, we know you do that." He lifts his chin toward the house. "Move things around, try to freak people out." He cringes when he says it, still not looking at me straight-on.

I narrow my eyes at his face, but he doesn't notice. I mean, yes, I do those things, but I still have no idea what this has to do with this moment, and Lydia's phone. I also had no idea they knew about it. I wonder if they're out here more often than I realize.

"Seriously," Lydia begins, emboldened by Marco at her side, *on* her side. "There's something wrong with you, even bef—"

She cuts herself off.

Before. My body language suddenly mirrors Lydia's. Hands on hips; self-righteous anger. A sting of bitterness. "Yeah, I remember. I've heard you refer to me as Child of the Corn, Lydia. Even *before*."

She cringes and shakes her head, like even she realizes she's gone a step too far. Which she has. Still, there's something I like about it, how she doesn't tiptoe around the things she thinks she shouldn't say. She lowers her voice. "You just appear sometimes, from nowhere. You make no sound. It's freaky."

I look to Marco, who stares at the side of Lydia's face, like he can't believe she's saying this.

She shrugs and continues. "Sometimes I would forget you were there. I'd be talking to Sutton and Marco, and then *boom*, there you were, standing in the corner."

I can feel my voice rising, the anger shaking loose. "So, basically, I freak you out because you *forget I exist?*"

"Well, this is a little different. This is . . ." She moves her hands, searching for the word. "Intentional."

"Kennedy," Marco says, like he's suddenly the voice of reason, "we're sorry, okay?"

Lydia puts her hands out, as if to calm me, to rationalize. "If this is to get back at me and Sutton and Marco for hanging out on your property, I get the picture. We won't do it again. Okay? But this is seriously messed up."

"I have *no* idea what you guys are talking about. I just got back."

Marco gazes at me from the corner of his eye. "You weren't in the house?"

"No." I fish my visitor badge from the meeting out of my pocket, try to flatten it out so she can see my picture, my name, the time stamp. "See? I was . . . here."

Lydia stares at the crumpled paper, her jaw still set. "Well, *someone* was here," she whispers, her eyes widening. Like maybe it's a ghost, who's eavesdropping even now. She steps back, staring at the house.

"Oh," I say, "the Realtors have been in and out. I saw a car before I left. I should've mentioned it. But I have every right to be here. I still own the house. They can't kick us out." Then I imagine being her, alone at *the Jones House*, and hearing someone else. "I'm sorry I didn't mention it," I mumble. But I don't get it, what she thinks I did with her phone.

"I thought it was you."

"Thought *what* was me?"

"The lights. They all went on. Every one of them. In the shed, in the house, like it was brighter than they should've been." She shakes her head. "And then everything shut down." She looks to the shed. "Everything."

Realtors, electric company, grid overload—there are a hundred possible causes. We live in an old farmhouse, after all. But she's staring at the shed like she believes it's haunted. I've lost her. "So where's your phone?"

She drags her eyes slowly from the shed back to me. "When everything came back online, just for a second, I swear I heard your voice through the headphones."

"The headphones?"

"Through the audio output? I had just plugged them in, hadn't done anything with it. Anyway, I just got the hell out in a hurry. Sorry, I feel ridiculous now."

But she doesn't step any closer, and her apology feels more for her own benefit, like she's talking herself out of something, calming her nerves.

"Seriously," I say, rolling my eyes. I enter the shed, move notebooks around the desk until I find her phone, facedown and silenced, in a pink-and-gold case. I pick it up, see my missed texts, my missed calls. I bring it out to her, and she mumbles her thanks, grabbing Marco by the sleeve, turning to go.

"Wait. Lydia. The date," I say. "Did you write it?"

They both stop, looking back over their shoulders. "What date?" Lydia asks.

"The numbers. On the pad of paper."

"Oh yes. I wrote that down right before the lights thing happened . . . and then . . ." And then she took off, spooked. "Look, that's all I can tell you. Whatever's running on that thing"—she points to the shed—"it originated December fourth. That's as far as I got."

"December fourth. You're sure."

She makes a face, like she's insulted I'd doubt her. "I'm sure."

Neither of them remembers. The date is just one more in a string of numbers. The crack that runs straight through my life: *12/4, 12/4, 12/4 . . .*

"Well," Lydia says, waving awkwardly toward me, toward the house. She turns on her heel, and Marco gives me some self-deprecating grin that I can no longer decipher, and it's like he's summing up our entire relationship with this one expression. I watch them go. I'm still not sure whether she believes me, but either way, I know she won't be coming back.

I duck inside the shed again to escape from the heat, sitting inside with the overhead fan, the computer humming. I stare again at the numbers Lydia has written on the pad of paper, as if they will tell me something more. The date repeats in my head, over and over, until it's all I can think. I close my eyes and see a flicker of the shadow house. Then I picture Elliot sitting in this very spot, maybe earlier in the night, fingers flying over the keyboard, with his headphones on. Music blaring and him humming along—

And then the scene splits and I see him in the shadow house instead, and I squeeze my eyes shut, until all I can really see are the spots behind my eyelids.

Alone in the shed, I take out my phone to log on to the forum to see if Visitor357 has responded to my request for more information, to see if I can piece together some explanation that makes sense. When a new message notification from Visitor357 comes up, I sit straighter, hyperfocused.

But he's responded to my request for more information with two short lines. His brother has disappeared. And that signal is coming from his room. That's it. That's all it says.

My heart sinks, because it's not the right direction, but also because I understand, suddenly, why the equipment. Why he's the ghost-hunting type.

I swivel back and forth in the chair, the noise cutting through the empty room.

Through the window, I watch as Marco and Lydia climb over the fence, one after the other, back to their neighborhood. I hit Reply.

> The person looking into this event for
> me disappeared, but it was just for a
> moment. But for that moment, I felt
> it. It was like anything was suddenly
> possible, almost like I was on the

edge of understanding something. Of
course, she came back, and it's not
the same. I guess what I'm saying is,
I think I know how the universe looks
to you right now. The not knowing,
where everything and anything is
possible. Even if it was just for a
moment.

Then I take the flash drive back to Joe's, with all the new data, to see if the signal is still coming through.

I don't think this guy is going to look at this the same way. He's looking for something else—something that isn't there. But after his last message, I don't have the heart to tell him.

And I don't have a way to explain what I've just started thinking. That this date means more than a random potential contact coming from somewhere in the vastness of space. That it was a signal meant for me to receive.

Like maybe whatever I'm receiving right now is not just a message, but a warning. And it's taken me this long to notice.

12

NOLAN

Agent Lowell has always seemed overly interested in my story of Liam's disappearance. It was a mistake, telling him anything when he came on board the case. But at the time, I still thought honesty could help. Unlike the others, Agent Lowell wasn't interested in the fact that Liam was wearing a maroon shirt, or that Colby had a brown-and-white coat but a tail that was solid brown—little details I gave while others nodded along in support. It had felt like we were all on the same side, until Agent Lowell.

Why did you start to panic, Nolan? He'd only been gone a handful of minutes.

I told him it was a feeling; I told him about the dream. He became convinced I knew more than I was saying. I had overheard another agent, months later, saying I had given a suspicious statement. I didn't know whether that meant *I* was suspicious, or that the statement itself wasn't particularly trustworthy, but I stopped talking after that. Kept my feelings and thoughts to myself. Kept a good distance from the actual investigation.

Now, standing eye to eye with Agent Lowell, I see he hasn't dropped this perception of me. But I no longer feel intimidated by his gaze. I've been through it. Straight through. An entire investigation, your whole world ripped apart, while you stand there, begging them to do it.

Abby says you're close—

What can you tell us about your brother—

How did you feel about him?

Offering up your belongings, and his, to try to track him down. Turning over your phones, your computers, your entire privacy, in the hopes of eventually finding him. Closing your eyes and imagining the sound of his music on the other side of the wall, the shake of a collar out in the hallway— imagining that everything would eventually lead us back to this.

"I'm going out," I tell Agent Lowell now, knowing better than to get involved once more. "If my parents are looking for me, tell them I'm not interested in wasting time with this."

He raises an eyebrow. "You think this—an email claiming to know what happened—is a waste of time? Why would that be, Nolan?"

Because the only explanation for what happened to my brother is that he was taken by something we can't understand. That something pulled him, against his will. Some crack in reality, and my brother slipped through.

When Liam first disappeared, the number one theory, in the absence of any sign of foul play, was that he had run away. There were several points in favor of this theory. He volunteered at a shelter that was rumored to be frequented by teen runaways—he would know what to do, how to do it. It's one thing to take a person, the police said. It's another to take a person and a dog. Same goes for accidental injury or death—both Liam *and* the dog? A tougher thing to explain, though my dad insisted that Colby wouldn't have left Liam's side if he'd been hurt.

My parents asked Mike if he agreed with the runaway theory—he said that at first he didn't think Liam was the type, but what he had learned was that there *wasn't* really a type.

So everyone agreed: Liam and the dog both disappearing was a sign.

This gave my parents a shred of hope, even though it was a ridiculous idea. Liam Chandler, running away.

He had the girlfriend. The social status. The college scouts. The future. And all the searching through his life turned up nothing—no reason, no explanation.

I could've told them that from the start. Actually, I *did* tell them that. I'd spent the previous year hearing Abby in his bedroom through the wall, watching his friends taking over the house, staring down the shelves of his trophies and awards.

Liam Chandler running away? No. Not possible. There was the dream, the feeling, and then he was gone. Never to be heard from again.

But there were sightings. Two hundred and nine the first week (a kid hitchhiking in Florida; another filling up a gas tank in Ohio with a dog in the backseat; one buying a lottery ticket in Maryland), followed by 330 the second week. Calls from people who meant well, and those who didn't. No leads panned out. Nothing real, anyway. The sightings picked up, spread across the country like his image was contagious, then shrank back in, slowly but surely collapsing on themselves. Like he was fading, just as we were reaching for him.

I saw him once myself, over a year later, when the investigation had slid to a halt. This past winter. I'd had the flu, and he appeared to me in the middle of a fever dream. I had been half-sleeping—that type of semiconscious state when you're sick, where you dream, but you're always right there, on the cusp of waking. I was curled up on the couch, blanket tucked around me, medicine on the table, half-dreaming of his voice, speaking to me. Then I opened my eyes and he was *right there.* Standing across the living room, in the same clothes he wore the day he disappeared: jeans, long-sleeved maroon shirt, mud-streaked blue sneakers with dirty laces.

Liam, I said, *we've been looking for you.*

It was my father who found me, standing in the middle of the room, in the middle of the night, talking to empty space. Who put a hand on my forehead and dosed me with Motrin and said, *Let's not tell your mother about this.*

But even as my father spoke, shaking me gently, washcloth on the back of my neck, Liam still stood in the corner, in front of the fireplace. His mouth moved, but no sound came out, like there was some boundary he was desperate to breach.

"Listen," I tell Agent Lowell, "knock yourself out. We used to get hundreds of emails a day. Why does one matter now?"

"Because, Nolan, the email included an encrypted attachment. Turns out, it's a picture."

My shoulders tense, and from the quirk of his lips, it seems he enjoyed springing this little piece of information on me. "A picture of *what?*"

"A picture of Liam. Your brother."

"From when?"

"Well," he says, taking a deep breath. "That's what we're about to find out."

I take a step back, so close to being pulled back in; a trap, a lure. A carrot on a stick, until we're back where we started. "Abby has a thousand pictures of Liam, sir. My guess, you're not gonna have to look all that hard."

"You think this is Abby's work, Nolan? That she faked an email to herself? Abby has always cooperated with the investigation." As if implying that I have not. "She seems pretty shook up to me," he adds.

But that was the thing about Abby. Everything shook her. It was just in her expression. Like she was always a step behind, surprised by where she found herself. The last time I'd seen it, she was in the car with me—the moment she realized what she was doing. Like I'd been the one to start it, instead of the other way around.

"Yes, I think this is her doing," I say, but my words have less force, less conviction. And I no longer feel I can leave the house; I feel like there's something holding me, against my will. I go upstairs to my room, leaving the agent to whatever he's doing downstairs. The answers aren't going to come like this, this simply. With a picture of my brother in an anonymous email, after all this time. Not to Abby.

No.

The truth was sent to me. Something has been trying to reach me, and now it's finally pushing through.

I never told my father the other part of the fever dream. The words I could just barely make out, Liam's lips moving too fast to make out the rest. *Help us. Please.*

I bought this equipment the very next morning.

13

KENNEDY

The first thing I notice when I upload the new data is that the signal is no longer there. I mean, it *was*, but eventually the signal went dead, around the time Lydia mentioned the power going out. It's not there after the reboot. I change views, change parameters, hit a thousand different random numbers searching for something more. But all that remains is the expected background noise of the vastness of space, exactly where it's supposed to be—a whole lot of nothing, in an endless expanse of nothingness.

"No," I mumble, something twisting inside. It was *right here*. I stare at the screen, scrolling through the data over and over.

"Kennedy? Can you come out here?" Joe calls, finally back from campus, but I'm not done checking, I keep hoping I'm wrong. It could be showing up somewhere I don't understand, some part of the program I don't know about—

"Hey, did you hear me?" Joe peeks his head into the

room, catching me off guard. "What's that?" he asks as I turn the monitor of the computer black.

"Physics," I say, and Joe nods. Like, of course it's physics. Not: *I think I'm receiving a signal from outer space, but I think it's a warning, and it's coming to my house, which, by the way, I swing by at night sometimes while you're sleeping.*

"Can you take a break for a sec?" He asks this though I've already obviously shut it down. But we're like this with each other, asking, always, before we step.

"Okay." I follow Joe out to the living room, where he sits in the center of the sofa, his arms braced against his legs, leaning forward.

Oh God, we're about to have a talk. This is the demeanor he exhibited when: we went over the ground rules; we discussed our living arrangement; he sat across from me in the hospital, trying to find the words. The police had taken me there, in the ambulance they had no use for otherwise, because they didn't know what else to do with me. I sat there, alone, in a white-walled room, with white sheets, a white curtain, everything shadowed beyond the bed. I have no idea how long I was there, only that, by the time I left with Joe, it was daylight.

He's gotten better at the words. Not so much the demeanor, though.

I perch on the edge of a flannel recliner chair that I'm fairly certain he found at the side of the road somewhere on trash day. And I balance myself carefully on the ledge, leaning forward, so I can take off at any moment, depending on the direction of the conversation.

It's then I see he has a few sheets of papers beside him,

folded into thirds. He spreads them open in front of him, his fingers trembling, like he's prepared to give me some speech. "The district attorney's office," he begins, and I'm already standing.

Here I thought he was out having fun with friends. But he was probably just working his way up to *this*.

He puts the papers aside. "Kennedy, sit down. We're supposed to do this. I promised them."

"Joe, come on."

"The trial starts next week, Kennedy."

"It's not my trial."

I see the muscle in his jaw clenching, but he must've taken up yoga or something, because he takes this deep breath and the muscle finally relaxes. So much different than the early days, when he'd slam a door, grab at his hair, look up at the ceiling, his eyes bone-dry but looking as if he'd been crying. He takes a deep breath. "I told him we'd go over the questions. Just you and me. None of that." He shakes his head, as if the problem were the office, the wooden table, the man, and not the crack running through everything.

"Joe, I know. I know. And we will, I promise. But I can't tonight." I scramble for any excuse, completely desperate. "Lydia asked if I could sleep over. I forgot to check with you, but I told her I'd be there after dinner." I look at my phone. It's definitely after dinner, whether we've eaten or not.

"It's a school night," he says, but his objection is half-hearted already.

"Right. But Lydia goes to my school. We're studying. We *were* studying, earlier, but then I had to leave." I stare directly at him, my eyes watering from not blinking. I've never lied to him so directly. I hold my breath.

"This is important," he reiterates, though I can see he's losing steam. Joe wants me to have friends, to have a social life. To move on. He wants me to do this.

"Tomorrow," I say. "After school. I can do this tomorrow." I gesture to the papers, the couch and chair, whatever this whole thing is.

He nods. "Do you need a ride?"

"No," I say, "she's close enough to take my bike."

"Leave me the address. And a phone number."

"Joe, come on," I say, even though my mother would've said the same. "*I* have my phone." But still, I jot down the address, knowing he won't look it up. Because his mind is already somewhere else. "Go out," I tell him. "Have some fun."

Joe used to be surrounded by an ever-changing stream of girls. I'm not sure if they were girlfriends, but there was typically some girl. I'd met at least three different ones in those first six months when we all lived in the same town. When we moved last year for my mom's new position at the university, my mom said it was because she wanted to keep the small family we had together as much as we could—at first I thought for Joe, since my grandparents died while he was in college; but now I thought it was really for us instead. But I haven't seen any girl—or really, any friend at all—in the six months I've been living with Joe. As if, in solidarity, he's adopted the same ground rules as me. "The house is yours again," I say, gesturing with my arm in a flourish.

He smiles faintly. When he stands, I retreat toward my

room, to get ready to spend the night at my old house, excited that I won't need to sneak out to get there, for once.

When I'm almost at my room, he calls after me. "Kennedy, I miss them, too. I'm on your side. Always."

My throat tightens. "I know," I say, but I'm already closing the door, and I'm not sure if he's heard me.

I need help. I need help from someone who is definitely on my side with this. Joe wouldn't be. Joe thinks he is, but he wants to sell the house, and he wants to go over questions. He wants to sit in the past, dealing with the minutiae of what's left of our lives.

My bag is packed for my fake stay at Lydia's, but I'm not quite ready to go yet.

Visitor357 hasn't responded, probably because I sent some embarrassing message rambling about disappearing people, totally downplaying the fact that his brother is gone. So I send an addendum:

```
      I meant to say, I'm sorry about your
brother.
      But also, I'm sorry, because I
don't think this is related to your
brother.
      I know you're looking for him.
But I think, I think, you've stumbled
upon something else. We're missing
something. Because it's not just your
room. It's also a radio telescope at
```

my house. I hate to ask this. I know
how this will sound. The Internet, I
know, predators, creeps, etc, etc.
But. Locations would help.
    I'm on the 37th parallel, north.

14

NOLAN

Etc, etc.

I was back in my room, locked away, fake-studying, when my phone dinged with a new message. I didn't know what to say to KJ's last message (the feeling, he explained, like you're on the edge of understanding something, even when something is gone, and the not knowing, where everything and anything is possible. Yes, yes. But you can't just write back *Yes, yes*, to some dude on the Internet who's looking for aliens. You can't write back *Something was taken from me, and I keep searching the emptiness, and I think I see something else, not just emptiness, something* else), and I figured that was the end of that. But now there's this new one.

What. The. Hell.

The 37th parallel? As in, latitude and longitude lines? What am I even supposed to do with that?

I pull up a fresh Internet window and search for a latitude and longitude grid. I find a site with an interactive map of the world, crisscrossed with labeled lines. I zoom in, finding the 37 north mark, and trace it across the screen. It bisects the entire country. The entire world. And okay, it's possible I'm on it, too. It cuts straight through Virginia. But it also cuts through California, Asia, Europe. I get that he's trying to let us keep some anonymity, but I don't think this is helping.

We're missing something, he says.

Well, I'll add it to the ever-growing list of things I'm missing right now. Whatever's happening next door, and downstairs. The stack of textbooks on the side of my desk, my untouched math study guide beside the pile.

I stare at the study guide I haven't yet started and probably won't—circles, angles, degrees, equations. Answers that require calculations.

We *are* missing something. We keep focusing on the fact that this is *happening.* But the why isn't always important. Or: the why isn't always understood. That's how I've been approaching my search—not in the hard, scientific facts, but in the unpredictable.

So it's not just that it's happening; it's the signal itself. We've been ignoring that part, but there's definitely a pattern. I pull up the data from KJ's readout, which is much more practical than my own, with raw data. And I start plugging numbers in.

Count the time, KJ said. That's what's the same. The timing. Not the type of signal, not our exact location, but this. The pattern: the spike, the hold.

I'm only seeing a video of his data, so I can't get the

numbers exact, but I can get a rough estimate. And it looks like the spike happens every three seconds.

I wonder now whether the pattern means something.

I look at the math study guide again. A bunch of questions asking me to *Calculate the area*, *Calculate the circumference*. The hairs on the back of my neck stand on end, and my spine straightens.

The geometry of a circle. Pi. It's a universal ratio between the circumference and diameter of any circle: 3.14. The numbers go on and on from there, to infinity. Could it be?

I'm sure there's something more to pi than what I know from Algebra 2, so I look it up online, more convinced than ever.

It's an irrational number, unable to be expressed as a common fraction. Well, this is an irrational event.

It's a transcendental number, whatever that means. But also: this is a transcendental event.

I dump everything into my bag, preparing to go. My hands are shaking as I hit Reply.

I wish I were better at math. I hope KJ is better. I'm sure he is, with a radio telescope pointed at the sky. I'm guessing astronomy requires a lot of math.

I'm hoping he's open to suggestions on this, though, because there is no way this signal in my house is coming from outer space. It's my brother's room. KJ is wrong. It's related, but he's wrong.

My brother trying to tell me something. With the fever dream. With this.

I need to go back to the scene of his disappearance, where he must've slipped through. If this is a clue, this pattern, this pi, I wonder if Liam's trying to tell me something about how he disappeared, or why. If he can't breach the barrier with language, but with math.

I write quickly:

```
I think I know what we're missing.
Like you said, it's the timing. Every
three seconds or so—could it be pi?
3.14, etc, etc. That's some universal
constant, right? For something to do
with circles? Wouldn't it make sense,
if something was trying to speak to us
but they couldn't just speak to us,
they'd do it with math?


PS—Has it occurred to you that maybe
the signal isn't coming from space?
(Could it be something closer? Say,
whatever's in my house?)


PPS—I don't know what the 37th
parallel north is exactly, except
I think I'm on it, too. But for
clarity's sake, I'll say this instead:
I'm in Virginia.
```

I read it over and laugh at my use of *etc, etc.* Maybe he'll think I'm smarter than I am, talking like that. I don't know why this is funny. The moment feels irrational. Transcendental.

As if I, Nolan Chandler, am finally onto something.

15

KENNEDY

The one thing I wanted to do at the house tonight was to look through Elliot's notes, to try to understand. To see if I could figure out what was happening on December fourth, while I was gone.

By the time I arrive at the house, though, and hide my bike under the shadow of the front porch, I have a new message on the forum. But I can only check with my phone, since the house no longer has Internet.

I read it on the way to the shed around back, where I've left the box of Elliot's notes, with my bag slung over my shoulder.

There are two things that stick out in the message. That make me freeze. That make the goose bumps rise across my arms.

The first: *pi*. How did I not see that? I'm practically running to the computer out back to see if he's right, when I notice the second part of his message: *Virginia*.

Holy. Crap.

So what if he doesn't want to think this is coming from space? I'll deal with that later. There's no way this radio telescope picks up something from his house. It's pointing *at the sky*. Anyway, he's mapping electromagnetic fields, and I'm documenting radio frequencies. We're not even looking at the same *thing*.

There's something more important here. The location. And the pattern itself. *Pi*. Holy crap, I think he might be right.

I write back immediately, telling him I'm in the process of confirming, and then I tell him the name of my county before I can stop myself and think about whether this is a good idea or not.

For a second, I wonder if he's some master computer hacker or something, who has hacked into my forum account, has seen where I was sending my message from, and has responded accordingly. If he's doing this to play me, prey on me. But then I think of his notes about his brother, the video with the blue wall, and no. It's not possible.

We have something here. Something real.

The problem with Elliot's equipment is that it isn't exactly the highest-tech equipment in the world. This began as some independent project last summer, before the start of his freshman year of college, and it took on a life of its own after that—he brought at least one friend back from college to see it: I saw them at night after, lying on their backs, looking up at the stars.

It's an old satellite dish, plus scraps he acquired from various old electronics, and a computer program I think he partly copied and partly made himself, and I'm having difficulty pulling the exact times from the readout. But I think Visitor357 is right, even with my inexact calculations. It's definitely right around three seconds. And he's right; that's close enough that it could be pi.

I kick myself, that I didn't think of it first.

Elliot told me that when *Voyager* was sent into space with a message for any extraterrestrial life that might come upon it, our mathematical definitions were included, possibly as a way to communicate.

The signal has to mean something. And yes, it makes sense: this is what you'd send. Math is universal. The ratio of a circle would be the same anywhere. The universe operates by certain laws that are bigger than all of us.

This is one of them.

My eyes have gone dry and the numbers on the screen are starting to go fuzzy when I hear footsteps out back—several people's footsteps. And then, underneath, the familiar mode of speaking among the group of friends I've come to know so well since we moved in last year.

Sutton is leading them across the field behind the shed; I don't even have to look out the window to know it. His voice is the most distinct. Marco and Lydia are following a step or two behind, interjecting periodically. I can't make out any of the conversation, but their presence here is enough to be suspicious.

They were here on Friday, when the signal started coming through. Lydia and Marco said they know what I've been doing at the house, messing with the inside to scare prospective buyers off. It made me suspicious then, and it makes me suspicious now that they're here again. I need to know what they really do around here.

I quietly step outside the shed, picking out their darker shadows heading to the other end of the field. To Freedom Battleground State Park.

They move in a pack, each anticipating the other's moves; all my time hanging out with them, and I never felt I fit in, because I didn't. As Lydia said, she would literally forget I was there. I wasn't meant to be a member. I was always just a visitor.

I met Marco almost right after we moved into this house, the summer before starting at a new school. And I hitched myself to their group when we started hanging out, never making myself a separate set of close friends. Friends who would call me up, rally around me after an eventual breakup.

Well, lesson learned and then some. The friends I made here were all friends-of-Marco first. There is no rallying group remaining.

I keep about fifty yards behind them now, and Lydia's right—they never even notice me. I'm right *here* and no one turns around. If they spotted me now, it *would* be creepy, I'll give her that. But it's their own fault.

They duck between a row of trees, following a path deeper into the park. Their voices stay low, as if they're trespassing and afraid of getting caught. It's a Sunday night, and Sutton's got a bag with him, and every once in a while someone shines a light on the path with their phone.

Eventually they veer off the trail into a larger clearing,

and Sutton lets out a cheer as he climbs on top of a tire swing, swinging like a pendulum in the dark night. He swings back my way, where I'm standing behind a row of hedges, but he never notices me. I feel the rush of air as the tire brushes by me; I'm close enough to reach out and touch him. We're in a playground in the middle of the park, next to some picnic tables. I think there are probably grills around; I've been in here before, but only in the daylight.

Marco opens Sutton's bag, pulling out a can of beer.

Wow, mystery solved. Apparently they need to trek from their neighborhood, across my property, into a state park, off hours, in order to carry a backpack full of beer to the center of a playground in the middle of the night. Completely logical. Completely.

Marco sits on top of a wooden table, his feet on the bench, focused on the now-opened can of beer in his hands and nothing more.

"Where are you, Lydi?" Sutton says, his voice coming and going as he swings.

"Here, you idiot." He reaches forward for her in the dark but she jumps back, laughing.

He swings back in my direction once more, and I get a whiff of coconut hair product. What to say about Sutton: He's got locks. Like, not hair, but locks. Like a hair commercial, and he knows it. They trail behind him in the wind. Sutton always makes sure there's some sort of wind blowing in his direction. And if there's not, he creates it, like now.

"Sutton," Lydia says, but he ignores her. "Sutton." Louder now, until he drags his heel in the dirt, bringing himself to an abrupt stop.

"Someone's here," she whispers.

I freeze, trying to decide between running away and letting them find me, and I'm not sure which would be more embarrassing. Except Lydia tips her head in the other direction, away from me.

It's then that I see him.

A fourth person, in the shadows. I can tell he's taller than the rest of us—except for maybe Sutton. And he's got a backpack on. I quickly run through the list of possibilities: hitchhiker, drug dealer, teen runaway. Serial killer. Killer.

Instead of getting quieter, Sutton gets louder. "Who goes there?" he calls, like nothing can touch him. Like the chance of there being a knife (or a gun) is so outside the realm of possibility. Six months, that's all it's been. Six months, and everyone's gone back to believing themselves untouchable. That the evil is behind bars and can no longer exist out here.

The belief, once more, that they are the center of their universe.

That this story is theirs.

16

NOLAN

Sutton Tanner is an asshole. "Who goes there?" he calls, like we're actors in some Shakespearean play, and the play is about him.

I raise my hand. "Hey. Sutton?" I ask, even though of course it's Sutton. Of course. We don't go to the same school, but every winter there's this tri-county baseball clinic, and so I've sort of half-known him for years. He has this easy demeanor that everyone loves in the dugout, something to lighten the mood, something to distract from the cold, or the crappy play. But the act never really falls away, and then it's just grating. Either way, he's easy to pick out, I'll give him that.

"Hey, man. Nolan, right?" He smiles, his teeth glaring white in the moonlight.

"Yep." I don't know what to say. How to explain what I'm doing here, if he asks. But he doesn't.

"Welcome," he says, stretching out his arms, like he owns the place.

God, they don't even know. Where they're standing. What they're doing.

They're drinking beer in the middle of a state park, and I don't get it. What the allure is of meeting up to drink beer outside on a hot night in the dark, when the mosquitoes are eating you alive.

Get a little more creative, I think. Sneak inside someone's room. A basement. Something with air conditioning. Maybe use a cooler. A refrigerator. This cannot be the peak of adolescence.

He hops down from the tire swing and steps closer, the two other people with him drawing nearer. There's a guy, tan and skinny, kind of sullen-looking. Though maybe it's on purpose; from what I can gather from the girls at my school, the moody look is in. And there's a girl with brown skin and long, dark hair, who stops to look at something over her shoulder every few steps.

"Marco, Lydi," Sutton says by way of introduction, rapid-fire.

"—ah," the girl adds. "Lydi-ah." She looks me straight in the eye, and even in the dark, I can tell: she's beautiful.

Sutton smiles wide. "You can only call her Lydi if you've—"

She swings her arm in the direction of his head, but he catches her wrist, laughing.

"You're such a jerk," she says, but she's smiling.

I don't get it. I really don't. Sutton Tanner is an asshole, and she can't get enough.

God, I have to get out of here.

"Want a beer?" he asks, fishing through a backpack. From

the way he can't keep still, there's like an eighty percent chance that can of beer explodes if he's the one who carried it in here.

"No thanks, I'm . . ." I'm *what? Trying to find out what pi has to do with my brother's disappearance, in the middle of the night, believing he's sent me some sort of clue? Searching for the paranormal, and this is the prime spot?* They stare at me, waiting.

A twig snaps in the distance, and Lydia jumps again, her head twisting.

"Did you guys hear that?" she asks, her voice shaky.

"Calm down, babe," Sutton says.

Marco peers over his shoulder into the dark. "She's still jumpy from this afternoon."

"What happened this afternoon?" Sutton asks, looking between Marco and Lydia. You can tell, even now, he doesn't like to be the last to know something.

Lydia shrugs. "Kennedy happened. Wanted me to take a look at something for her, and then she left me there."

"She left you at the house?" he asks, shuddering.

"No, the shed."

"Just as bad," he mumbles.

"Right, and then I . . . heard something. I could've sworn she never left. Only she says she was at the police station, meeting with the prosecutors or something. She had the paperwork and everything."

Sutton frowns. "Why were you even *at* Kennedy's house?"

"She asked me to, Sutton. God. But really, you didn't hear anything just now?"

"*I* heard something," I say.

They both look at me, surprised. Like they'd already forgotten I existed. Forgotten that they had just thirty seconds ago called me nearer, introduced me to their group, offered me a beer.

"Sutton, come on, I want to go," Lydia says, tugging his arm.

He presses his lips together. Shrugs. "All right," he says. *Okay, not a complete asshole*, I think.

Then he turns the whole thing around with a wicked grin. "Always give a girl what she asks for, my friend." Nope, definitely an asshole.

Lydia nudges him as he walks past, then quickly falls into step. Even Marco trails after them. Back down the path, out of the park. No one really cares what I was doing here. No one wonders. It should probably feel more like relief.

Their voices carry, and I wait for silence. Sitting still, in the dark, with my eyes closed, I can feel the memory of the signal in the palm of my hand, the way it buzzed, in a rhythm. I picture a circle, myself at the center.

And then I try to listen for my brother. For whatever he's trying to tell me. I focus on the way he looked during the fever dream, his mouth moving, trying to decipher the words he was saying: *Help us. Please.*

It takes a minute for everything to still around me, for every sound to have a place, until I feel it. Something else. Some*one* else.

I open my eyes.

17

KENNEDY

The voices fade in one direction, but I remain behind. At first, the three of them were like a pull, like I could see my own shadow, see where it should be as I followed them. The hole left behind, an ebb of darkness. But the farther they get, the less I feel the need to catch up.

But now I'm stuck. I don't want the guy in the clearing to notice me—since Sutton knows him, I'm assuming he's not going to abduct me. But I also don't want him telling Sutton that some girl was out here, watching them all. By reasonable deduction, they would probably realize that it was me.

I crouch lower behind the row of bushes, peering between the branches near the ground, watching the guy in the clearing. He's lying back on the table, staring up through the circle of trees. It feels like I'm witnessing something I shouldn't. Or maybe I'm witnessing something I *should*. Someone should be here, other than the nothingness, to bear witness. How many things happen to us in the dark, alone?

There's a bag at his feet. It looks like he's asleep, but his eyes are open, the whites reflecting in the moonlight through the clearing.

I imagine his story: running away, using his bag for a pillow, hiding out in the park at night. Sutton called him *Nolan*. Sutton didn't really care, though, didn't think it odd that some guy was in the park alone.

Behind the hedge, I open my phone for comfort. There's a new message from Visitor357, sent sometime during the last hour.

> I'm not in that county, but close.
> Next one over.

I pull the phone closer to my face, my heart racing. So, this *is* a location thing. I think about asking Visitor357 to meet up with me at the college. I'm thinking of how to explain that I don't know much about the instrumentation, or how to decipher it on my own.

I write back:

> Do you know anyone else who could
> analyze this signal? My contact didn't
> exactly work out.

I stand, ready to retreat from the scene, imagining that the situation is reversed and there is someone watching me when I want to be alone, when the guy on the table suddenly darts up. I panic, thinking he's heard me. I stand perfectly still, in hopes that I will blend into the surroundings.

But he doesn't look my way. Instead, he feels around beside him, and I see the light of his phone illuminate his face. It's the first time I'm getting a good look at him, but the light cuts him into angles and shadows. Like he's half here, half gone. His hair is dark, and sort of messy, and he runs a hand quickly through it, pushing it to the side, before bringing the phone close to his face for a few moments, his fingers darting across the screen. Then he places it on the table as he lowers himself again.

Maybe he's meeting someone. A girl. Or a guy. Or the second person of some drug-deal-exchange thing.

I'm still holding my phone, so I see it light up with a new alert. Another message notification. The message says:

```
No. But I'm trying to get some more
info tonight.
```

I look back up at the boy on the table. *No,* I think. It can't be. But . . . the next county over, he said. This park runs the line between two counties. Still, it's most likely a coincidence. We all live and die by our phones. It wouldn't be too unusual for someone to send a message at the same time I happen to receive one.

Visitor357 is not some teenager in the middle of the woods at night, looking for ghosts. Not some friend of Sutton's. Not some kid who won't know any more than I do. He can't be.

`Test`, I write back, then stare across the open space of the clearing.

He sits up again. Types something, lies back, and then I have a new notification.

The message is blank, except for three question marks.

Oh my God. My hands are shaking as I type.

```
Please tell me you aren't sitting
on a table in the middle of Freedom
Battleground State Park right this
second.
```

He sits up slowly this time, turning his head in every direction. His eyes are wide, and his mouth hangs open, and he grabs his bag, like he's afraid, like he's got something in there to protect himself. As if I am the thing, suddenly, to fear.

"Oh, you've got to be kidding me," I say.

18

NOLAN

I've got my bag in my hands, ready to make a run for it—someone's watching me, *right now*—except the voice doesn't sound like the voice of a killer. It's soft, but cutting. I assume it's one of Sutton's friends, who was supposed to meet up with the group. But then a girl steps out from the hedges, and she looks just the slightest bit familiar.

"Please tell me you're not Visitor357. Please."

I'm still holding the phone in my hand, and she's got one in hers, the screen lit up, and everything clicks. She's the one who just sent me a message asking if I was in the middle of the park.

"What the hell," I say, narrowing my eyes. "You're *KJ*?"

KJ. I was picturing a man. A much older man, maybe a professor, a scientist, someone with graying hair and wire-rim glasses and a crooked bow tie, just *somebody*—someone who might have some real information I could use.

She tips her head up, like she's angry at something. "I said *please*," she mumbles.

"Wait, but I thought you had a satellite dish. I thought you—"

She puts a hand on one hip and leans into it. "Yeah, I do. In the field, on the other side of the park. Where I live. KJ. Kennedy. Jones." She spells it out for me, like I'm a moron. And maybe I am. Kennedy Jones, of the Jones House. The stories Sutton told us. The girl who must've been there when I showed up yesterday morning, taking readings. The girl who must've decorated my back car window with her hand-prints, trying to spook me.

I hop down from the table, stepping closer. "Were you following me? Tracking me or something?" I ask.

She makes a face that in any other setting would have me running, regardless of the fact that she's practically half my size. "No, I wasn't following *you*. I was following *them*." She tips her head in the direction of Sutton's crew.

"That's not any less creepy."

She shakes her head. "They cut right through my yard. I was just . . ." I feel her grasping for something, not just the word, but some way to explain. Her face shifts, and she shakes it off. "What's it to you? I live nearby. I should be asking if you were following *me*."

I give her a look right back, and she raises an eyebrow. "Well, what are you doing out here in the middle of the night?"

I gesture around me, in a circle. "This is it."

"This is what?"

"Where my brother disappeared. You never heard of it? Liam Chandler? Two years ago? You live right there. . . ."

Her mouth forms the word *oh*, but no noise comes out. "We moved here last year. I'm sorry, I didn't know."

"It was on the news."

"Not by me, I guess. I lived near DC most of my life. People disappeared a lot. Or worse."

As if missing brothers happen all the time. As if this isn't the defining moment of my life, and everything that's happened since.

"So . . . ," I begin, looking her over but trying not to seem like I am. She's smaller than I realized at first. Her legs not as long, when she's standing in front of me. And her hair, it's hard to tell in the dark, but it's not quite as wild. Her eyes are wide, and dark, and unflinching.

I've obviously failed in keeping my observation of her a secret, because she does the same to me, only she doesn't try to hide it. I try not to shrink into myself as her eyes skim over me slowly. She presses her lips together. "So, Visitor—"

"Nolan," I say. "Nolan Chandler."

"Nolan, Nolan Chandler," she repeats, "what were you hoping to find out here?" She gestures to my bag. "Is that what I think it is?"

I open the top and show her the contents, but she doesn't move to touch it. Just nods slightly. I remember, then, this girl is looking for aliens. I think she mentioned that someone was looking into it for her. "Wait," I say, remembering the conversation that just happened between Sutton and his friends. "Was that girl—Lydia, right?—was she your, quote, contact?"

Kennedy crosses her arms over her chest. "She's smart. She knows computers. She knows that stuff almost as well as anyone else. Besides, doesn't sound like you have anything to add. So far, you've sent me a *No* and three question marks. At least I'm trying something."

"Fair enough. I'm trying something, too, though."

"I think—" she starts, just as I say, "Want to know what I'm thinking?"

We both grin. "You first," I say.

She shakes her head, looking up at the sky, then back at me. "I don't know. I don't know what it means. Any of it. The signal stopped happening, and I never would've thought it was anything real if it weren't for the fact that you were seeing the exact same thing."

I smile then, without even thinking about it. Because I suddenly don't feel so out of my element. I feel exactly in my element. I have been living in uncertainty for two years. "Me too," I say. "But it's not happening at my house anymore, either. And if I hadn't taken that video, I would've thought I was just remembering it wrong."

She wrinkles her nose either at me or at the equipment, I'm not sure. But it turns her suddenly vulnerable. "There's someone else. I know someone else who can help, who might be able to tell us what it means. I'm going to talk to him tomorrow."

"Who?"

She looks at me as if to say she doesn't trust me yet. Well, she ran into me in the middle of the night, in the middle of the woods—who can blame her? The silence eventually reaches peak awkward levels, and I clear my throat. "Okay, well, on that note, I think I'll be heading back to my car now."

She steps back at the same time, like it's a race to see who gets away the fastest. "Okay, well, guess I'll be making my way back to the house now."

"I thought—"

She turns around. "You thought what?"

"I thought no one lived there anymore."

She smiles, and it catches me off guard. "They don't." And with that, she's gone.

19

KENNEDY

The next morning, I end up getting on the bus at the same stop Marco and I both used to use, before he got his license, and a car. I sneak on between two students, head down, headphones on, but the stealth mode is unnecessary—the driver doesn't even look my way.

This was my bus at the start of the year, anyway, before I moved in with Joe. My seat is still empty, third row from the back, where Marco would sit beside me. The whole row is abandoned now, like we've just vanished and nobody noticed.

I spent last night reading articles on my phone about Liam Chandler, to make sure this Nolan guy was who he said he was. Most of the articles are older, from early spring two years ago. Liam Chandler was a senior when he disappeared, and, according to the articles, great at *everything*. Sports, academics, involved in community service, with plenty of friends, from what I can gather by the number of people interviewed, claiming to be his best friend.

The articles stopped for the most part by summer, except around graduation, where there was a tribute to him in the student paper, lest anyone forget.

After that, crickets.

I've been trying to figure out what to write to Nolan, to explain. And also, to apologize for jumping down his throat, for being angry at him just for being someone like me, with no more answers than I have. Instead, I decide to just skip that part and hope he doesn't notice. Nolan said yesterday that he had a car, and suddenly everything feels more possible. I told him I had a plan about today. The truth is, it was only half a plan. He doesn't realize it, but he's just provided the other half.

In the middle of first period, when the teacher tells us to use the class to prepare for our finals, I slip my phone out from under my desk and send him a message.

> Hey Visitor, hey Nolan,
> Sorry getting used to that. Any chance you're free this afternoon, say around 3pm? I need a ride. It's in both of our best interest. Someone who can tell us about the signal, help us decipher it. But I also need you to not ask any questions.
> Also, here's my number, probably easier than going through the forum, right?

I refresh my messages over and over, but eventually, two classes later, a text comes through instead.

Hi KJ, sorry, Kennedy. Make it 3:30 and I'm in. Where should we meet?

I smile, then try to think of a neutral meeting place. I get home at three, and we're already cutting it close, timing-wise. In the end, I justify sending him Joe's address by the fact that Sutton knows him, and a quick Google search gives me his address, too. The whole way home I'm thinking about this—about Nolan and the car and answers—because we're so close, and I know just where to get them. I'm not thinking clearly, and I'm so fully distracted that I walk into a complete ambush, with Joe waiting for me at the kitchen table.

It's 3 p.m. and he's got a two-liter bottle of soda in front of him, half empty, and he's peeling at the label. It looks like he's been there awhile, a condensation ring forming on the table, his elbow resting on a wrinkled sheet of paper.

"Oh," I say, suddenly remembering. The papers in front of him. The questions. I close my eyes. "I'm sorry, Joe, I made plans. Can we do this another time?"

But he's already shaking his head. "This was the time you gave me, Kennedy. And you promised. We're doing this now."

I look at the clock, drop my bag from my shoulder, and perch on the edge of the kitchen chair. "Okay," I say. Best to get this over with, make it quick, be done with it.

But it looks like Joe doesn't want to start, either.

I drum my fingers on the table. Joe looks at me over the edge of the page, then focuses on the questions.

"'On the early morning of December fourth,'" he reads, and then he puts the pages down. "You know, you were right. This is pointless."

I sigh, my entire body relaxing.

"They're going about this the wrong way. Pulling at pieces. Why don't you start instead," he says.

This was not part of the deal. Not part of our agreement. "We can just tell them we did it," I suggest with a small grin.

He closes his eyes and picks up the paper again. He speaks faster, robotic, like he doesn't really want to hear my answers. His fingers tremble, and he readjusts the papers to try to get them to stop. "'On the early morning of December fourth,'" he says in a gravelly voice, "'what time did you leave Marco Saliano's house?'"

I close my eyes. "Just tell me the answer, Joe. Tell me what to say."

He looks up, fixes his eyes on mine. "The truth, Kennedy."

The truth. It's hard to remember now. It's hard to tell the difference between what I remember and what I want to remember; what I was told versus what I saw. "The thing is," I begin, "I don't remember looking at a clock. I don't *remember*, Joe. I've spent six months trying not to think about it, and all these details, they're just not *there* anymore." I shake my head, both trying to remember and trying not to. "There was a storm, and I was waiting for it to let up before I went home. We went over all this, with the police. And *they* gave me the time, based on that. Based on what Marco said."

"And," Joe adds, "based on the nine-one-one call. At one-eighteen a.m."

I nod slowly. "Right."

He nods at me. "Okay, you're doing good," he says, even though I'm not. He moves his finger down the page, to the next question. Truthfully, this is already going better than expected. He's not going to force an answer from me where no answer can be found. His pointer finger stops at the next line. "'How did you enter the house?'"

Easy question. "My bedroom window." The house was originally a ranch, before the second-floor loft addition. All our bedrooms were on the main level, accessible through the windows with a few strategically placed steps—either via the deck railing, or a bench pulled below.

As if anticipating this answer, he moves to the next one. "'Was the window already open?'"

"The window was how I left it," I say, my eyes feeling wide and dry, like I'm in a trance. "Mostly closed, so the cold air wouldn't come through. But cracked open so I could get my fingers underneath and push it up when I got back home."

I'm there, suddenly, kneeling on the back railing, my fingers drenched from the rain, slipping on the glass, trying to wedge it open—

"'What made you . . .'" He pauses, the line between his eyes deepening, his brows furrowed. "'What made you leave your room after you got back home?'"

I shoot my head up, my eyes meeting his. "I don't understand the question," I whisper.

He shifts in his seat, clearly uncomfortable, not wanting to take this trip down memory lane any more than I do. "I think it means, I think they're trying to understand . . . you got home after sneaking out, sometime around one-ten or one-fifteen in the morning. So you climbed through the window and you were in your room, and you kept the door closed, right? So no one would know you were gone?" He cringes. "So, they want to know, uh, what made you leave the room after you got back."

I don't answer. I'm frozen.

"Was the door already open, Kennedy? Did you see something? Were there lights on?"

And then I'm back outside the window again, peering into the shadow house; it's raining, and my fingers shake from the cold.

"Kennedy." His warm hand is on my arm, and I flinch. Joe looks down at my hands—I didn't realize they were shaking now, too. Joe puts the paper down, the air suddenly charged, and he tips his head just slightly to the side. "What happened that night? Is there something you're not telling me?"

I close my eyes, shake my head. "I hid," I say.

"I know."

"I tried to call for help."

"You did, Kennedy. You did. They have the nine-one-one call. We all heard it. You did everything you could."

Our voices are so low, and his eyes are my mother's and the shadow house is here. It's right here, so close, like suddenly there's just the thinnest film between us and the blurry other side, and there's a tear, the plastic pulling apart, so I can see—

His phone rings, jarring us both. The moment is broken. The shadow house is gone, Joe is Joe, and I am just me.

He doesn't move to answer, doesn't move at all. "It's okay," I say. "You should get it." I stand from the kitchen table, the blood rushing from my head, the room tilting momentarily.

"Kennedy," he says, reaching an arm for me.

But I'm already halfway to my room. I'm behind the door, my back pressed up against it, trying to slow my heartbeat.

I hear him answering the call, moving farther away, until the sound of his voice disappears.

I'm alone, and I'm safe again.

20

NOLAN

The house at the address Kennedy sent me is a sharp contrast to the Jones House. I should probably stop calling it, capital letter, implied italics, *the Jones House*. But that's how it was introduced to me, like something haunted, a landmark from which ghosts and stories originate in equal measure. It's not that large but looks larger rising up out of the center of a huge field. And it's distinctive, with a wide porch and wooden steps and this feeling it's missing a pack of farm animals or something.

In contrast, this house I've just pulled the car up to is a small ranch, set in a row of near-identical ranches, mere feet apart from one another. They differ from one another only in the color, or the presence or absence of a fence. But really it just looks like someone stuck a row of Monopoly houses down and called it a day.

The address is displayed on the mailbox, sticker numbers pasted on. At one time I'm guessing the siding on the house was blue, but it's faded to a worn gray, lighter in some sections than others. And no one seems to give two craps about the yard.

She hasn't answered my texts.

I'm here.

Outside your house.

Still outside your house.

I decide this is almost as creepy as telling her I'm texting her from inside her house. So eventually I get out of the car and ring the bell.

There's a flurry of footsteps from the other side, and a man opens the door. I see Kennedy racing behind him; the look on her face one of *oh crap*. The man is about my height, with Kennedy's coloring—dark hair, sort of messy— but his eyes are blue to her brown. He's looking me over in a way that makes me uncomfortable, like he's assessing me for danger. And Kennedy looks between us like she wishes one of us weren't standing in this doorway, and I'm not sure which of us that is.

"Um," I say, looking at my phone, "I thought . . ." Because I can't figure out who this guy is, and whether I should pretend I have the wrong address.

"No, sorry, my fault," she says, elbowing the guy aside so he's no longer taking up the entire doorway. "I told you I had plans," she says to him, looking at the side of his face.

But he hasn't taken his eyes off me. "What kind of plans?" he asks.

"The studying kind," I say, on instinct, which is my go-to answer to my parents, and from the look of relief on Kennedy's face, it seems like the right answer in this situation, too.

"Joe, this is my friend. Nolan," she says, smiling, like she's only just remembered my real name. "Nolan, my uncle, Joe."

Joe nods, but he doesn't extend his hand. Instead, he looks at Kennedy with one eyebrow raised. "I know, I know," she says, fake-smiling, "two friends in less than twenty-four hours, must be some sort of record, right?"

"Kennedy . . . ," he warns.

But she sidesteps. "What? Is this because he's a guy? I know you said no boys, I know. But I didn't think that was an across-the-board rule. Not that I couldn't study with someone who happened to have a Y chromosome. I thought you just meant, like, no boys in your house? As in, italics, *no boys.*"

I'm trying not to smile, watching this exchange. Her whole face changes when she talks to him, and she moves her hands to accentuate her points.

Her uncle—it feels weird thinking that, since he can't be that much older than us—has turned almost scarlet by now. She stares up at him, and he stares back, and it's like watching the most passive-aggressive game of chicken in history.

When Joe doesn't answer, she puts a hand out in my direction, in the universal *stop* signal. "Nolan, to be safe, please keep both feet on the other side of the doorway."

Joe cracks the slightest smile then, and he opens the door wider. "Take your phone," he says as she disappears down the hall, presumably to get her things.

When she's gone, his expression turns serious again.

"Nolan *what*?" he says, like he's planning to run a background check on me.

"Chandler," I say. "Sir."

He almost laughs.

She breezes back out again, just as quick. "Bye, Joe," she says.

"And *answer* it if I call you, please."

"I will!" she calls over her shoulder.

"The library closes at eight!" he yells as she's getting into the car. "I expect you back here at quarter after!"

She slides into the passenger seat of my car and closes the door like it's her own, and she's smiling so wide at something Joe said, but I don't even get it. She gives him the thumbs-up as he watches us drive away.

She rubs her hands together and looks at the clock on the dashboard and says, "We'd better hurry. We don't have much time."

I'm going about five miles per hour, inching down the street. "Um, I know you said no questions, but it would help if I knew where to turn."

"Ha, yeah, that would help. Sorry." She holds up her phone and turns up the volume, and it starts directing me. *Right on Wilson. Left on Stenton. Merge onto highway. In twenty miles, take the exit.*

"Twenty *miles*," I say. No wonder she mentioned the time. I have a thousand questions I want to ask. Namely: Where are we going? What are we doing? Who *are* you? But I've grown comfortable in the unknown. Everything takes time. And so will this.

On the way, she grills me on *the Event*. That's what she's started calling it. "Did you pick up anything related to the Event in the park last night?" she asks.

How to explain that I wasn't out there testing things with machinery. I was out there trying to listen for my brother. "Eh, I think your friends kind of ruined the setting."

"Those aren't my friends," she says.

"You just follow them?"

I can *feel* the look she's giving me, and I smile to let her know I'm kidding. Sort of.

She sighs. "Marco was my . . . Well, when I moved here last year, he was my boyfriend, so I sort of fell in with that group. But it was more just like they kept me around because they had to. Now that Marco and I aren't together . . ."

I try not to scrunch my nose, picturing her with Marco. "The skinny, sullen-looking one?"

She smiles. "I guess. Well, compared to Sutton and Lydia, at least. To be fair, everyone looks sullen compared to Sutton."

I grunt. That probably sounded sullen.

"How do *you* know Sutton, anyway?" she asks.

"Baseball."

I feel her looking at the side of my face, then her eyes trailing down my neck to my arm. I try not to fidget. "Makes sense," she says.

"Are you saying I look like a baseball player?" I smile and peer over at her from the corner of my eye, but she looks away, out the window.

"I'm saying you move sort of like Sutton."

I scoff. That hair. The expression. The mannerisms.

"It's hard to explain," she says.

I'm about to make a comment about what she moves like (a ghost, something fast, something I feel like I'm trying to catch, but that slips from your grip just when you think you have it), when her phone directs me to the exit.

"Finally," I say. But Kennedy has gone uncharacteristically silent.

Her phone directs me through three more turns, and the road becomes wide and deserted at the same time. I hit the brake when I see the sign up ahead, just stop dead in the middle of the road for a second—and I'm glad there's no one behind us.

Then I veer off to the shoulder and put the car in park. The engine rumbles underneath our seats, but she doesn't say anything. I stare at her until she looks my way. "What are we doing here?" I ask.

"You promised, no questions."

"Well, I changed my mind. I'm not going any farther until you tell me what we're doing here."

She stares at me like she's daring me to look away first, but I don't. "Pretty sure you already know the answer to that," she says.

I frown, because she's right. Out the front window, the sign on the side of the road says PINEVIEW REGIONAL DETENTION CENTER. I put the car in drive again, because of course I know exactly what we're doing here. And I don't know how to tell her this is a terrible idea. I'm sure she knows that.

It is. For the record. An absolutely terrible idea.

I pull the car into the lot beside the high metal chain

fence, facing the large concrete building beyond. The sun feels especially brutal out here, amid the area cleared of trees, with nothing but metal, pavement, and dirty concrete. We walk to the entrance, and the security guard at the gate looks us both over.

"You don't have to come in," she says, but I follow her anyway.

At the gate, we're instructed to leave our phones and keys, so I turn my cell off before leaving it in a locker. We don't speak. Not during this part, and not when we walk through a metal detector on the way to the registration area. And not while she's standing in line.

There's a line of people in front of us, and another group waiting to be let inside, and I start to get a really bad feeling.

I want to tell her to forget this, offer to take her somewhere else, anywhere but here. But before I know it, we're at the front of the line, and she hands over her ID.

"Inmate's name?" the woman behind the plastic window asks, without even looking up.

"Elliot Jones," she says.

21

KENNEDY

The woman looks up from her computer screen and shakes her head. She looks way too friendly to be working here, asking for inmate names all day, from behind a plastic shield. "You're not on the list."

"I'm his sister," I say. "Family." I point to the ID so she sees the name. Last name *Jones*.

Her face softens even more. "I know, honey." She pivots the computer screen my way so I can see. There's a column of approved names: I see his lawyer's name and Joe's name, not that Joe has ever visited, to my knowledge. And then a column marked *Unapproved*. There's only one name on it. She taps her purple fingernail against the screen. "There's a note here, with your name. It says, specifically, you're not approved."

My teeth grind together, and I can feel the people behind me in line growing restless. "Who would do that?" I ask, thinking of Joe. Or Elliot's lawyer. The police. "Let me talk to someone—"

She shakes her head. "It won't help. Also, darling, you can't come in regardless without a guardian present. You're a minor."

"A *guardian*." I almost laugh. "That's *him*." I point to the computer screen. I have no guardian anymore, not one that counts. Technically, Joe is the person to put on the school forms, and he can probably claim me as a tax deduction or something. But my true guardians are either dead or locked up behind that wall. Elliot, at eighteen, *should* be my legal guardian.

"I'm sorry, I can't help you," she says, already looking behind me, to the next person.

I pull the envelope out of my pocket, the one with the readout from the radio telescope inside. The thing, I'm sure, only he can decipher. "Can I get this to him? Please. He won't . . ." Call, accept my letters, anything. I need him to see this. To tell me what it means. He built it; he would know.

She seems to be debating something, and it's awful, the hope that precedes her words. "No, Ms. Jones. The inmates set this list." She waits for me to understand, and when it seems I haven't gotten the point yet, she lets out a sigh. "This list, this decision, is from him."

I shake my head, not understanding. Elliot won't see me? *Elliot* won't let me visit? Not the lawyers, or Joe, but *Elliot*? Elliot, who never acted like I was a pain in his butt, even when I so obviously was. I don't understand. I *need* him to give me answers.

Suddenly I feel a hand at my elbow. A voice at my ear. "Come on," he says. It's Nolan, beside me, the line of people growing louder behind us. They're completely unsympathetic to my cause, and I get it, I do. Look where we are; everyone's got a problem. We're at a *jail*. They're probably immune to scenes like this. To people like me.

He leads me back into the sunlight, against the barren landscape. I hold the paper out to him so he understands. "He built it. The satellite dish. The computer program. He'll know what it means."

Nolan frowns. "Can't you email or something?"

I feel my jaw clenching. "He doesn't have email. He doesn't use the phone. I don't know if my letters get to him." I used to send them, but eventually they were returned, unopened. I didn't understand. I *don't* understand.

The lawyers, Joe, none of them would let me see him. I thought it was because of *them*. Or because I'm working with the district attorney. For the facts. Just the facts. That's what I told them. When his lawyer starts in on cross-examination, I'll be able to tell them there must be another explanation. Elliot, who had never hurt anyone in his life, not even me. Elliot, who once tried to help me clean a cut on my knee (a slip off the railing, the first time I tried to sneak out), and who almost got sick just from looking at it. Mom called me her wild one, which made Elliot the stable one, the reliable one.

Elliot with his prints on the gun; Elliot, covered in blood. Elliot, running from the house, running away.

My nails dig into my palms.

"Maybe there's someone else who would understand . . . ," Nolan says.

But I shake my head. "When Lydia looked at the program,

she said something about the date," I explain. "The date the program began."

"What date?" Nolan asks.

"December fourth," I say, and I stare at him until I see the information process.

December fourth. Before. After. The split in my life, in the universe.

Something happened then. Elliot Jones was not himself.

"Don't you see? This signal has to be some sort of warning. Something happened that night," I explain. "Something dangerous."

He's shaking his head, but then he stops. He looks me over carefully.

"You see, don't you?" I ask, but he seems to be somewhere else. I can tell from his expression, though—he does. He must.

22

NOLAN

December fourth. The day, according to the papers, that Elliot Jones killed his mother and his mother's boyfriend, and then ran; schools remained closed in both their county and ours, for safety, until he was found the next day.

The story was this: Elliot's mother and her boyfriend, Will Sterling, another professor at the college, were at some holiday event. Something happened when they came back to the house after midnight. The daughter—Kennedy, arriving home, sneaking back inside—saw Elliot running from the house. And then she found the bodies on the stairs.

It was a near miss, Sutton said. That Kennedy wasn't home. That Kennedy was late. He knew her, he said, the girl who survived it. She was at her boyfriend's house when it happened. Marco, I now know.

I'd seen the pictures in the paper, on the news: the two professors—the woman, with dark hair, smiling in her photo, with the sky and ocean behind her, and the rest of the photo cut away; and the man, with salt-and-pepper hair and a graying beard covering a square jaw.

But Elliot's photo is the one that haunts me the most: the dark, hollow eyes; the expressionless face as he stared back through the lens of the police camera.

The next day, while the search parties were still out, Elliot suddenly appeared, walking up the driveway, like nothing at all had happened, seemingly with no memory of the event. He was allegedly in the same clothes, dirty, shaken, the blood still under his nails. Sutton said Elliot made it almost all the way to the crime scene tape across the front door, asking, "What happened?" before someone stopped him.

He had no idea there was a manhunt under way for him at that very moment.

There were a lot of rumors: that he was high; that he was furious, that it was a chaotic attack; that he was completely calm and collected and carried out the crimes with a chilling precision. No one knows what really happened, only that he did it. But his trial is starting next week, so I guess we're about to find out.

I tap my fingers on the steering wheel in the silence. "Um, are you hungry?" The clock gives us more time. A few more hours until she needs to be back, and I can see she does need something else. Something not in that ranch house with her uncle and the overgrown yard.

"Yes, actually," she says. She sighs, like she's irritated at her own hunger.

"Pizza?" Right at that moment, there's a sign just off the highway for the World's Best Pizza, which I think is probably optimistic, considering we're in the Middle of Nowhere, Virginia, half a mile from a jail. But who am I to judge?

"Pizza," she repeats, which I guess could be taken as either a *Yes, pizza, please* or a *Pizza, are you serious?* but I'm choosing to see it as the former, because I'm starving.

At the pizza place, we stand in line together, and she's silent. I'm seriously the worst person for this. I'm terrible at knowing what to say, finding the right words in a crisis. *Sorry your brother is in jail, but would you like extra cheese?* She saves me from the awkwardness by ordering for both of us, only looking at me after the fact to make sure it's okay. Well, I was right about one thing: she likes to be in charge.

I pull out my wallet. I have no cash, like seriously none. Like right now I have to decide between gas and dinner. I have a credit card for emergencies, though, and this suddenly feels like an emergency.

But she offers to pay instead. She insists, actually. "No, you drove, I'll feed."

I carry the drinks, and she takes our order number and props it on the table, where we wait for our pizza (pepperoni and sausage) to be delivered.

"So," I say, waiting for her to continue. It may seem odd—I know it probably does to anyone else, to the me who existed before all this—that I have just accompanied a near stranger to the jail where her family member awaits trial for the death of another family member. It seems so much, so intimate.

But something happens after a big event like the ones we've both been through. Something we can both understand. A brother disappearing, followed by a thorough investigation into all of our lives. I'd imagine it's the same sort of thing that must have happened to her. She was a witness to a crime that happened in her house, a death.

Sorry, I have trouble just saying it: a double homicide. A murder.

Anyway, this is what tends to happen to us: a recalibration of sorts. Of what embarrasses you, versus what you try to hide. I mean, I live in a house covered with the faces of other people's missing children. Her house is a crime scene, her brother the alleged guilty party. There's a reordering of what matters.

She needed a car, so she asked me; we needed answers, so we went to the jail.

"I was with Joe already," she says, unprompted, "when they found Elliot. When he came back to the house. We never got a chance to . . . he didn't tell me what happened. It doesn't make sense."

He's been awaiting trial; the evidence, according to the papers, was pretty cut-and-dry. A witness who puts him at the scene when the crime occurred, his fingerprints on the weapon, the blood under his nails. He hasn't denied it, not that I've heard.

But that can't be true, because it's going to trial. It's going to trial, to prove he's guilty, because he hasn't admitted to it, either. And Kennedy is the only witness.

Oh, I think.

"I'm sorry," I say, because what else is there, really, to say? *Sorry your brother is in jail for killing your family. Sorry you have no one else. Sorry he won't see you, still.*

"My mom and Will used to go out every weekend.

Started out as once a week, then turned into twice, after Will convinced her we were too old to need her around all the time. It was just . . . routine," she says, like she's trying to get me to understand. "That night, it was the same as every other time. Nothing was different. There was no reason. It doesn't make *sense*."

I sit back and listen, trying to picture it—the faces I've seen in the paper, all in the same room, with Kennedy. Talking to one another, maybe laughing. She's right, it doesn't make sense. None of this does. It doesn't make sense that, at a house one county over, my brother was here one day and gone the next, with no reason.

She sighs. "Elliot is seriously the most patient person. The most logical. Meticulous." She shakes her head, as if because he's logical and meticulous, he could not do such a thing.

"There was nothing logical or meticulous about it," she whispers. I see her eyes widen and wonder what she's imagining. The staircase, the lightbulb changed, the scent of paint. Chaos. Now I'm imagining it, too. The staircase. The horror of it. I wonder how a person can recover from that. From the knowing.

I'm not sure which is worse anymore: the not knowing, or the knowing. Her hand trembles as she reaches for her cup, and she moves the ice around absently with the straw before taking a drink.

"My brother," I say, "was perfect."

She's got the straw in her mouth, but she stops drinking, just freezes.

"Not the perfect brother. Not that. Just how everyone else saw him."

She nods, like she knows. Then moves the ice around with her straw again.

The pizza is finally delivered, the scent practically intoxicating. While waiting for my slice to cool, I decide to map with my phone how long it will take to get home. "Oh crap," I say, my cell in my hand. My phone has been off since we arrived at the jail. Since we turned them off and left them in the locker before walking through security.

I turn the phone on, holding my breath. Three new messages. I groan, holding the phone to my ear. The first is from my father, asking me where exactly I am, because they need to talk to me. The second is my father again, this time agitated, telling me to call him as soon as I get this. *As soon as,* he repeats. And the third message is static—nothing there. Time for my parents to get a new line. I can only imagine the state of my father during that call, though. How things might have escalated when I didn't respond.

Sorry, I mouth to Kennedy, hitting the call-back button for my dad's cell.

"Nolan?" he asks right away, as if my number hadn't just shown up on his display.

"Sorry, Dad, I didn't realize my phone had lost charge."

Kennedy makes a face at my lie. Like I didn't just see her do the same to her uncle, coming up with an excuse about who I was and where we were going.

My dad talks so fast I can't keep up. "What? Dad, calm down. What?"

"The *picture,*" my dad says, and I can hear his breath, the restraint in his words. "You need to come home and look at the picture, Nolan."

Kennedy raises her eyes to mine. His voice is so loud that she must've heard.

"You need to go?" she says, the pizza slice inches from her mouth, propped up in both hands.

"Sorry, I do," I say. I grab a box from the counter behind us so she can take it to go. "There's something happening at my house. My brother's case."

She holds up one finger, takes a bite, closing her eyes. As if the fate of the universe can hold on for just one moment. One simple moment where the only thing either of us is thinking about is the state of the world's best pizza.

She starts to laugh then. "Nolan," she says as I'm gathering my things. "I don't know how to say this, but I think it is."

"What?" I'm already mapping the course home. She pushes the half-eaten slice my way.

"The world's best pizza. I'm not lying—it's really good." She's really laughing, and it makes me pause. It's the first time I've heard her laugh.

I take a bite to humor her, feel the warmth, the flavor, the grease in my mouth. "Oh shit," I say around the bite, and she laughs. I can feel my eyes bugging out of my head. I change my mind, finishing the slice.

"We should come back here one day," she says, "just, one day."

"Yeah," I say as she grabs the to-go box. "Let me know, though, if it's as good reheated."

She shakes her head. "Come on, you already know the answer to that."

23

KENNEDY

Joe is sitting at the kitchen table when Nolan drops me off, much like when I got home from school. I wonder if he's moved at all since then, except I see a beer there instead of a soda, so . . .

"I come bearing dinner," I say, the rest of the pizza still lukewarm in the box.

"I thought you were studying at the library?" he says, half question, half accusation.

"We took a dinner break," I say, sliding the box onto the table. I open the top, contort my hands into the best impersonation of a magician revealing her tricks. "Ta-da," I say.

Joe picks up a slice halfheartedly, not realizing he's in the presence of the self-proclaimed World's Best Pizza. He takes a bite, puts it down. Takes one more, then chases it with a beer. I frown. I make a note to tell Nolan: *Not as good. The subject is unaffected.*

I get myself a paper plate from the pantry, to join him.

"Who was that, Kennedy?" he asks as I sit down across from him.

"Nolan, I told you."

"I'm just wondering if . . . you know."

I raise an eyebrow. I *do* know. He wants to know if this Nolan is my boyfriend. As in, have I broken his *no boys* rule officially. "He's just a friend of mine, Joe. I am allowed to have friends, right?"

He nods, and I take a slice from the box. I scrunch my nose, chewing carefully. It's missing something, outside the restaurant. It's not just the heat. It's something else, and I can't put my finger on it.

Joe puts the bottle down, spinning it on the table, not meeting my eye. "The call that came in earlier," he says, "it was the Realtor."

I stop chewing. Wondering if they told Joe I've been messing around with the house. That I'm spooking the prospective buyers.

"There's an offer," he says.

"What?" I say around a bite. Not possible. No one would want to live there. "Who wants to live in that house? *You* don't even want to live in that house, Joe, and it *belongs* to us."

He shakes his head. "From what I understand, they want to take it back to its roots." He spreads his hands out, as if this is something that should clarify everything. It doesn't.

"What does that mean, *take it back to its roots?*"

"Turn it back into a working farm. I guess."

"And how does one do that, exactly?"

He takes a deep breath. "They just want the land, Kennedy."

The acreage, stretching from the road to the fence to Freedom Battleground State Park. It's what drew my mother to it in the first place. That, and the fact that we'd never had land before, growing up closer to a city. She said it would be good for us, the space, the air. The house, quirky and charming, was full of history, which she loved. But she'd given me and Elliot control over the paint, the furniture, deciding what each room would be used for. That first summer, we painted it ourselves, steamed the carpets, hung the porch swing, dug the garden. Before the start of the school year, Will showed up with flowers—the kind ready to plant—and helped us transfer them to the side yard himself, the knees of his khaki pants covered in soil afterward. It was the first time we met him, the first time he'd asked Mom to dinner. It worked; they left us there to finish the garden ourselves.

"And what will happen to the rest of it?"

He doesn't say. He doesn't have to. They intend to level it. Take it all down. "No," I say.

"Kennedy."

"Joe. No. It's my house. I say no." We hadn't built it from the ground up, but it felt like we had brought it to life. I picture Elliot with white paint on his knuckles, dirt under his nails, his eyes unfocused, his cheeks flushed red from the sun. So different from the Elliot I was used to seeing. I think maybe that's what Mom meant, when she said it was good for us. In the middle of that summer, it did really feel like a house could change us.

"It's not that simple—"

"Except it is." It's mine—in my name, but in Joe's trust.

He raises his eyes to mine, and he looks immeasurably

sad. Worse than the first day I was here, when he cleared out the TV room, pulling furniture out into the hall to make room for me, while I watched. "Kennedy, who do you think is paying for Elliot's lawyer?"

I open my mouth, then close it again. I didn't. I didn't think about that at all. Elliot gets a lawyer, I testify for the DA; these are opposing forces, opposing motivations. "I don't . . ."

"Look, I don't want you to worry, but . . ."

"But what, Joe? What?"

He shakes his head at the table. "We need to make a decision here, and we're running out of time."

I'm staring out the window when he says it. At the dusk, settling to dark.

"Do you hear me, Kennedy?"

I'm breathing heavily, and it's the only sound I can hear, and the room feels charged suddenly, like something's about to burst.

"Did you know he won't see me, Joe? If we're paying for the lawyer, shouldn't he have to see me?"

He freezes. "Why do you know this, Kennedy?"

I can practically see the wheels turning in his head. "Because I wanted to see my brother." The brother I remember from the summer, not the one stuck inside a cell with nothing to do. I can feel the claustrophobia. My stomach hurts.

He sighs, but his shoulders remain tight, fixed. "That's not a good idea right now. The trial starts next Tuesday."

"Well," I say, "don't worry, Joe, because it seems like I don't have a choice anyway."

He's looking at me like he's missed something major, and

he has. He's trying to find out when I went to the jail, and how I got there. What happens in this house when he's at work. All the things I do when he's sleeping.

Maybe it was a mistake, telling him, but at least we're not talking about the house anymore.

"It's for the best," he says softly.

"It's bullshit, Joe. And you know it." I storm down the hall, and I slam the door. He didn't even notice that I brought him the world's best pizza.

I take out the folded-up sheet of paper with the readout, the signal.

And then I send Nolan a text.

What are you doing tomorrow? We need answers, and we're running out of time.

24

NOLAN

There's not even a place to park in front of my house. My parents' cars are in the driveway, and there are several dark cars parked along the curb, so I end up at the corner of the street, walking the rest of the way home.

"Where were you?" my dad asks as soon as I open the door. There's a group of them gathered in the dining room—my parents, men and women in suits, Agent Lowell. But no one waits for me to answer. They make a space for me and beckon me forward.

Agent Lowell has a hand on the back of a chair at the table. "Here, take this," he says.

My mom paces behind me. My dad, in contrast, is completely still. Once I'm seated, Agent Lowell places a photo directly in front of me, on top of the wooden table.

The picture is of my brother. They don't really need me to confirm this; it's obvious. In the image, he's walking sort of diagonally away, but his head is thrown over his shoulder so he's almost looking straight at the camera. Like someone called his name and he's looking for the source.

Still, it's a punch to the gut, seeing this. Something new. A moment, an image I've never seen before. I'd just about given up on seeing any such moments ever again.

I lean closer to the image. At the edge of the frame is the solid brown tail and a hind leg—Colby, beside him.

I can't figure out where he is, though. Only that the dog is with him, and it looks like he's in the woods. *Colby would never leave him,* my dad told the investigators, and he's right. We lost my brother and our dog that day, but I'm really only allowed to admit to missing the one. But here they both are, and something tightens in my throat, seeing them again.

Agent Lowell places a second photo in front of me, this one zoomed in on Liam's face. "In your best estimation, is this an accurate picture of Liam the day he went missing?" he asks.

"Yeah," I say. "It is." I can feel my heart racing.

"His clothes, the details?" he asks, and then I understand my role. I'm confirming the clothes he wore, the dog, the way he's looking over his shoulder. His dark blond hair is a little longer than it usually was, because he was due for a haircut, so it sort of falls over his forehead from the weight of it, instead of staying up and to the side, like he styles it. Styled it.

The jeans, the long-sleeved maroon shirt, the blue sneakers. All of it is Liam, all of it the details we gave over and over about that day; remembering, pulling things from his closet so we were sure. These details are now ingrained in our memory.

But, I see, there are some things we had forgotten, that I only remember now, by looking at him: the way his left arm bends slightly, held at his hip, from an old injury that never healed right. A broken bone brought to the doctor too late, already starting to ossify around the crack on its own. And a cut against the underside of his jawbone, from shaving. I'd forgotten that, completely, until they show me the photo of his face, zoomed in.

I remembered hearing him hiss in the bathroom that morning, the razor dropping, clattering against the sink. A bead of blood on the porcelain, left behind.

Why did I never mention that, in the days that followed? It's like that detail completely slipped my mind—like I was too focused, instead, on the feeling in the dream, the knowledge that, somehow, his disappearance was inevitable.

"It's him. It's that day," I say. More definitive now. There's no *best estimation* here. It's him. In that moment. The small, chaotic details leading to only that day, and no other day.

My mother whispers, "Oh my God." The room has otherwise gone silent.

"Thank you, Nolan," Agent Lowell says, a hand on my shoulder.

"What does this mean?" my dad asks. I'd leave, but the hand is still heavy on my shoulder, as if holding me in place.

"There's a time stamp in the image file. The date and time lead us to believe it was taken around four in the afternoon the day of his disappearance," Agent Lowell responds. "Though we know these things can be fudged with."

Nothing is definite. Still, it was taken that day.

"Do any of you recognize the location?" he asks.

I don't. None of us do. It's just trees, and Colby's tail, and my brother. "Couldn't this still be the park?" I ask.

"That would be highly unlikely," he responds after a pause. "This is almost four hours after he disappeared, and we had plenty of officers patrolling the park. It seems unlikely he would've been there all along without giving himself away. Especially with the dog."

Everything changes. I slip from his grasp, from the table, from that room. Their voices rise, and I continue up the steps, trying to make sense of things.

I feel sick. My brother, in a photo with Colby, at 4 p.m. He'd disappeared around noon—12:10, we decided, the best estimate after going through everything, over and over again, with the police. From the sun in the sky, to the temperature of the food, to the witnesses who saw us entering the park, and the cameras on the road before the entrance. We didn't have a clock to consult, until my dad went back to the car for his phone, to eventually call the police. It was a rule that we left our phones behind on family outings. It was a rule that we never followed again.

Inside Liam's empty room, I pace, trying to think.

I remember that night my brother appeared to me, across the living room, a boundary he could not breach. *Help us. Please,* he said.

When was that?

I stop moving, the room charged. The hair stands up on the back of my neck, because the date . . . the when . . . it was when I was sick, with the flu. I remember, I was sick when the news came through about some double murder nearby. I remember, because I was on the couch that day, my

154

computer setup in my lap, the noise of the morning news on in the background—but I had been focused on something else.

I bought this equipment the morning after my brother appeared to me, asking for help. I bought this equipment while the news anchor reported the details about some terrible crime. I remember thinking: *At least they know what happened; at least they know.*

The phone rang then, because school was canceled—a suspect on the loose—but it didn't matter anyway because I was sick.

Am I making it up? Putting the pieces together because I *want* them to connect? The memories blending together in my mind?

I have to be sure before I tell Kennedy.

Back in my room, I log on to my computer and pull up my credit card history, scanning back month by month until I find it. The order for the EMF meter, the Geiger counter, and more. I trace my finger to the date listed beside the purchase: *12/4.*

December fourth. My God, I was right. I bought this equipment December fourth.

It has to mean something.

I go to text Kennedy, but I already have a message from her. It must've come through while we were all sitting around the table, staring at the image of Nolan.

We're running out of time, she says.

I can feel it, too. The men in my house, the case reopened. My brother, the sound of his imagined voice whispering in my ear: *Help us. Please.*

25

KENNEDY

We have plans to skip school. Well, I'm pseudo-skipping school. I showed up for first period, because Joe doesn't get out of the house until after the bus rumbles by, shaking the thin windows.

I don't have any finals until next week, and apparently neither does Nolan. Besides, what do finals really matter when there's something else out there?

He said he'd pick me up out front at 9:30. Which is why I'm standing outside on the concrete pavement with the sun beating down at 9:28, squinting against the summer sun. A teacher walks by behind the glass doors. He looks at me with a face of concern, and I wave. I wave because I don't want him to think I shouldn't be doing this. People leave all the time, for appointments. I just don't want him to see someone *definitely not Joe* picking me up in the circular drop-off zone.

I look back once into the front office windows to make

sure no one is reporting this, and thankfully no one seems to be paying attention. Except for a face at the corner of the window: it's Marco, standing at the front desk, looking back. And of course, of course, it's him.

Marco pulled a disappearing act last winter, in the weeks following the crime. When he finally did show up to see me, he pretended he hadn't gone AWOL, pretended that everything was fine and he was the supportive boyfriend, though by then there was a hard and impenetrable wall between us.

And now finally he's paying attention, exactly when I don't want him here. I look away, pretending not to notice.

At 9:29, Nolan's car stutters into the lot. It's hard not to notice. It's not exactly quiet, and it's not exactly clean. I'm practically bouncing on my toes by the time he makes his way through the lot to the entrance, meeting him halfway so as not to draw any more attention.

"Go, fast," I say, and he listens.

The humid air funnels in, and it's hard to hear him when we're moving fast. "Sorry," he calls, "the air conditioner didn't kick in this morning. It's like that sometimes."

I don't complain. I like it, really. Reminds you how fast you're moving, the air pushing back against you, tears in the corners of your eyes.

The car slows when we pass the sign for Freedom Battleground State Park. "The turnoff for my house is easy to miss," I say in warning.

"I know," he says. "Sorry, not to be creepy. But I've been

taking readings around the park, and I saw your house from the distance. I knew what happened, and I . . . well, I don't know what I thought. That maybe I'd sense something? But when my device started picking up the Event, I could only think about the one thing I did differently. So I came back."

"I see," I say, though of course, I already knew he had been there. It was my handprints that had plastered his car's back window, after all—I'd assumed he was the Realtor then. I'm guessing he knows by now that it was me. He passes the turnoff, and I laugh. "Seriously, Nolan, you just missed it anyway."

He mumbles to himself. "You guys need a sign."

"Keeps the spectators away," I joke. Except I'm not. After the killings, people did one of two things: They either avoided our house to an extreme, not even looking as they drove past. Like Joe, going ten miles out of the way so we could pretend the road didn't even exist. Or they were sucked in like it was a magnet. The horror of it all; like they could taste it in the air. Like they could look at the house, peer in the windows, and see evil as an observer, from a safe distance.

Nolan drums his fingers on the steering wheel, over and over. "I have something to tell you," he says.

"Shoot."

"I was going through my credit card statement from last year, because I had this feeling about something that happened. Last winter, when I was sick, I saw my brother, talking to me."

"Uh-huh," I say. Even to myself I sound disbelieving.

"Right, so, that's when I decided to buy all this equipment."

"Okay." I don't know what else to say. It seems Nolan believes in ghosts. I don't.

He sighs heavily. "Anyway, I bought the equipment December fourth."

"Wait. What?" I twist in my seat, staring at the side of his face. My eyes scan his expression for a tell, for a giveaway. "For real, Nolan?"

He nods, his fingers tight on the steering wheel. "I saw my brother in a dream. Well, I was awake. I was sick. You know, a fever dream? Where you're not sure whether you're awake or not? I saw my brother, and I thought he was asking me to help him." He shakes his head. "I couldn't really make out what he was saying."

I can hear my heart beating inside my head. "December fourth, you're sure."

"I'm sure. I just double-checked with the receipt."

This program originated December fourth. Nolan bought the equipment December fourth. That split in my life, through the entire universe.

"Lydia said she heard something," I say. "When the power rebooted at my house. Something when the audio was hooked up to Elliot's computer."

She said she thought she heard *me*, but I don't mention that part. She must've been mistaken. Imagining me there, and trying to make sense of things.

He slows the car on the drive in, the wheels unsettled over the grooves in the packed dirt and gravel. He brakes suddenly, idling the car before the clearing, the house just visible between the trees. "Someone's here," he says.

I have to crane my neck to see, but then I do. At least two people—a man and a woman, from what I can make out—and two separate cars. It seems like someone is pacing, taking measurements. "Ugh, no," I say.

"Do you know them?"

My hands are clenched so tightly that my fingernails dig into my palm. "Not exactly. Someone put an offer on the house. Well, on the land." I turn to Nolan. "They want to tear it down. All of it."

Nolan shakes his head fast. "They can't," he says, and it feels so good, so necessary, to have someone on my side, finally. It feels like something else is possible. "Should I say something?" he asks, putting the car in park.

"Like what?"

"Like, get the hell off your property?"

I feel a smile forming, unexpectedly. Then I press my lips together, looking away. "No, if Joe finds out I was here, he'll flip. Can we head to your place instead? So I can see where the signal was coming from?"

But he stares out the windshield, mouth a straight line. "Depends," he says, drumming his fingers again.

"On what?"

"On how stealthy you are."

When we pull up to what must be Nolan's house, he's staring suspiciously at the front of the house. "That's odd."

"What's odd?" The house looks so *not-odd* I worry we're on the set of some television show. Everything seems fake. The perfectly lined-up yards and shrubs, the fronts of the houses all differing *just slightly*, but there's an underlying uniformity to everything. My mom loved houses with character. Which is why we were in an old house in the middle of farmland, with a shed that had once been an old stable. *History is important*, she always said, and then we lived within it so we wouldn't forget it.

"No one's here," Nolan explains. "Yesterday, we had like half the state investigators at our house."

I remember the phone message, calling him home. "What happened last night?"

"Long story. Basically, two years later, there's suddenly a picture that was sent to my brother's old girlfriend that shows him at four p.m. on the day he disappeared. Which is four hours *after* he supposedly disappeared."

"Couldn't he have gone missing and, like, officially disappeared after?"

"Yeah, but then, what was he doing for those four hours when we were looking for him? We were all together when he . . ."

I see it then, in his face, in his words. The first crack. Uncertainty.

"The date means something, Nolan," I say. "December fourth, right?"

"Yeah," he says, nodding to himself. As if he needs to convince himself. My stomach twists, but I follow him through the front yard.

He leads me inside the house, and I was wrong. There is nothing normal about this house. At first, there's the living room, which seems normal enough. But it doesn't take long before you realize *something is definitely weird here.* Only part of the downstairs looks like a *home.* The den on the other side of the living room doesn't have any couches. Instead, it has a long table with a row of computers and a cluster of phones between each monitor. There are whiteboards covering the walls, instead of family portraits or paintings.

Oh, but then I see the pictures. In the dining room, in the kitchen, they line the walls. It looks like what I'd imagine the inside of a police investigation room to be like, except this is a house, and they seem to be looking into dozens and dozens (hundreds?) of cases all at once.

"Right, so, my parents run a nonprofit for missing youth," Nolan says, as explanation. He walks straight past it all, like it's normal. And I guess for him, at this point, it is.

Missing children lining the walls, in place of family photos, or paintings of fruit baskets or something. It puts me on edge, but I nod, like it's cool, totally normal, no big deal.

I try not to look as we head for the stairway. There are so *many* of them. Which means, there are so many people like Nolan, too. Left behind. Searching for answers. For signs of what happened.

As I pass them by, the words keep hooking me from the corner of my eye. *Last reported seen at a gas station in Cedarwood, NC; Missing since February 23, 2015.*

All these people, where do they *go?*

At first, they blend together, in a mass; regardless of age or sex or race or features. But step closer, and the eyes look back, one by one.

"Don't look too close," I hear from Nolan behind me. "Or

else you'll keep seeing them." And then I understand. It's not normal for him, either. It's inescapable. This is what greets him, every morning. I have the shadow house. And he has this.

So I take his advice and turn away. But then my eye catches a single photo, alone on the wall of the kitchen. Like they've run out of space and are just beginning a new section. I step closer. Blue eyes stare back, straight into my own. Freckles across the nose and cheeks, all the way to the narrow chin, the forehead. High cheekbones.

I take another step, until I can't see the face all at once, but only features, one at a time.

The hair is dark, wrong.

The hair is wrong, but.

My hand reaches out, my fingers tracing the words below. *Hunter Long . . .*

"Nolan," I say, in warning. He circles back slowly as I cycle through the features again.

I never thought that much of Elliot's friends. In high school, they were sort of like him—quiet, studious, building things in the basement together in their free time. When we moved to West Arbordale last year, he didn't really know anyone until he started college in the fall, and most of them lived there. Campus living was unnecessary for Elliot, since our mother taught history there. They commuted in together most days, or Joe would give him a lift, or Mom would leave him the car keys for after school and Will would drop her home later in the evening. So I remember this face. I remember Hunter Long. This is the kid he brought back home from college.

He stuck out, I noticed, because he was the only friend of Elliot's I'd seen at the house. I'd gotten home from school, and they were in the kitchen, raiding the fridge. Neither noticed me as I walked by.

It was later, when I was alone in my room, and my door opened slowly—he stood in the entrance, like he was surprised to see me there. His hair was bleached pure white, a sharp contrast to his eyebrows, and the dark roots growing in.

I jutted my thumb to the left. "Bathroom's that way," I said, and he shut the door again.

By the time I came out of my room later, they were both gone. But they must've been looking at the radio telescope, because later that night, I heard Elliot's laughter, and when I peered out my window, they were lying back and looking up at the sky.

I didn't mention it to Elliot; he didn't mention it to me. It was a brief, forgotten moment. But looking at the image, I'm sure now.

"I know him," I say, my finger pressing into the photo, to make sure it's real. "I've seen him."

And suddenly, the room fills with a warm, prickly feeling. Like I'm surrounded by static. Like everything's connected somehow.

"You're right, Nolan. Something's happening. Something here, too."

His brother, the signal, me, him—all of us, connected. After, before. There, here.

This signal sent me here for a reason. So I would see this. It's right here. *This* is what I was supposed to do, where I'm supposed to be. The pattern was so I'd find this picture. It's not a signal for anyone else. It's for me.

"What do you mean *you've seen him?*" I ask.

Kennedy stares at this new photo on the wall, and her hands are shaking. The statistics are listed below: last reported seen; location; date of birth. He's seventeen—just barely making the youth list, just barely getting the attention of an organization like this. And he's from North Carolina, not close enough to make our news, as he didn't disappear from the middle of a picnic, like magic; but in the middle of the night, with a bag.

Her hand lingers on the letters of his name, and the fine-print details below. "Last fall. With my brother. I thought he was a friend from college."

But he's too young for college. And the details don't fit.

She turns to me, suddenly, looking me over slowly. Her eyes searching my face for something. I try not to look away. "Do you believe the universe can talk to us?" she asks.

I open my mouth to say no, then instead I remember the

image of my brother in the corner of the room, his mouth moving. "Maybe." Maybe not the universe. But *something*.

"Maybe," she repeats, like for the first time, it feels almost possible to her, too. "Because I'm thinking that *maybe* I was supposed to come here."

I look to the wall, at the image of the missing kid. "For this?" I ask, jutting my thumb in his direction, but she doesn't answer.

Her eyes widen, and then I hear it, too—a car engine turning off, the beep of the door automatically locking. I gently push her toward the steps. "Go," I say, my voice low and urgent.

"Where—"

"Upstairs, first door on the left. My room," I whisper quickly, knowing no one will look in there.

I brace myself for my parents' return, but instead the key turns twice and, realizing the door is already unlocked, Mike pokes his head inside tentatively. "Hello? Nolan?"

Well, my car is parked out front.

"Hey, Mike," I say, stepping out from the kitchen.

His eyes narrow slightly. "Shouldn't you be at school?"

I nod. "Forgot a project due after lunch. Rather take the skipped class than a zero on the assignment." He makes a face, like he knows I'm lying, but he also won't turn me in. Mike was Liam's volunteer supervisor at the shelter and has been working with my parents since they moved the headquarters of their foundation to our house. He sees what it's like for me here, day in and day out. And I know he's been through it, too.

He steps inside, shutting the door behind him. "Your

parents called me," he says, as if he needs to defend himself for his presence as well, "to cover the lines today. The interns should be here any minute. What's been going on?"

"Hey, Mike," I say, cutting him off, gesturing toward the wall. I don't want to talk about the picture of Liam. "What can you tell me about this newest face on the board?"

"What?" He's confused, and I don't even blame him. The number of times I've expressed an interest in any of these faces, in any of the things my parents have gotten involved with, can be summed up to a grand total of zero.

Mike steps closer, answering anyway. This is what he does, why he's here. Bringing the missing to life. It consumed his own life, the not knowing—he's dedicated his life to this. As if he can atone for what he missed in his own history.

There's a spark in his eyes now, even as he doubts me. "Hunter Long. New case. Just been added to the system. I did it myself last week." He shakes his head. "He up and left his home sometime in the fall, but it wasn't reported until much later, in the winter."

"So, over six months ago? And it's just being added now?"

"It's complicated. It wasn't reported for weeks because he had a habit of doing this; of leaving home for a while and then coming back. Had some issue with the stepfather, spent some time crashing with friends. The investigation, it seems, was sort of half-assed." He cringes at his language, but I nod.

Children are children, is my parents' philosophy. Danger is danger. It's not our job to judge the circumstances; no one is to be seen as worthier than anyone else. I'm glad this kid eventually made it onto our wall, because sometimes I'm not so sure if that statement is true.

Still, he's here now. Every day, reminding us, just like all the rest.

"Thanks, Mike. I'm just gonna grab my stuff now."

Mike settles in front of the long table, puts a headset over his ears while I bound up the steps, two at a time, to my room.

Kennedy isn't in my room. The door is open, but I can tell it's empty even before I step inside. Down the hall, the door to Liam's room is uncharacteristically ajar, and a shadow stretches out the door. I watch her from the doorway—she's standing in the middle of the empty room, surrounded by the moss-green walls, her hands at her sides, staring straight ahead, as if she's in a trance. I'm scared to spook her.

"Kennedy?" I whisper.

She jumps anyway before spinning around. *Sorry*, she mouths.

I ease the door shut behind us. "It's okay. The guy downstairs works for my parents. He's got headphones on, so he's not going to hear us. But more people will be showing up soon."

"Is this it?" she asks, frowning.

It. My brother's room. The source of the signal, of everything.

"Yep, this is it." She's staring at the room the way I did, like she's looking for something that isn't there. I'm too embarrassed to mention that I actually whispered his name, looking for him.

I clear my throat. "I told Mike I was on my way out, back to school, so . . ."

She raises an eyebrow, and it turns her more carefree, like I can picture the girl inside, underneath everything that's happened: the signal, the house, her devastating history. "Is this why you questioned my stealth mode?" she asks, and I laugh.

In the end, I have her sneak out the back door, behind the kitchen. Mike was right—the interns arrived right after him. Dave and Clara (or Sara). Clara/Sara looks at me when I come downstairs, notebook in hand. Her face pinches into both recognition and pity, and I can't stand it. She smiles warmly. She reminds me of Abby: pretty, friendly.

"Hey there," she says. "Nolan, right?" Dave runs a hand through his red hair, looks from her to me, and lowers his eyes again.

I half-wave and walk by the table. I can't stand that still, two years later, I am something to be seen in relation to an event. It's the only reason she's looking at me like that. Head tipped to the side, mouth pursed, *so tragic.*

Like Kennedy said, the spectators do come out, drawn to the scene. Like there's something alluring about our tragedy.

"Sara, right?" I say, pressing my fingers into the surface of the table, waiting for Mike to look up.

"Clara," she corrects.

Dave has inched closer, but he's fidgeting with the papers, like he's hoping I won't notice he's totally eavesdropping. "I remember you," I say, and he flinches.

Dave nods slowly. "I was at your school when . . ." When it happened. When Liam disappeared. He looks back down again. "I didn't really know him. But he was always friendly."

"Uh-huh," I say. As if I didn't know this about my brother.

Mike's talking on the phone and barely notices the exchange. He probably wouldn't have noticed if Kennedy had walked right by him, either.

"Well," I say, channeling my parents, "thanks for your help."

Clara leans across the table, just as I'm backing away. "You know, Abby is a friend of mine," she says, and I feel my cheeks start to heat. I wonder what Abby told her, about Liam, about me. I wonder if she knows about the email. Dave looks up again. Maybe everyone knows. Abby's friends, the police, Dave, who thinks he knows us.

"Late for next period," I say, turning away.

I'm out the door before anyone can call me back.

I wait for Kennedy in the driveway, weaving past either Clara's or Dave's black SUV and Mike's blue car, which is much nicer than my own. It only makes it more obvious that mine is in desperate need of a cleaning. They've both got a decal of my parents' organization in their back windows, whereas I've always refused. I felt like a walking billboard as it was—no need to add a sticker for people to know.

I like to avoid the attention magnets as much as possible.

Kennedy slips into the passenger seat, and she's looking at me in a way I can already interpret: she wants to boss me around. "Okay, Kennedy," I say. "Where to?"

"Well, I sort of need my bike back. Maybe you can drop me at my house and I can take it to Joe's? As you can see,

I'm pretty stealthy. I'll sneak around back when the buyers aren't looking."

"That's kind of a long bike ride."

She shrugs. "I do it every couple of nights."

"Wait, when do you sleep?"

"Naps, Nolan. Give them a shot. I'm big on the after-school nap before Joe gets home for dinner. At this point, I think I have him convinced it's just a normal part of female adolescence."

"You know, I can just drive you instead."

She twists in the seat, not responding.

I repeat the offer, only this time I make it a statement instead of an offer, so she will just accept it already. "Stop biking. I'll drive you over there tonight to get your things. And then whenever you need a ride. At least until we figure this out. Okay?"

"Are you going to try the nap?" she asks, and I think that means she's agreed.

She asked me if I believed the universe could talk to us, and the truth is, I do think it's something. The fact that we both received the signal and it linked us together; the fact that she came to my house and recognized a photo. All of it means this was not chance, but purpose.

I think it's this: The signal isn't the message. It's the sign. A clue, from my brother maybe, trapped somewhere beyond this world, telling me where to go. And right now, it's telling me to follow Kennedy Jones on her mission, and somewhere along the way, it's going to lead me to the next sign, or the next, and we will *find him*.

27

KENNEDY

Now.

Wait, no.

Now. For real.

Okay, my texts to Nolan are not the most eloquent. Not that his are any better.

Here, he wrote five minutes ago.

I mean, at the corner, he amended in the next text.

I'd just spent the last five minutes making sure Joe was really sleeping, and not just staring at the ceiling in the dark. Joe didn't come home until after dinner, when I was crashing—a nap in preparation for tonight. When he knocked on my bedroom door—to apologize for being late, *got caught up,* etc, etc—I tried my best to look like I hadn't just been sleeping.

I must've failed, because he frowned and asked if I was feeling okay.

I've been watching the clock since then. Joe didn't go to bed until just after midnight, when the house was dark and quiet. I gave him twenty extra minutes.

When I opened his bedroom door to check on him, he didn't move.

It was time.

Without my bike, the routine feels off. I'm more on-edge than usual, sneaking out in the middle of the night. Once I'm outside, I make a dash for the corner of the street, where Nolan said he'd be waiting.

The overhead light inside his car turns on as I pull open the passenger door, and he squints. "Hey," he says.

"Geez, find the creepiest spot on the street, why don't you."

He rolls his eyes, and it looks like he just woke up. Like he's only half focused, and it turns him softer at the edges. "Better than having someone call the cops on me because some beat-up car is parked under a streetlight outside their house."

"Okay, okay," I say as he drives off.

"Hey," he says, nudging me in the shoulder with one hand while he drives. "Breathe, Kennedy."

I smile at him, at the slow grin that forms as his eyes adjust to the dark again.

The street is quiet at night, winding through forest and farmland, no sidewalk on either edge. "I can't believe you bike this in the dark," Nolan mumbles.

The shoulder of the road is pretty narrow, dropping off to a grassy ditch, but from this angle it looks worse than it is. "Barely anyone ever drives this way at night."

"That doesn't make it any better," he says, tightening his hold on the wheel.

This time, he slows down early enough to turn into my driveway on the first pass. "Turn off the headlights," I tell him when he pulls off the road.

"What? No way. I'd really rather not end up wrapped around some tree."

"Just go slow. I don't want someone to call Joe and tell him someone's here."

"It's almost one in the morning, and this is your property, right?" He looks my way and lets out a sigh. "When we're closer to the house and I'm sure I can see, I will, okay?"

I hold my breath until we reach the roundabout in front of the house and he flicks the lights off. The house is a shadow in the night, with the moon hidden behind clouds. We exit the car as quietly as we can, which isn't really quiet at all with the rocks and dirt kicking up in our wake.

I've got my flashlight with me, like usual, and keep it aimed low to the ground so no one will notice unless they're already here. My bike is still hidden underneath the porch, and I mumble a thanks to whatever higher power was looking out for it while the prospective buyers were here.

Nolan is not nearly as good at stealth mode as he thinks, closing his car door too firmly, stepping too loudly, kicking at a pebble with every other step. "Shh," I remind him.

"What?" he says.

I gesture to his feet, to the ground. The problem is sort

of . . . all of him. He makes an impression. He leaves a mark. I give up and continue on, hoping for the best.

At the shed around back, the door squeaks when I push it open.

"I thought we were coming for your bike," he whispers.

"While we're here, I might as well check the new data," I say, stepping inside.

Nolan flips the switch on the side of the wall, on impulse, but I flip it off again. "Trust me," I whisper, thinking of Marco and Lydia and Sutton, who've been spending a lot of time out there.

Instead I turn on the computer screen, which illuminates us in the dark. Nolan's face glows an eerie yellow, and his eyes keep darting around the room. "What is this place?" he whispers.

"A computer shed. That used to be a storage shed. That used to be a stable."

"I see," he says, like that makes perfect sense.

I download all the data we can get, storing it on my flash drive, then gesture to the box of Elliot's things, left behind from when Lydia was in here. "Can we bring that with us, too?" I ask. I want to take advantage of the fact that we have a car. I want to spend some time looking through everything.

"Sure." Nolan scoops it up, then pauses at the door, and I realize he's waiting for me. Or he's waiting for the flashlight.

"Just a sec." I finish up, shut everything down, and follow him back outside, illuminating his path with my flashlight. I shine the light under the porch and wheel the bike out, walking it back to his car.

He pops the trunk, and I see a baseball bat wedged in the

corner, along with his gear. He pushes it to the side, making room for Elliot's things, then takes out a couple of bungee cords to secure my bike.

"Ready?" he asks as he closes the trunk.

But I stare up at the house, then back at Nolan's car. "There are a few more things I want to grab. In the house."

He pauses before nodding once.

"You don't have to come in," I add.

"I've already been in there," he says, and I narrow my eyes at him over my shoulder. I knew he had been *at* my house, not *in* my house.

"I know, I'm sorry." He puts his hands up, surrendering.

"Okay, well. I left handprints all over the back window of your car to freak you out," I say, since we're in the confessing spirit.

"I sort of figured," he says, and even in the dark, I can tell he's grinning.

He follows me around back, but he pauses at Elliot's window, like he's considering changing his mind. I'm expecting him to tell me he'll wait for me out front, when he finally climbs in after me. He doesn't move from Elliot's room at first, once we're inside. It's different in the dark, I get that. Instead, he stands across the room from me, a shadow in the dark house.

"Come on," I say.

"I can't see."

"Sorry. No lights, or someone will notice."

"Are you trying to freak me out again?"

I cross the room and grab his hand, pulling him behind me, his dry palm pressed against mine, fingers locking, like it's nothing. I'm thankful for the dark as we walk, tethered together. And I'm thankful for his hand, which at the moment is for me and not him. The scent of paint, the stairway before me—the shadow house is here.

My free hand grips the banister, and I hear nothing—no breathing behind me. Nolan knows what happened here, too. He must. His steps follow mine, in grave silence.

At the top of the stairs, I finally turn on the flashlight, shining it back and forth. To the right is the loft area. To the left, the room for storage, with the boxes of Elliot's things. My eyes meet Nolan's. "Do you think this will all fit in your car?"

The backseat is full of Elliot's boxes—if Elliot won't talk to me, maybe I can still decipher his intentions, his thoughts. Maybe there will be a note about the program on December fourth. Maybe I can figure out how he knew the kid on Nolan's wall. There must be answers in here somewhere.

I know this isn't everything, that the police took things from his room, as evidence. But this had all been left behind, or stored in the shed behind the house, until the cleaning company was called in, followed by the stager and the Realtor.

We leave Nolan's car at the corner where he picked me up earlier and slowly transport my bike and the boxes, one by one, to the base of my window. I decide I'll move them later, once Joe is up and in the shower and won't hear me banging around in the next room. Except when we're depositing the last boxes, the outside light turns on. The back door swings open and Joe is there, staring at us both. He's in gym shorts and a T-shirt, and his eyes look bloodshot, and I can't tell if I've just woken him or if he's been awake for a while now.

He stares from me to Nolan. Nolan puts the last box down. "I should go," he says, taking a step back.

"Yes, you should go," Joe says, in a voice I've never heard before.

Nolan looks at me and cringes, mouthing *Sorry*. I'm still watching him stride toward his car on the corner when Joe's booming voice cuts through the night. "What the hell is all this?"

"Elliot's things," I say, even though surely he can see this for himself. The boxes are labeled in black marker, with his name.

"Where did you get all this?"

When I don't answer, he throws his hands in the air and spins around, retreating into the house once more.

"Joe," I say, following him inside.

He stops walking down the hall but puts his hand up, cutting me off.

"You sneak out, sneak out with a *boy*, and what, take a joyride to your old house?"

"He's not some *boy*, Joe. It's not like that."

"Oh, I'm so glad to hear it's *not like that*, Kennedy. What's it like, then? Go ahead. Tell me. Is he the reason you've been skipping school?"

I stare at him, frozen.

He nods, every movement tight. "Yeah, the school called. They called, and I thought you were sick, thought that's why you looked tired when I got home. I told them you weren't feeling well. Thought it was *my fault*, that there was something I missed, but you were just planning to meet up with your boyfriend—"

"Nolan," I say. Joe looks at me, confused. "I was planning to meet with *Nolan*, Joe. Because something's happening. At the house, something isn't what we thought."

"Kennedy, stop." He puts his head in his hands. "I don't know how to help you."

"Well, you can start by not selling my house, Joe!"

He takes a deep breath and lets it out slowly. "You're grounded. For the week. School and back, that's it."

I shake my head. "You can't do that."

"Yes, I can. I can also take your phone, if you want to push it."

I clamp my mouth shut. These were his rules: no skipping school, no boys.

As if this is the source of the change in me.

Not the signal, not the photo, not Elliot at the jail. But a boy in the night.

"Joe, please."

"Kennedy. Go to bed. Now."

I listen, but only because this is not the right time. And before that time comes, I need my phone.

28

NOLAN

Grounded for a week

That's all I hear from Kennedy the next day. Meanwhile, if my school has called about me skipping a day, it doesn't seem to register. Or else no one has checked the messages. Though from the way my parents looked this morning, my guess is it wouldn't make their Top 10 list of Things That Require Attention, either way.

When I arrive home from school, Dave, Clara, and Mike are there, along with the remainders of their day: three energy drinks on the desk, two sandwich wrappers, and an open bag of Doritos. I can feel Clara's eyes on me as I walk past, but I don't look. I have to tap the table in front of Mike to get his attention. He reminds me of a college kid pulling an all-nighter, only he's in his forties and he does this all the time. Sometimes I wonder if this is my future, the sibling left behind, a life dedicated to searching.

God, I have to find him.

Mike looks up but doesn't remove his headphones at first. "My parents?" I ask.

He holds up one finger, then points to the headphones, like maybe he's listening to a message.

"They left," Dave says. "With some dude in a suit." I close my eyes. Agent Lowell. "Think it was about the picture," he continues, obviously the master eavesdropper.

Clara perks up, opens her mouth to talk just as my parents walk in the front door, clearly disoriented.

They thank the group working in the living room, then excuse them for the day. They drift through the downstairs, my mom tossing her purse onto the couch as she wanders to the sink and sticks her mouth directly under the faucet. That is, for the record, the most un-Mom-like move.

I'm transfixed.

I jump when my dad puts his hand on my shoulder, and then tense. This is the parent move I *am* familiar with. I'm even more shaken by this than by the un-Mom move. Because I know what this means. *Nolan, we have something to tell you.*

"Dad," I start, before he can say something, sucking us back in. The reason I was looking for him when I got home from school. I pull him to the kitchen, pointing to the new picture up on the wall. "That kid on the end. My friend was here yesterday, and she says she saw him around here."

He narrows his eyes, steps closer to see the details. If he thinks anything of me having a girl in the house when they were gone, he doesn't say, doesn't seem to care. "Hunter

Long," he says slowly, like he's pulling the file up in his brain. "Here? Is she sure? When did she see him?"

"In the fall."

He nods slowly. "Seems unlikely. But we'll make a note. Give me her name tomorrow."

But he's not paying attention. Usually, when they get a bite of promising information, their movements quicken, their eyes brighten, fueled by the hope.

My dad turns away from the photo, letting out a sigh. "Nolan, we have something to tell you," he says, and my stomach continues its precipitous plummet. No point in prolonging this, but still, I plan my escape route.

I back out of the room so I'm hovering between the dining room and living room. "Uh-huh," I say.

"The photo of Liam appears to be authentic," my dad says. "The photo is proof."

My mother appears then, her eyes glassy, her weight leaning slightly to the right, and for a second I wonder if she's been drinking.

"Proof of what?" I ask.

"Proof that the park wasn't where he disappeared from," she says, the faraway look still in her eyes.

I shake my head. It has to be the park. It's where I've centered everything. Every test. Everything I've been looking for. My brother and his dog disappear without a trace. A forest of ghost stories and legends. Some crack in the universe. Everything happened against his will; he didn't choose to go anywhere, without telling us.

I feel sick, like the world has tilted. I can't orient myself. *No.* They're wrong.

"They've enlarged the photo for us," my dad says, gesturing to the living room. "Agent Lowell is asking all of us to take a good look again. To think about where it was taken."

The room is practically spinning. It feels like I'm falling, like something is slipping from my grasp—

"Nolan," he says, like he's repeating something he's already said.

It's then I notice the printout on the living room table. Enlarged Liam, in the center of the room.

I picture my brother, in the corner of this very room. The fever dream. His mouth moving. *Help us. Please.*

I picture him over the sink the morning he disappeared, the drop of blood. The hiss of pain, the razor clattering in the sink.

"Someone went to a lot of trouble to disguise where the email was sent from," my dad adds. "They're still working on it, at the field office."

It's then I think: *They won't find anything.* It's a thought that suddenly feels absolutely true: from somewhere beyond, my brother did this. He's been trying to reach me, with the dream, the email, the signal; and now he has.

When my parents leave the room momentarily, I snap a photo of the printout with my phone, and I text it to Kennedy.

This is the photo that was sent to my brother's old girlfriend.

And then I walk up the steps to my room, staring at the photo on my screen, at the grainy pixels. It's just trees. Trees, and my brother, and Colby's tail in the corner.

My phone rings in my hand, but it's a video call. When I hit Accept, I see Kennedy sitting cross-legged on the floor of her room, with notebooks and papers spread out all around her, empty boxes in the background. The phone must be propped up on one such box.

She leans closer to the screen for a moment, then shakes her head. "You don't look that much like him." Then she looks down again, shifting a few papers around.

"So I hear," I say. I've been told that most of my life. Liam really was the golden child, both in actions and looks. We were like opposite sides of the same coin: his hair was a dark blond to my fully brown; his eyes blue to my brown; his face perfectly symmetrical, whereas my nose still bent slightly to the left after getting too close to a swing in Little League. I bet I'm as tall as him now, though. The thought hurts my stomach.

She stops moving then, looks up from the work around her. "That wasn't a slight. I was just picturing someone more like you." Her eyes flick away and she turns her face to the side, her hair falling over her features so I can't read her expression.

She goes back to multitasking, or whatever it is she's doing. She called me, but it's like she's expecting me to lead the conversation here. "Uh," I say, "what are you up to?"

"Well, there's definitely no signal coming through any-more. So I'm looking through all of Elliot's things, seeing if I can figure anything out. See where it came from. Trace it back."

"Any luck?"

"Not really. I wish I could get back there, though. I want to try rebooting the electricity. It seems that's what knocked it out the first time. You?" She pauses, tipping her head over, twisting her dark hair up into a haphazard ponytail on the top of her head, as if she needs it out of her way to think clearly.

"Well?" she asks, still upside down.

When I forget to answer, she flips her hair back and looks at me head-on.

"Sorry, was just waiting for you to finish."

She gives me a look like I'm ridiculous. "Can you not do your hair and speak at the same time?"

"I don't really think about my hair all that often."

She smirks, then flips her hair back and forth, like a joke. But now it's all I can think about. Dark hair, cascading over my vision. I clear my throat.

"Sorry, nothing here, either. I told my parents about the photo of Hunter Long, but he was reported missing this past winter. Still, can I give them your name?"

"Sure, though I don't think I'll be much help. I saw him in the fall."

"Sorry, Kennedy, about last night. I hope I didn't get you in even more trouble."

She winces. "I'm in trouble, but it's not your fault. My idea, my plan. Sorry you got caught up in it." She smiles then. "Could be worse. At least I still have my phone."

She goes back to the papers, but I don't want her to hang up. "Can Lydia find out what's in the signal?" I ask.

"Eh. She's, like, a computer expert. Heard she got

suspended in middle school for hacking into the school email and sending out a snow day closure alert. So yeah, she's crazy talented, but I don't think she has the right equipment."

"And Elliot won't talk to you. Do you think he would talk to someone else?"

"No, I don't. His trial is coming up, and the lawyers are focused on helping him remember. . . ." She sighs, her thoughts drifting. But then she sits straighter, leaning closer to the screen so her brown eyes look twice their normal size. "There are people at the college who can do this, though. My mom worked there. They know me." She looks quickly over her shoulder and lowers her voice. "But I have to talk to Joe first."

Her head twists to the side, and she leans even closer so all I see is the side of her cheek, half her mouth, as she whispers, "I have to go."

And then the screen goes black.

Long after everyone should typically be asleep, I hear my parents across the hall. My mom's voice, high and fast. My father, trying to calm her. The tension fills the house, until it reaches my shoulders and I need to act.

They don't hear me walking by their room, past the closed door. They don't hear me on the stairs, or heading out the back door. If they notice the engine starting, they don't come out to stop me.

• • •

There's no one at Kennedy's old house right now. All the lights are off, and the front door is locked. I go around back, let myself in the way Kennedy taught me yesterday, keeping a flashlight low and away from the windows.

Tell me what to do, I think, closing my eyes. "Liam," I whisper into the emptiness. Nothing comes. I thought my brother wanted me here. I thought he was sending me a message, to come.

Nothing answers. Not even a flicker of a sign. The air conditioner kicking on, or a gust of wind rattling something in the vents. It's just an empty house, in an empty field, under an empty sky.

I pull out my phone instead of my equipment and make a call. Kennedy's face appears, barely decipherable in the grainy dark surrounding her. She sits upright. "Nolan?"

"I'm here," I say. "Tell me what to do."

She rubs her eyes, runs a hand down her face, then tucks a strand of hair behind her ear. I've woken her. She's still in bed. "At my house?"

I nod.

"Okay," she says, keeping her voice low. "Reboot the house. Let's see if we can restart things to pick up the signal again. It's the only thing I can think to do. There has to be something more. Something more than just pi, if that's even what it is."

She leads me with the sound of her voice to the garage, even though I've been here before. Still, I give myself over, letting her lead the way. When she instructs me to shut down the fuse box and flip it back on again, I listen. She sends me to the shed next, to make sure the computer is back online. "It should—running—and then . . ."

"Kennedy?" I shake the phone in the dark, as if I can jar her back into focus. "Hold on, you're breaking up."

The feed continues to cut in and out as I walk in the dark. But even as she disappears, I think I hear her voice.

29

I need to find a way back to my house this afternoon. Nolan rebooted the electricity and sent me a text to let me know it was done.

I haven't slept since. I'm already sitting at the kitchen table when Joe emerges from his room.

He does a double take when he sees me. "Morning," he says, sticking his head into the fridge. "I'll get milk on the way home."

"Okay." I'm eating my cereal dry, crunching the Cheerios between my back molars.

"After school, the Albertsons invited you over. Until I'm back."

I drop my spoon. "What?"

Something in my voice must resonate, because he shuts the fridge door, turning slowly. "To and from school, that's it." As if he could sense that I was already planning for Nolan to pick me up from school, drive me by our house, where I could pull the data and be back at Joe's before he realized it—hopefully even before the school bus.

"Is this a joke?"

"No, Kennedy, this isn't a joke."

"Joe, okay, tomorrow I'll do that. I'll go to the Albertsons' and stare blankly at these kids I don't know. Totally fine. Just not today."

He narrows his eyes. "What's so important about today, Kennedy?"

I grasp for anything frantically. "You know I have finals. How am I supposed to study with a bunch of people I don't know around?"

"How are you supposed to study when you spend all hours of the night running around with some guy?"

"Nolan," I repeat, for the tenth time.

"Right. Nolan who is not your boyfriend, but who drove you to the house in the middle of the night so you could get these boxes. Nolan, who I literally never heard of a week ago, but who has been to our house to see you at least two times that I know of. Was it this Nolan who took you to see Elliot, too?"

I don't answer right away. "Joe, haven't you ever done something nice for a friend because they needed your help?"

He shakes his head. "Not like this, Kennedy. This is not a list of normal things you do for a friend. Especially not one you just met. Trust me on this."

I glance at my phone, trying to sidestep him, but he puts a hand out. "And the second you leave this house, you're going to be on the phone with him, am I right?"

I stop midstride and look up at him.

"Like I said, Kennedy. Not a friend."

"I feel sorry for you, Joe. That every relationship you've ever had is only surface-deep."

As soon as I leave the house, I'm on the phone to Nolan, just like Joe accused. Only this time, when he picks up, I can't get Joe's words out of my head. It's true, Nolan is the first person I thought of this morning, the part of the day I was looking forward to the most. He asks me for my email so he can send me something, and it's immediately something else to look forward to.

Is it normal to talk to someone first thing each morning and last thing each evening? To hold their hand in the dark in the house where your worst nightmare happened? To hide out in the room of their missing brother?

Is it normal to drive a girl you just met to a jail? To skip school because she asked?

Maybe not. But I wasn't about to tell Joe the reason: *It's not that he's into me, Joe. It's that we've both simultaneously stumbled upon proof that the world is more than it seems.*

A text arrives at lunch: **Check your email.**

Nolan came through. My email is full of scanned images. It's the information on Hunter Long. His address in North Carolina, his pictures, the brief overview of the case, and his parents' contact information.

I write back: **Thanks. What are you doing? Are you at school?**

I'm scanning through the documents in the school library,

eating lunch in the corner, when my phone vibrates under the table with a new text: **Sort of. What are you doing?**

**Eating lunch in the library. Reading through
the file.**

I'm halfway through my banana when the library door pushes open. I look up, and Nolan's there, hands in the pockets of his jeans, standing near the entrance like he's lost—because he is.

I'm already smiling when his gaze finds me at the corner table, and his face mirrors mine. He walks toward me and my stomach flutters, and *Oh crap*, I think, *Joe was totally right*. He must've been able to read it on my face, whenever I mentioned Nolan's name. I try to hold it back so Nolan doesn't see. Though from the way the girls at the next table are watching me, smirking, I have a feeling I'm a little too late.

"What are you doing here?" I ask when he sits in the chair beside me. Not across, beside. Pulling the chair even closer so he can look over my shoulder at the documents I'm reading.

"This seemed a little more pressing than gym today," he says. "And I figured I won't get to see you later, what with the whole grounded thing."

"Joe's making me go to the neighbors' after school. I think I'm being babysat."

He cringes. "Sorry about that."

"It wasn't your fault."

"No, as you pointed out, I'm not that stealthy. It was probably because of me."

I don't argue, because it's true. He's not. Even now, people at the next table are looking at him. It's nothing you can really put your finger on—just the way everything comes together. The slight bend of his nose, the crinkle at the corner of his eyes, the angles of his cheekbones, the downslope of his lips. I noticed the very moment he walked into the library.

"How'd you get into the school? And find the library?" I ask.

"Just walked straight in when some adult got buzzed in. They held the door for me and everything. As for the library, you're not going to believe this." He lowers his voice and grins. "I asked. Turns out the average high schooler is not nearly as suspicious as you."

"Well, welcome to West Arbor-Hell," I say, smiling, which is how Marco introduced it to me.

He pulls the papers out of his backpack. "Figured it would be easier if you had the hard copies to look through. Better than on your phone, anyway."

He sets some paper and pens between us. "Wait, did you bring a highlighter?" I ask.

He grins. "I came prepared."

We spend the next twenty-six minutes highlighting relevant information and dates, seeing where the investigation into Hunter's disappearance petered out, trying to track his whereabouts. Eventually, the overhead bell rings and my shoulders tense. "I can skip," I say.

"No. Go. I don't want you to get in any more trouble."

"It doesn't matter—"

"It does, though, if I don't get to see you after school."

He looks down at the papers then, as if embarrassed. I can feel my cheeks heating. I let my hair fall over the side of my face as I pack my bag so he doesn't notice.

The bell rings again, and I'm officially late. He still doesn't look up.

"Nolan," I say.

"Yeah?" He's shuffling papers, still looking down.

I put a hand on his shoulder until he turns his head. "Thank you for coming today," I say.

I watch as his smile forms, and then I dart for class.

Marco catches me at my locker after last period. "Hey," he says, angling his body between me and my locker door.

"Hey," I repeat, tipping my head so he gets the picture to move out of the way.

He frowns and steps aside, but he's still hovering over my shoulder. "What are you doing with that kid?"

"What kid?" I say, slamming the locker door.

"Uh, the kid who walked into the library, looking for you, even though he doesn't go to our school."

I had no idea Marco was in the library. "What's it to you, Marco?"

His expression shifts, like I've somehow hurt him. Impossible. Marco didn't care enough to be hurt. "You don't have to act so mean, Kennedy. I didn't do anything to you. I didn't mean to hurt you. I just didn't know how to . . ."

I wave him off so he'll just stop. He didn't. He didn't know how to act, or be, and I didn't know how to tell him what I needed. We were young, and then we weren't. Things got hard. He disappeared.

It wasn't surprising, but it was telling, and it left me with no one, on my own. My friends were his friends. And when he left me alone, that was it. I was *alone*.

"Stop acting like this was my decision," he says. "You seem so angry at me all the time."

"I'm not *angry*. I'm . . ." I can't find the word. Indifferent. Empty. Bitter. Maybe there's a part of me that *is* angry, a little. Maybe it's easier to be angry about things like that—my boyfriend didn't come to see me after—than the other parts.

"Well, be careful, Kennedy. That's all I wanted to say. That kid? Nolan? Two years ago, his brother disappeared. Did you know that?" I nod and keep walking. Marco hurries to keep pace. "Well, there were a lot of rumors. A lot of stories." He looks side to side before leaning closer. "Including one about his brother's girlfriend."

I turn on him, narrowing my eyes. He holds out his hands, backing away. "I'm just saying. No one knows what happened, still."

He keeps moving until he's swallowed up by the crowd. But his words keep echoing inside my head.

After school, I head over to the Albertsons', and I stare at their children, and they stare back at me.

They're twins in the freshman class—Lacy and Riley, but I don't know which is which. Only that one has shorter blond hair than the other. They wear identical bathing suits, wrapped in identical towels, and they whisper to each other in some coded language, like I'm some specimen to examine.

Their mother brings a bowl of fruit to the patio table out back, overlooking the pool. "Can I get you anything else, Kennedy?" she asks, but I shake my head, my gaze fixed on the surface of the water, the way the sunlight reflects sharply off a subtly moving current.

"Are you coming in the pool?" the one with shorter hair asks, a spear of watermelon visible in the corner of her mouth.

I start to say no, then think, *Why not?* I take off my shoes and, still in my shorts and shirt from school, I step off the edge. I sink under the cold water, and I scream.

I'm underwater, looking up at their blurry figures above. I see them standing side by side and hear their voices in unison, muffled by the water: *One, two, three*—and then their simultaneous splash pushes me farther away. I stay that way, near the bottom, until they get too close and my lungs burn.

Joe comes to get me when he arrives home, thanking Mrs. Albertson, like I am a child who must be watched. I walk home, dripping wet, daring him to say something. Daring him to ask. But he doesn't. He disappears down the hall and comes back with an old beach towel, frayed at the edges, wrapping it around my shoulders. His hands stay there, firm, like he's holding me in place, scared I'll disappear like the rest of them.

"I'd ask what you've been up to," he says, "but that seems like a stupid question."

I crack a grin despite myself. He steps back, arms hanging loosely at his sides. He takes a deep breath. "Sorry I sent you there. I don't know what I'm doing half the time here, Kennedy. In case you couldn't tell."

"Joe, you have to trust me. I'm not a child."

"Except, technically, you *are*. And I'm the one responsible for you." He runs a hand through his hair. "We have to trust *each other*."

He waits then, until I silently nod.

Joe sighs, like he's relieved. But his moment of calm seems short-lived. "I'm having trouble sleeping, too," he says. "With the trial. The lawyers wanted to try hypnosis, in the hopes of filling in some of the gaps that night, but I don't know what's best. I don't know whether that will make it better or worse." I know what he's implying: whether Elliot's memory of that night will destroy him; whether the not-knowing is for the best.

Standing in front of me, while I'm drip-drying just inside the front door, Joe looks suddenly younger, out of his depth. Alone.

"Did you know any of Elliot's friends?" I ask.

"Not really," he says, refocusing on me. "Why?"

"I'm just wondering. I'm wondering if they'll be called up for the trial. To talk about the type of person he was."

He looks me over slowly from the kitchen beside the foyer. "You're only going to be asked about the facts, Kennedy. What you saw."

I nod slowly. "But what if there was another explanation?"

He shakes his head. "Don't do this, Kennedy."

"No, Joe, listen, please. You wonder, too, right? Why would he do it? Have you talked to him? Has *anyone* talked to him?"

He spins away from me, walks to the kitchen, places his hands on the counter. Shutting down, again. Then he breathes deeply and turns to face me. "Okay, come sit down."

"No, I don't need to sit—"

"Things are going to come out in the trial, Kennedy. Things you need to be prepared for."

I half-listen, not sitting, but at least standing in the kitchen. "What sort of *things*?"

"The sort of things that tighten up the case. Listen, it's not just that his prints are all over the weapon. There was a large amount of gunshot residue found on him. You know what that means?"

I shake my head, but not because I don't understand. Because I don't believe it.

"It means they have even more evidence that he fired the gun, Kennedy. An expert will testify to that." He sighs. "The police believe he shot . . . her. And then Will tried to wrestle it away from him. And then he shot him, too."

I shake my head. It's not possible. My brother studies and builds things. He's funny in a self-deprecating way. Of the two of us, he's the rule-follower. The responsible one. He goes to school, and he comes back home, and he tolerates my presence when I have nothing better to do. My brother pales at the sight of blood. He has never hurt anyone. Let alone our *mother*.

"That makes *no sense*. Come on. It was the same as every

other night. There is no reason he'd get Mom's gun *just because*. There has to be another reason. Maybe someone else was there, and he was protecting—"

"Kennedy, stop. Everyone at the college . . ." Joe runs a hand back through his dark hair, but he doesn't continue.

"Everyone at the college *what?*"

Joe sighs. "Everyone at the college noticed the tension between Elliot and your mom. They weren't getting along. There are several witnesses who heard them arguing in her office in the days leading up to . . . Come on, you had to notice. *That's* what people will say, if called to testify."

"No, that's not true," I say impulsively. But what did I really know? Did they avoid each other at meals? Walk silently to the car in the mornings, with a telling gap between them? Did I hear Elliot's voice cutting down my mom while I was talking on the phone with Marco?

I was busy with the things I thought mattered then, with Marco, too distracted to see what was happening in my own house. Literally alive, they say, because of this. Because I snuck out to Marco's when everything turned upside down.

"So? So what if they weren't getting along? Is that really a motive for killing her? For killing *two people?*"

He frowns. "You know how Elliot was taking one of Will's classes?"

"Yeah, I know that already," I snap.

"Well, he was failing the class."

I shake my head. I keep shaking it as I back away, out of the room. It seems like the very stupidest thing to do, the worst reason to kill someone. Over a grade? An argument? Had he been fighting with my mother about that? Elliot is smart. I can't imagine him bringing home anything lower than a B—but so what if he was failing? Was that really a reason? That, enraged, he would hear Will come inside, go into the linen closet, where my mom kept the gun hidden, and take it?

But what was I expecting? A good reason? I can't think of a single one.

"He wouldn't," I say from the hall.

"*Except*, Kennedy . . ." Joe trails off, not needing to say the rest.

The gun, the residue, the blood, Elliot running from the scene. I am testifying *as a witness*. The police have no doubts about what happened next.

I snuck out that night because my mom was going to a department holiday party with Will. She wore a black dress and a red scarf. I saw her readjusting it in the hallway mirror while she looked out the window, hearing the sound of Will's car.

If I'm not home until after you're asleep, good night, she'd said, swooping down for a quick kiss on my cheek.

Goodbye, Elliot, she called over my head. Had he responded? Did she frown?

I can't recall it clearly. Instead, I had been counting the moments until she was gone so I could leave.

I assumed they wouldn't be home until after midnight. And then I was held up by the storm, and Marco. I didn't notice how late it had gotten, and I was worried she'd notice I was gone.

But she didn't.

It was horrific, the simplicity. The police knew what time

they'd left the party. They figured she'd only been home for a handful of minutes before everything went wrong.

I didn't know Elliot had a motive, albeit a terrible one.

This trial is not going to be what I thought—a chance for me to offer another explanation. They already have the details, the reason, and I'm just providing the proof.

30

NOLAN

Back at home, my parents and Agent Lowell are speaking in the kitchen quietly. I've had it with the ambushes, the looks, the hopes that will inevitably be shattered again. It's just a photo, taken two years ago. Sent to Abby, not to us. What was she supposed to do with it?

I try to sneak by them up the stairs, but the second step squeaks, the traitor, and the voices in the kitchen abruptly halt.

Agent Lowell pokes his head out of the kitchen and announces, "Nolan. We've been waiting for you."

"I have finals next week. Kinda busy." When the investigators for your brother's case are in your own home, it's hard to justify avoiding them. But this is the point I've reached. Invoking the lie that studying is currently more important than finding out what happened to my brother. If only they knew about my own search.

"Sit down." It's my father, then, emerging from the kitchen, and his voice is rough and unfamiliar. My mother,

I can tell, has been crying. Her eyes are red and the skin is swollen underneath. She doesn't look at me as she stands beside my father.

My father gestures to a chair in the dining room, and I drop my bag and sit, as instructed. Something about his voice keeps me silent. Something about the way they're standing twists my stomach.

My mother does not sit. No one else sits. And there's nothing in front of me, no picture to look at, or clothing to confirm, just three adults standing over me. I start to feel sick, claustrophobic.

"We've traced the email with the photo," Agent Lowell begins. Then he stops, as if expecting me to continue for him.

"Nolan," my father prompts.

I hold my hands up, confused. What do they want from me?

"Your father tells me you work most weekend mornings at the Battleground County Library."

I don't answer, because that *is* what I tell my father. But it's a lie. I have been there maybe three times in my entire life. Enough to know the name and location. Enough to use it as an excuse. I pass it every day on the way to Freedom Battleground State Park.

"The IP address," Agent Lowell continues, "was from the library."

"What?" I push back the chair abruptly, facing them all.

My father repeats it, in case I haven't heard. "The email to Abby's college account with that photo of Liam. It was sent from there."

My mouth drops open, and I'm shaking my head,

desperately trying to process. "I'm sorry, and you all think *I* did this?"

My mother still won't look at me. One freaking suspicious testimony, and two years later, I still can't escape it.

The problem with a missing-person investigation is this: Everyone is under suspicion. If they were taken, it's most likely by someone they know. A disappearance could be reported in order to cover something up, something worse. Some of those children on the wall are probably dead. I know that. This is what I've learned after being at the center of this house for two years.

But this is different. Liam was there, and then he was gone, along with the dog. Like he slipped from this dimension, like something took him from us. It's *not* the same thing.

"It wasn't me," I say. "I don't really go there. I don't use the computer. I swear. Check the cameras."

Agent Lowell shakes his head. "They don't have cameras, which I'm assuming you realized."

I feel sick. The library. I pass it every day, and someone else was sitting there, sending this picture. . . .

"Mom, Dad, I was lying, okay? I don't tutor. I don't go there—"

My father reaches out to grab my arm, and his grip is too tight. It's not kind. He's angry. "Where did you get this picture?" he says, his voice sounding hoarse and raw.

"I didn't," I say, yanking my arm back.

Even Agent Lowell looks alarmed by the change in my father's behavior.

My mother looks from him to the agent to me. There

are so many levels of worry going on right now. We were all together when Liam disappeared. They should vouch for me. They know. They *know*.

"It's a mistake," I tell them. "We were all together. During the search. We looked for Liam together."

"Listen," Agent Lowell says, "we're not implying anyone did anything. Only that you might know more than you've let on. If you sent this picture to Abby to get our attention, Nolan, you have it. Even if you didn't take the photo, did someone send it to you, after the fact?"

"No one sent this to me," I say, practically yelling myself. "I've never seen it before."

It's then I hear the footsteps overhead. Two men come down the steps, carrying boxes in their outstretched arms. "What . . ." I stand, stepping closer, until I can see into the boxes as they pass: my computer, my bag, my *things*.

"Dad? Mom? What did you *do*?"

Agent Lowell steps into my path, preventing me from getting any closer. "They didn't do anything, Liam. It's our job to track down anything that might help us. We're going through your computer and electronics right now, to see if there are other copies of the photo."

I moan. What they will find on that computer is a mapping of the park where my brother disappeared. Articles about the Jones House. The documentation of my search for the unexplained in Freedom Battleground State Park, and more. It should clear me, but I worry it will seem like something else. Like I'm looking for something instead.

"One more thing. We need your phone," he says, holding out his hand.

"No," I say.

"Nolan," my dad says. "It's not yours. It's ours."

I have no more connection to the outside world. The bathroom fills with steam from the shower, my image disappearing in the glass. I catch a glimpse in the fog, and it's Liam instead.

I look down at the sink and imagine him that day.

Standing in the bathroom, the drop of blood in the sink. The hiss. The razor clattering.

The tension rises, like there's static, like something's going to burst through this room. I keep picturing it, over and over. Like Liam is there, showing me something.

I'm cold and shaking by the time I leave the bathroom, my hair nearly dry, like I've lost a gap of time.

I feel like a prisoner in my own home. My things are gone. My connections to the outside world are severed. No one here wants to believe me.

I need to talk to Kennedy.

I'd call her, but my phone is gone. I don't know her number by heart. At least I have my car keys. The sky is dark, and I'm only half-concentrating, and by the time I park in front of their ranch house, it's almost ten at night.

But I'm not of sound mind to stop myself. I ring the bell, and it's Joe who answers.

"I need to see Kennedy," I say, but he stands firmly in my

path. "I know she's grounded. I'm sorry. Please, I need to see her." My voice cracks on the word *please*.

But she's already there, pushing Joe aside. In pajamas, hair wet and braided down her back.

Joe steps aside, and her hand is on my elbow, pulling me in.

31

KENNEDY

Nolan stands in my doorway, looking terrified. There's no other way to describe it. His eyes have gone hollow, and his skin is pale, and his hands are trembling. There's this desperate yearning in his eyes, and I think it struck Joe as well, because he doesn't object. This is clearly an emergency.

"Are you okay?" That's my first thought, over anything else, but then I feel ridiculous because he's obviously *not okay*.

Nolan, now in the house, seems to calm slightly. "They took my phone. I would've called first but they took it. They took everything."

Joe gives me this look over Nolan's head like he's worried about his behavior, or what he might do, so I sit him at the table. "You're not making any sense, Nolan. Who took everything?"

He shudders, then finally seems to realize where he is, and who is listening. "The email with the picture came from the library," he says, lowering his voice. "The library they think I work at. They think I sent it from there." His words are fine as razors. His eyes wide and pleading. "They took all my electronics, to check."

"Oh." I open the fridge to get Nolan a drink, then look at Joe, still standing in the foyer, watching us, and give him this eye signal like, he needs to leave us.

Are you sure? he mouths, and I nod. We need to trust each other, and he is. He's trying.

"I'll just be in my room, if you need me," he says loudly, like he's speaking to make sure Nolan hears.

I wait until Joe disappears down the hall, but he leaves his bedroom door wide open.

"Tell me what happened," I say.

"They think it was me," he whispers, and my hand shakes as I pour the can of soda into a glass in front of him. I tighten my grip so he doesn't notice. Nolan's on edge, coming apart. Marco's words briefly echo in my head: *Be careful.* I remember him telling me about Nolan and his brother's girlfriend. A motive. A quick zing of unease passes through me, but I shake it off.

Marco doesn't know him. None of them do.

"They think I sent it. That I know where Liam is. What happened to him. But I don't."

I nod. "I know."

He looks up, his eyes meeting mine, our faces inches apart. "Do you believe me?" he asks, and it's so open and pleading that I think I could ruin him with one word.

"Yes," I say, without hesitation. It isn't about evidence, or proof, or a balance of pros and cons. It's simpler than that. It's Nolan, and I believe him.

Most people see something, some evidence, and then they believe. But I think maybe it's the other way around. Maybe you believe first, and then it changes you, so you can see what else is possible.

Nolan stays until midnight, talking at my kitchen table. He claims he's rarely even been to the library. I used to go plenty, meeting up with study groups in the fall. Marco and Lydia used to head there after school sometimes, and I'd join them. College kids, home for the weekend, earbuds in to block out our noise. I don't recall ever seeing Nolan there. The library is built into a slope and set up for privacy—books with reading areas on the main level, cubbies with computers, all arranged at angles around the downstairs.

It could've been anyone. They're focusing on him because they were looking at him to begin with. But I also get a chill, realizing that someone nearby sent that picture. If not Nolan, then still *someone*.

I haven't realized how much time has passed until Joe comes out of his room and says, "I think it's time to go. As long as everything's okay." He looks at Nolan then. "*Is* everything okay?"

"Yes," Nolan says, pushing back from the table. "Sorry. I'm sorry for intruding."

"It's all right. Get home safe."

I walk him to the door and we linger in the doorway, like

neither of us is sure what to do now, to break the moment. And also, Joe's watching. So I just go with my gut and weave my arms around Nolan's shoulders, pulling him close. I can feel the sigh that escapes when his arms circle me back.

"I can email you, when I get to school tomorrow," he says.

"Okay."

I watch him walk all the way to his car, and I watch until the car drives down to the end of the street, just to be sure of him.

When I close the door, I turn around, and Joe's there, arms crossed over his chest.

"It was an emergency," I say.

"I know, I could tell. But, Kennedy, I heard what he said—weren't you both just at the library together?"

I look away, remembering the lie, and his face darkens.

"I need to know, Kennedy, how you know him. I need to know what's going on. The trust has to work both ways here."

I fidget with the braid running down my back. This isn't how I was planning to explain this to him. But the panic is tightening something in my chest. Something's happening, and we're running out of time, and if I can't trust Joe, then who do I really have left?

"We met because of something we both found," I say.

"I'm not following."

"There was a signal," I say. "On Elliot's satellite dish."

Joe blinks slowly, trying to process. "What are you talking about?"

"The dish, pointing out at space. Here, wait." I race to my room and fish through my backpack for the flash drive. It's in my hand, extended toward Joe, as I walk toward him. He hasn't moved from his spot in the hall. "Here. It's all here. Last weekend, I pulled a signal. Only it's coming through where no signal should be. I've been trying to see if I can replicate it."

He stares at the flash drive in my hand but doesn't take it. "Back up a second. You've been by the *house*?"

I push the flash drive at his chest again. "Joe, you're not listening. There's a *signal*. And Nolan's been receiving it, too."

He doesn't answer. I wonder if he's debating something. If he believes me. I hold the flash drive in my open palm, begging him to see.

"I know who he is, Kennedy."

"What? Who?" My arm drops to my side.

"Nolan. Nolan Chandler. I know who he is, what happened to his family."

"This has nothing to do with—"

"This has *everything* to do with this. Listen to yourself. Two people receiving a signal. Two people who—"

He stops talking, turning to face the window.

Quietly, I ask, "Two people who *what*, Joe?"

He fixes his eyes on me then, his jaw moving softly side to side. "Two people who have suffered a terrible loss, Kennedy. Two people who have endured something horrible, much younger than is fair. Two people who both want something desperately."

My hand tightens on the flash drive, gripped in my closed fist. "What is it, exactly, that you think I want?"

He opens his mouth, then closes it again. "Well, for starters, you don't want me to sell that house."

I shake my head. "You think I'm lying? To keep you from selling the *house?*"

He runs his hand through his hair and winces. "I don't know. I'm just saying. You don't want to sell the house, and now there's apparently a . . ." He searches for the word. "A signal? From space?" He says it like it's impossible. Incredulous. And coming from him, it suddenly sounds that way. Like everything we've been doing is for nothing.

"What happened to trust, Joe?" Was it just a word, an empty promise, to keep me in line?

"It has to be *earned.* Look, Kennedy, I believe that *you* believe this, I do. But—"

"Elliot could tell us what this all means. That's why I went to see him."

"Kennedy!" he yells. I've pushed him to yelling.

"Please, Joe. Please, I know you can bring this to the college. I know there are people who can read it, who can figure out if there's something there."

"Kennedy, you don't know what it's like there, at the school right now. . . ."

I frown, confused. "What's it like?"

"They're reeling from . . ." From the loss of my mother, and Will, both professors there. From the fallout of my brother. From a student who turned a weapon against his teacher, and his mother. And where must that leave Joe? I've never even thought about it. What this must be like for him now.

I nod, feeling like everything is slipping from my grasp.

Fingers shaking, I leave the flash drive on the laminate tabletop, an offering. I go to my room, to bed, but I don't sleep. I think of Nolan, and everything he's feeling, and how cut off from the world he must be, over there right now, alone.

"I know," I whisper to the dark night.

The next morning, Joe has uncharacteristically beaten me to breakfast. He has the flash drive in his hand, twirling it between his fingers. "I will take it to a guy I know, Kennedy."

I suck in a gasp, reaching for his arm. "Thank you, Joe. Thank you."

He stares at my fingers on his sleeve, and he nods. His throat moves as he swallows, but he slides the flash drive into his pocket. "I will do this one thing for you. And then, after, you will do something for me."

I step back, already leery. "What?"

"You will let the house go."

I open my mouth, but he puts up one hand.

"Kennedy, you have to let it go."

I tip my head in the faintest nod. If it can even be perceived as that. But once he sees the signal, he'll believe me. Once we do the first part, he won't demand the second. He'll understand.

The house is important. *This* is important.

32

NOLAN

At school, I can finally log in to my account, ready to send Kennedy an email to apologize for last night. In the stark light of morning, I think about what I must've seemed like, showing up at her house unannounced, on the edge of panic, or worse.

I only know that I felt calmer as soon as I saw her, and by the time I left, this felt like a problem we would deal with together, like everything else. That is, if her uncle will ever let me near her again.

But as soon as I log on, I see I've already received a note from Kennedy.

8:03 a.m.: **Joe's finding someone to check the signal at the college. Stay tuned.**

The *stay tuned* makes me grin. Half the time, I can't decide whether she's being ironic or serious.

PS—please let me know you receive this. AKA that you made it home last night.

I write back: **Got it. Will do. And yes, made it.**

    PS—thank you

At the end of the day, I log on again and see a string of new messages.

1:22 p.m.: Joe says he's picking me up after school. Says the guy he knows wants to show us something.

But I didn't see that message earlier, and there's a follow-up now:

2:12 p.m.: Meet me at the campus at 3 if you can. I'll wait for you in visitor parking.

I look at my watch. It's already 2:48. I send her a message, hoping she'll get it, but I'm definitely going to be late:

on my way

I race to my car, and I honk at the pickup truck in front of me, sitting in the back of a long line of cars waiting to exit the student parking lot. The two girls rammed into the front seat with some guy turn around, and both of them give me the middle finger through the back panel. I give up, K-turning out of the line of cars, hooking it around the back lot of the school, where I make an illegal exit from the bus lot.

I drive right by the teacher lot on the way out. I'll deal with the fallout from that later.

I don't know the college campus well, but figure I can't go wrong by following signs for visitor parking. I ease my car into a spot under a giant oak tree in a half-empty lot, trying to figure out if Kennedy got my last message, but she's nowhere. There are maybe four other cars scattered around the lot, and I don't know which of these cars belongs to her and Joe.

Looking around, I see that the campus is an expanse of green grass and leafy trees and brick buildings. There do not appear to be any signs directing me.

It's 3:03 and she's probably already in there, meeting with some guy, and I'll have to hear about it secondhand, filtered Kennedy-style.

And then I faintly hear my name in the background, from the direction of one of the brick buildings. Her image comes into focus next—dark hair loose, wearing shorts and a bright blue T-shirt, waving frantically as she races into view from farther down the brick path. "Come on!" she shouts.

She waits until I've caught up, then drags me by the hand as she veers onto a paved path, toward a nondescript building up ahead. It's not until we're climbing the wide front steps that I see the name of the building carved into the stone above, barely noticeable until you're already upon it.

Inside, the building feels colder, and empty. The halls are dark, and our steps echo. Kennedy finally lets go of my hand, clearing her throat, as if she just noticed. "The students are on summer break," she says. "It's just the researchers. Faculty, postgrads. We're on the second floor."

We pass a wall of windows, which look into classroom lab spaces. Behind the glass, there's a robotic device in a darkened room. In the next, there's a flat table, a mechanical arm hovering, immobile, over the top. It's obvious this is a building for engineering, or physics, or something.

My hand shakes when I grip the banister in the stairwell.

I get this feeling that everything's about to change. I try not to get my hopes up. But I can feel my heartbeat in my palms, down to the soles of my feet.

Inside room 243-A, the first person I see is Kennedy's uncle—Joe. It's obvious from the way he frowns at us, hands shoved in the pockets of his jeans, that Kennedy did not tell him I was coming.

The second thing I see is a man sitting in front of a massive display of computer monitors. Cables running over the desktop, and a few larger unknown electronic things set up around the room. I realize the fact that I refer to them as *unknown electronic things* means I am probably not cut out for this endeavor. But the signal was coming to me, and so here I am.

The other man turns around, looking over all of us. He looks eerily similar to Joe, as if there's some dress code that people here have to adopt. Or maybe it's just because they're friends. But they both have this overlong hair, not quite professional. And this casual way of dressing. And they're both skinny, with angular faces. But Joe has darker hair, more like Kennedy. And he seems older in the way he acts. Maybe just because he's had to, as guardian to a teenager.

"Everyone here now?" the other guy asks.

"Yes," Kennedy says. "This is Nolan."

I wave. The man doesn't wave back.

Kennedy sighs. "This is Joe's friend, Isaac. He said he found something in the readout."

Isaac swivels his chair back and forth, chewing on an overlarge piece of gum, looking decidedly uncomfortable. "Look, I don't know exactly how this was set up."

"My brother did it," Kennedy says, and the room changes. Isaac looks quickly off to the side, and Joe shifts on his feet, and I remember that her brother, Elliot, was a student here, while her mother and the boyfriend were both professors. It's a tragedy that has affected the entire campus—teachers and students alike—with everyone looking for some sign of what was to come, in hindsight.

"Right." Isaac scratches his head, sliding his chair in closer. "I'll just get right to it, then. It's an audio signal?" Except he says it like a question, which doesn't instill the greatest confidence.

"What?" Kennedy says, and Joe steps closer to the machinery.

"What does that mean?" Joe asks quietly.

"Like, radio signals. There's plenty going right by us all the time. I don't know what happened with this one, why it's displaying like this in the program, but anyway, it's really broken up." His hands fly over the keyboard. "But I pieced it together." He gives Joe a meaningful look, which could be interpreted as a warning.

"Do you want me to play it for you?" he asks.

"Yes," Kennedy answers before Joe can get a word in.

Isaac takes a deep breath and turns back to the computer. A second later, the sound fills the room.

There's some static first, and then we hear a voice. *"Is anyone there?"*

My head jerks up. The air chills. It's Kennedy. It's her voice, except faster, higher-pitched. Panicked.

All the hairs on the back of my neck stand on end. The whole room narrows to a point, and that point is Kennedy. She tenses, becomes a statue, her eyes empty.

The static cuts in and out. *"Can anyone hear me?"* Then it's just the sound of her breathing, like her mouth is pressed too close to a microphone. Then movement, like things are being slid across a table, or a floor. More static, and then her voice again. *"Something's happening in my house. Something terrible. Help us. Please—"* The transmission cuts off, and the sound of static fills the room, until a robotic voice gives the time stamp in stilted syllables. *"December fourth. One-oh-three a.m."* And then it starts back up again, on a loop. *"Is anyone there? Can anyone hear me?"*

"Turn it off," Joe says, his tone furious.

Isaac presses a button, and the room falls silent. We remain silent. Isaac turns in the chair, looking at the floor. "Did your . . . uh, was the setup, did it have, like, a radio transmitter?"

"I don't know," Kennedy says, speaking in a whisper. She's practically out the door already. I think she's going to be sick. I wonder if this is what I looked like when Abby told me about the email.

Isaac continues, like it's not a big deal. Not *enormous*, the size of the universe. "Was there, like, you know, an antenna . . . ?"

No one answers him. I've seen the antenna on the top of the shed, though. I'm guessing the answer is yes.

Isaac takes a deep breath, moving the gum to the side of his mouth. "What I'm guessing is that you transmitted a signal. And this is the bounce back, playing."

Joe steps toward her. "Is this some sort of joke?"

Isaac frowns. "Depending where it was transmitted, it could bounce back off the moon. Or off something closer. A satellite, even, the atmosphere . . . I don't think this was intentional. . . ."

Her eyes are wide, panicked. She shakes her head, but she doesn't speak. There's something familiar, like a sense of déjà vu, itching at the back of my head.

"December fourth?" I ask. "Are you sure?"

"That's why I called you in," Isaac says to Joe quietly. "It must've been transmitting on some sort of loop."

Joe whips his head from Kennedy to Isaac. "Is this the nine-one-one call? She made it at one-eighteen a.m."

Isaac presses a button, to start replaying the message. But we've already heard it once. Kennedy is moving back, like she can't possibly sit through it once more. I reach an arm for her, but she doesn't notice me there. "*One-oh-three a.m.*," the recording tells us again, at the end.

Fifteen minutes before the call to 911. We all turn to look at Kennedy, but she's gone.

"Dammit," Joe mumbles under his breath. And then he takes off after her, and it's suddenly just me and this dude in the room. I hear her words again. So familiar. I close my eyes, and I see my brother, as I saw him in the fever dream, standing across the room, moving his mouth: *Help us. Please.*

"Play it again," I say.

33

KENNEDY

No.

That's the only thought in my head. *No.*

That cannot be all that's out there. Nothing but my echo, reflecting back.

Standing outside Elliot's window that night, I peered into the shadow house. And then I ran. Soaking wet, under the storm, I took shelter in the shed.

And that's all this is: my shout into the abyss, when I hid in the shed, when I tried to get help, when I had no phone but saw the microphone. I knew Elliot had added an antenna to the shed over the summer, when he was out here working. I hoped it would work like a radio transmitter, like those things truck drivers use. That someone would pick up the signal and call for help.

A shout into the abyss, and no one answered. *Is anyone there?*

The answer is the same as it's always been: No.

...

I've run clear across campus. I have no idea where I am. The trees cover the ground in overlapping shadows. I want to sink into the earth.

And then I'm back, with the smell of dirt and dust, inside the shed with the computers running over the top, the wires trailing under the ground, my back pressed against the wall while I'm sitting under the desk, shouting those words. *Help us. Please.*

I said them to myself even after I stopped broadcasting. I said them over and over, in case anyone, anywhere, was listening.

Joe has called me four times in the minutes it has taken me to sprint across the campus. I look around me, but it's only more of the same. The ground curving away, in every direction, at the horizon.

There's no place to go. The earth is finite, I can't escape my existence here. Or the things I did, and the things I didn't do.

Eventually, I stand, brushing the grass from my shorts, and I circle back. There's nowhere else to go. Run forever, and the earth curves back around.

On and on it goes. The same thing over and over.

I head back to the parking lot and see a shape waiting for me there. When I get closer, I see it's not Joe, but Nolan. He pushes off his car, standing there, looking at me like he doesn't recognize me.

I stop in my tracks, halfway across the lot. "I didn't know," I say. "I didn't do it on purpose."

"I know," he says.

He opens his mouth to say more, but we're cut off by a booming voice in the distance.

"Kennedy!" It's Joe, jogging down the path from the other direction.

I turn back to Nolan. "You should go," I tell him.

"No, I want—"

"Please, Nolan." Because I don't want him to hear this, the things Joe is about to ask me. I don't want him to know what really happened that night.

At first, Joe doesn't say anything. He just gestures to his car, and we drive in silence, except we're not heading toward his house, or mine. We're just on a highway, signs designating east.

"Where are we going?" I ask.

He taps his fingers on the steering wheel. "You know, the first week you were at my house? I'd wake up in the middle of the night, and I'd see you sleeping, and I just . . . I didn't know what to do. I would get in the car and just drive. For hours."

I twist in my seat. "You snuck out?"

He presses his lips together, but it's almost a smile. "It's not sneaking out when it's your own house. I even left you a note on the kitchen table in case you woke up." He cuts his eyes to me. "A courtesy you might want to take into consideration next time."

"I'm sorry."

He lets out a slow breath and merges onto some other

road, less traveled, nothing but trees surrounding us. "Me too, Kennedy. Truth is, I didn't know what to say to you." He grips the wheel tighter. "I still don't. Right now, I want to ask you what happened, but I don't even know where to start."

"I tried to get help," I say to Joe again, and this time, he understands. He pulls the car over onto the shoulder, in what feels at that moment like the middle of nowhere.

He takes a deep breath, then turns to face me. His voice low, and calm. "It's just us, Kennedy. Just me and you, for real this time. Anything you say to me, it stays right here. And we're nowhere. Okay?"

He's right; it feels like nowhere. I didn't think I'd be able to find this exact spot ever again. There were no mile markers. Just road and trees and a sun dipping lower on the horizon.

I stare out the front windshield, my eyes watering from the glare.

It had been dark and raining that night, and I was waiting for the distance between the lightning and thunder to spread out so it was safe to race across the open field, to my house. And then I ran, sprinting through the storm.

"When I was coming back home," I tell Joe, "I could see, from a distance, a light was on. In Elliot's room. I was all the way across the field still, though."

I heard a loud *boom*, and then, a little while later, a second one. The first I could explain away, as a trick of thunder, and the distance. But at the second sound, I jumped. The noise felt closer than the storm. Sharper, something that gripped my heart, turning everything still.

It was enough to keep me from going to my room, sliding

open the window, and crawling inside. Some deep-buried instinct. It was like, even then, I knew.

"When I reached the house, I looked into Elliot's room first—where the light was on. His desk chair was empty, but the light over the desk was on." The headphones had been sitting beside his laptop, like he'd just been sitting there a moment ago. His bedroom door was open, and I could see the hallway. "Out in the hall, I could see the handprint on the wall. Red, a streak of blood below." I shiver, and Joe closes his eyes. "And I could see Elliot, crouched down, but I didn't know what he was doing. I hit the window with my palm." Fast, an open slap, to get his attention. "When he stood up, he was holding a gun. He was covered in . . . his hands were . . . And he was pointing it straight at me."

Joe doesn't move. He doesn't breathe. I want to come back from the shadow house, but I need to say it all now, or I never will.

Elliot's eyes were dead. His face was pale. There was so much blood I thought he would've passed out.

I didn't know if he could see me, in the dark. Or if it was just his own reflection in the bedroom window. I like to think he didn't know it was me, standing on the other side. That it was just a reflex.

"I ducked down quick, and I ran. I hid in the shed." Not yet processing. The blood, my brother with a gun. The shots I'd heard. My phone was still in my room, left behind in case my mom checked my location, and the other houses were too far away, and I knew we needed help. He was Elliot, and he was not Elliot.

I picture the headphones on his desk and wonder what

he was listening to. If there was something that made him . . . if there was some other explanation. Because there has to be. He's my brother, and he wouldn't do this.

Joe grabs my hand. He doesn't ask first, he just does it. I squeeze back.

"I tried to call for help. The Internet was hooked up. But Elliot built everything. I didn't know how to do it. I tried. Joe, I tried."

"I know you did," he says, his voice barely a whisper.

"I stayed there until I heard his footsteps racing past. I could tell he was heading for the park. I counted to two hundred, just to be sure. Then I went inside." I crawled back through my own window, got my phone off my dresser, and called 911. "I never left my room, Joe. I didn't open the door. I didn't see. They asked what made me leave the room when I climbed back inside, but I didn't. Not until the police arrived. And even then, I never looked."

The police believed I saw them on the stairs and called for help, but I didn't. From outside Elliot's window, I could see the handprint, out in the hall. The one we've now covered with fresh paint. And I could see Elliot. There was so much blood. That, I could see.

I don't know if I could've saved them. If I lost my mother because of my own fear, my own inaction. I don't know if it was too late from the start. But I didn't leave my room until the woman on the other end of the phone told me the police were at the front door. I kept my eyes closed, my hand on the other wall, as I made my way to the front.

It will always be a shadow house, kept hidden from my memory. Full of the horrors I can only imagine.

34

NOLAN

The net is closing in, everything slipping from our grasp. I can feel it, like something coming for me. In the email, tracked to the library, where I was supposed to be. In Kennedy's words, echoing back in the signal. Like we're stuck in a loop. Like the circle is us.

I sneak in through the side door behind the kitchen without my parents noticing. But I hear them talking to Agent Lowell in the dining room. Snippets of conversation filter up the stairs. *Nolan's computer. Library. Evidence. Official statement.*

It's wrong. It's all gone so wrong. I can't explain any of it. I am sure of nothing. None of the things happening in my house, surrounding my brother's case, make sense.

But this is what I am sure of: My brother's image appeared to me in the living room at the same time Kennedy was making that call for help. Her words reached me. I don't know how, I don't know why. That connection is the proof;

yet there's also nothing I can hold in my hands and show someone. Just this feeling, and December fourth. Everything circling around it.

I don't know where to go from here. How to prove all the things I believe.

There's only one lead remaining, and we have to follow it.

My room feels empty without my computer, and I keep looking for my phone, thinking I've misplaced it, before I remember that it's gone. I pack a bag, stuffing it full of clothes, a toothbrush, the essentials. I sneak out the side door and drive off before they notice I'm home and take my keys. Before they bring me in for some sort of official questioning.

At least without a phone there will be no way to trace my path. I can disappear for a bit. I'm used to no one noticing the things I do, but now their focus is turning on me. Now they're looking closely. They're wondering what they've missed, these last two years, when they were looking for Liam instead.

It's the kind of dark where even the animals have gone silent. The moon is covered by clouds, and the streetlights have gone dim in the haze. I worry, at first, that nobody's home, but then I recognize Joe's car in the driveway.

I'm not sure which window is Kennedy's, but there aren't too many options. There's a light on in one of the rooms, and I'm going to have to take the risk that this one is hers. The blinds are pulled shut, but they're vaguely familiar, like I've seen them on a video call, from the other direction.

Still, I tap gently before ducking below the glass, so I can pretend it was the wind, or some giant bug, if Joe looks out through the blinds instead.

But it's Kennedy's eyes peering out from between the slats, shifting side to side. I stand from my hiding spot, raise a hand sheepishly, hoping she'll smile.

She frowns, raising the blinds. She pushes the window open so I can feel a gust of the air conditioning from inside, but the screen still separates us.

"Nolan?" she asks, even though of course it's me.

"Hey, hi," I say quietly. Then I'm at a loss. I don't know what I expected, what I wanted. "I just wanted to tell you, I'm going to North Carolina."

Her face scrunches up. "What?"

"North Carolina. The photo on the wall, of the missing kid. Hunter Long."

She shakes her head sadly. "What's the point?"

"Excuse me?" I say. The point is answers. The point is there was a signal, sent to both of us. The point is my brother, whispering across some impenetrable divide. And Kennedy's voice, filling up the classroom.

She lets out a long sigh, resting her chin in her hand. Her gaze shifts behind me, but I can't figure out what she's looking for in the darkness. "Have you heard of the Fermi paradox?" she asks. I haven't, but she must know that, because she continues. "In the history of the universe, there's been more than enough time for life to develop somewhere else, and to advance. But there's no evidence that any exists." She frowns. "A scientist postulated years ago that the reason nothing has made contact with us in four billion years, the reason that there is no evidence that anything has colonized the universe, *ever*, in *fourteen billion years*, is simple, really." She waits for that to sink in. "It's because nothing else exists, has ever existed, or will ever exist. We're a fluke, and we're alone."

"No," I say, "my brother."

But she continues as if she hasn't heard me. "We're in an echo chamber, Nolan." I remember, then, her own voice echoing back. "A vast expanse of nothing, nothing, nothing. There's no one out there. This is it. Even my call for help. It just . . . bounced back."

But that's not true, because it *reached me*.

Kennedy has changed somehow, like something's been taken from her today. Some belief. I don't know how to give it back to her, except with the truth. I need her to see.

"December fourth, my brother appeared."

She brushes the comment aside. "I know, you told me."

"And I couldn't make out what he was saying," I continue, my voice growing more animated. "Just the end. He said: *Help us. Please.*"

Her gaze shifts from the empty night, back to me. She blinks slowly. "What?"

"It sounds crazy, right? I had a dream, and he came to me, and he spoke in the corner of the room. *Help us. Please.* Just like you said at the end of the transmission. I think the signal was reaching out to me, even then." Not just the signal. "I think it was you."

She shakes her head. "That's not possible."

I place my hand on the screen between us, leaning closer. "*None* of this is supposed to be possible. That's the *point*."

"*What's* the point, Nolan? I think I'm missing it here."

I say the thing that's been itching at the back of my skull. This feeling that's been with me since that first day, when my device started moving against my brother's wall, driving me to the computer to see what it meant. "I think I was supposed to find you."

She doesn't answer for a moment, and I think she's mulling it over. I think she believes it, too, even if she doesn't want to admit it. "For what?" she finally asks.

I'm not sure. Not yet. But I think we're close. "For you to come to my house. For you to see that picture."

I can see her thinking it over. "I thought that at first. But I don't know, Nolan. I don't know what to believe anymore."

"What have we got to lose, Kennedy?"

"You mean, other than Joe completely freaking out?"

"Right. Other than that."

She thinks for a second. "Give me a few minutes. I need to leave a note this time."

35

KENNEDY

"Now I know why you wanted me to come," I say. "How were you planning to find this place, without me and my phone?"

Nolan grins, gesturing to the glove compartment. "Look inside."

I pull out a pile of maps, folded up and labeled in sections with a highlighter. "Oh my," I say.

"Yep. Stopped in a gas station to fill up the tank, bought these inside."

"Admit it, though. You're glad I'm here."

He turns his face from the road briefly, his eyes meeting mine. "I am, Kennedy."

It's a long drive, and the highway twists through the mountains in the dark. I keep worrying he'll fall asleep, or I'll fall asleep, but both of us are on edge, antsy in our seats. And I think I understand: instead of waiting for answers, we're driving after them. It fills me with adrenaline. I almost don't need the second coffee. Almost.

• • •

I turn off my phone when we arrive on the street of the Long residence, just after dawn. Joe will be waking up soon, and he'll see the note I left—*Be back by Sunday, promise*—and he'll immediately start calling my number. Whatever tentative trust he's placed in me, I'm sure I've shattered it with this move. But I hope he'll forgive me. That he'll understand.

Nolan's car idles at the curb. There are two cars in the driveway, beside a white picket fence. The porch light is still on.

"It's early in the day still. Maybe they'll leave soon," Nolan says.

"Let's get some breakfast and come back," I say.

"If by breakfast you mean more caffeine, then yes." It's then I notice the dark circles under Nolan's eyes—mine must be the same. A string of sleepless nights, ending in this.

The residential area of town we're in is just a scattering of streets in a grid. As we drive, the homes give way to brick buildings set farther back from the road. In the distance, a plume of smoke rises from the large chimney of a factory.

There are very few people, or stores, or restaurants. The sidewalks are half crumbled, the pavement buckling in sections. Beyond the residential area, this feels like a town of decaying buildings, with weeds pushing back through the concrete squares, like the earth is reclaiming it. There doesn't seem to be much in the way of food, just large, nondescript buildings with empty parking lots. But eventually we find a fast-food place with a drive-through on a corner next to a gas station, surrounded by nothing but empty space.

There are three other people inside the restaurant, all spread out, sitting at the farthest corners. No one looks up as I pass with the tray of food to join Nolan at the booth. Out the window facing away from the road is a ballfield surrounded by a chain link fence. But even the dirt has become overgrown with grass, like no one's used it in ages.

I'm suddenly queasy, unsure of what we'll find—unsure of what exactly I'm hoping for.

"You're quiet," Nolan says.

I guess I'm worried that everything means nothing. That there is no reason for anything, other than chance encounters, and chaos. The universe, heading toward more disorder.

But I smile at him instead. "Thought you could use the break," I say.

He smiles back, but it's like he knows I'm lying.

Two coffees and three breakfast sandwiches later, we head back to the house.

Both cars are gone. We linger at the curb, staring at the house. "I'm going to ring the bell," I say, since neither of us appears to have a plan. "Go park somewhere else in the meantime. If someone's home, I'll meet you around that corner."

Nolan leaves me at the sidewalk, and I enter the gate of their white picket fence, easing it shut behind me. It's a modest home—two stories, older, but kept up nicely. There are brightly colored flowers on either side of the porch. When I ring the bell, it echoes inside. No one appears after a few moments, so I use the brass knocker, just in case.

Still nothing.

I look over my shoulder to see if anyone's watching. It's a residential street, but the homes are hidden behind larger oak trees, and I hope that obscures the view of me, if any of the neighbors are watching. Eventually, I hear someone walking up the driveway, and I prepare to come up with some excuse—*selling something; looking for directions*—but it's only Nolan.

I shrug one shoulder at him and then check the obvious places for keys: under the flowerpots and the doormat. Out of luck, we circle around to the backyard. Here the curtains are pulled open, and I can see the darkened kitchen, the laminate surfaces, cleaned and orderly. Except for a coffee cup in the center. I freeze, wondering if someone's there, or whether someone has just forgotten it.

Nolan knocks this time, and I stare him down. "And what exactly will you say to explain why you're knocking on the *back door?*" I whisper.

He shrugs. "Lost Frisbee?"

Oh my God, I think, looking at the sky. *He's serious.*

Thankfully, no one comes to the door, and I resume my search, checking the downspouts and around the patio furniture. There's a metal planter on the patio, and tipping it to the side, I find a metal key, lined with dirt. "Hallelujah," I mutter, wiping it off on the side of my shorts.

The back door creaks when I push it open, and the downstairs smells like syrup and coffee. It reminds me, suddenly, of home. And I can hear my mother and Elliot talking at the table—only now I can't remember whether they sounded happy, or whether there was tension underneath. I remember Elliot saying, "You don't see the other side of him, Mom," but when I walked into the room, they stopped talking. I remember entering the room, my mother tucking her dark hair behind her ear, her smile when she saw me, the steaming mug in her hands—

"Kennedy?"

Stop. I have to stop. But I wonder if, even then, they were discussing Hunter Long.

"Coming," I say.

The first floor doesn't appear large—a kitchen, a dining room, a living room, maybe a bathroom out of sight. There's a family photo on the mantel of the fireplace—a mother, a teenage daughter, and a younger version of Hunter, without his hair bleached white. He looks just like the image hanging on Nolan's wall. There are other photos surrounding it, including a man, but Hunter isn't in any of those pictures.

Nolan completes a circuit of the downstairs. "Come on," he says, waiting for me at the base of a staircase. I follow him up the carpeted steps, the wood underneath our feet squeaking with every shift in weight.

There appear to be three bedrooms upstairs, all off a single hall—two with their doors open, which Nolan walks right by.

"It will be that one," he whispers, pointing to the closed door. Still, I peek in the other two doorways we pass—a room in purple and gray, clothes strewn across the floor, which must belong to the teenage girl in the family photo; the other room has a queen bed and an ornate headboard.

Pushing open the closed door, Nolan holds his breath, as if expecting to see something waiting for us.

But, as I could've told him, it's only the emptiness. You can feel it, that the room has been abandoned. Someone has been through here, cleaning, organizing, so all that remains is a bed, neatly made, with a pillow on top; a dresser, all drawers firmly shut; and a closet door, also shut. You can see the vacuum marks on the rug, and I know we're leaving a trail of evidence just by setting foot in here.

I'm thinking about how to cover it up—find the vacuum, maybe?—when Nolan walks straight for the closet, his footprints marring the pristine lines on the floor.

When he opens the closet door, an assortment of shirts faintly sways on the bar, disturbed by Nolan's presence. He lets out a long sigh. It's just an empty room, and I think he must be facing the truth, too: that there was nothing leading us here. This room belongs to a missing kid, but, like I learned when I was standing in the downstairs of Nolan's house, there are hundreds, *thousands*, of missing people, all over the world.

There's nothing on the walls. Nothing for us to find. Elliot and my mom were probably talking about someone else that morning, anyone else. We've driven through the night to look at the room of a random kid, who will end up meaning nothing to us. We've been trying to force the connection, seeing it everywhere, even in things that don't exist.

This room feels like it's hovering in the in-between, just like Liam's room felt to me when I hid upstairs at Nolan's house. Like it's the ghost of a room, waiting for someone, with all the life sucked out of it.

Nolan frowns, looking around. "When you don't have answers, you don't know what to do. . . ."

"Answers don't always make things easier," I say.

Nolan's face changes, and he reaches for me. "I'm sorry. I didn't mean . . . That was a terrible thing to say." But he sets his jaw, looking out the window. He means it, I realize. He thinks it's better to know, even if the knowing is horrific. What must it be like, living in that house, for him to think my life is the better option? What must it be like *here*?

"It's all terrible, Nolan," I say.

He nods once, and then his eyes widen. Downstairs, a door creaks open. We stare at each other, frozen. Nolan grabs my arm and pulls me into the closet, shutting us both inside. We're pressed together, chest to chest, the clothes and hangers swaying around us, and I can feel his heartbeat against his ribs, as fast as my own must be beating. His breath against my forehead comes quickly, and I try to slow my breathing, to calm myself. It isn't working. Someone's here.

Nolan grabs the clothes, to keep them still. I hold my breath.

The house is older, and I can track the person just from the creaks in the wood, doors opening, cabinets closing, water in the pipes.

I start to relax, thinking we just need to wait this thing out. Maybe someone forgot their wallet, or something else they needed, and they'll be on their way again. But seconds later, we hear footsteps coming up the stairs. I start to panic.

And then, as the steps get closer, they start moving faster. Oh God, we left the door to this room open. My entire body tenses, and I can feel Nolan's doing the same.

The steps stop at the door of the room. And then a voice. "Hunter?" She sounds younger, our age—I imagine the teenager in the family picture downstairs.

My hand tightens on Nolan's arm, and he pulls me closer.

The footsteps approach, and it sounds like she's mumbling, "You're such a jerk—"

I hold my breath, counting the seconds, hoping she turns away. Nolan's fingers are trembling against my skin. Then, in three quick steps, she storms across the room and yanks open the closet door.

I close my eyes, as if that can stop the inevitable. And I throw my hands in the air, as if that's ever stopped anyone.

36

NOLAN

"What the—"

The girl in front of us is probably around our age, and she's quickly backing away. Her blue eyes have gone wide, and her mouth, colored with bright pink lipstick, has dropped open.

"Wait!" I yell after her, thinking she's going to call the police, or worse.

But she has her phone in her hand, held out to us like a weapon. And she's still backing away, into the hallway. We should run, too. We should run before we're found by someone else.

"We're friends of Hunter's!" Kennedy shouts, and everyone freezes.

Oh God, I hope she has a plan.

The girl turns around, her grip still on the doorway, like she's about to take off at any moment. "Did *Hunter* send you here?" And then she no longer seems afraid. She narrows her eyes, holds out her hand again. "Whatever you took, leave it. Or I *will* call the police, and you can tell him that."

Huh?

Kennedy shoots me a look, as if she, too, is unsure where to go from here. "No, sorry. We went to school with him. And no one"—she clears her throat—"no one seems to be looking anymore. We just thought . . ."

"You thought *what?*" the girl asks, her knuckles still white from the tension in her fist.

I hold my breath, waiting. Her face is hard, unreadable. "We thought . . . we thought . . ." But even Kennedy is coming up empty.

The girl continues. "You want me to believe that Hunter didn't send you here? That instead, you decided to just break into his house, looking for clues?" She looks between the two of us skeptically. "How the hell did you get in here, then?"

"The key," Kennedy says, "in the backyard." She holds it out, fingers trembling. The girl stares at her hand, frowning. She doesn't come any closer.

"Nothing to see here, kids. The police have been through here already. There's no mystery. So how about you get the hell out of my house, before I call the cops?"

"You found him?" I ask. I don't get why his photo is up on our wall, if so.

She laughs. "Hardly. Hunter doesn't want to be found, so he won't be. But I don't need to see him when the money from the downstairs jar goes missing. When my mom's diamond bracelet goes missing, and also his favorite food from the fridge. I thought you were him, when I heard you up here." She rolls her eyes. "He is officially the worst, if he

thinks we don't notice." She shakes her head. "My mom re-
fuses to accept it, though."

"You think he ran away?"

"Think?" She starts to laugh, then stops. "He's done it before, but he always comes back. So yeah, I'm sure. Who else
would be stealing our things without breaking in?"

"I don't believe it," Kennedy whispers, though I don't
think she's talking to this girl. I think she's talking about the
search, how it's just led us here for nothing. A whole empty
universe that makes no sense.

But this girl isn't having it, Kennedy's denial. "Yeah?" she
says, leaning into her hip. "That building behind the old Rollins factory?" she asks, like we should know what that is. I
nod, an instinct. "Swing by at night. You'll see what I mean.
He's been here recently, and he never stays far from where
he can get money. And right now, that place is us."

I walk slowly toward the hall, pulling Kennedy along, because I'm starting to think we're actually going to get out
of here without her calling the police, when she grabs my
arm—no longer afraid, but pissed. "Hey, what'd you say your
names were?"

I scramble, panicked. "Liam," I say, the first thing that
comes to my mind. This is who I'm doing this for, after all.
Kennedy tips her head, like she understands, and says, "Elliot."

The girl's face scrunches up in confusion. "Oh. Huh.
Okay. Yeah, I've heard of you." I can see Kennedy tense beside me, her eyes widen. "I just thought you were . . ."

"You thought what?" I say. Kennedy appears stunned, and
unexpectedly short on words.

"His boyfriend. I thought Elliot was a guy. Sorry, I heard

him on the phone with you when he was back once this fall. I just assumed . . ."

Kennedy looks to me, her eyes impossibly wide, almost tearing up. Her mouth drops open, and I can see her processing, fitting the pieces back together. The connection, it's here. I can see her believing again.

The signal sent her to my house so we would find this boy. This boy who, we now have proof, knew Elliot Jones. Not only that, who might have been Elliot's boyfriend.

We *are* supposed to find him.

The girl steps closer before speaking. "I hope you're not mixed up with whatever's sent him running, Elliot. Really. If he won't show his face, there's probably a reason, knowing him. I'd hate to see you disappear, too."

Then she takes the key from Kennedy, eyeing us slowly. "I will call the police if I see you here again."

Kennedy nods, and we head down the stairs. But before we're out the door, we hear her call after us. "If you find him, tell him it's time to come home already."

As soon as we're back at my car, out of breath, Kennedy grabs my arm. "Holy crap. Did you get the address?"

"The old Rollins factory? Yeah, look it up on your phone, see if you can find it."

She turns her phone on and cringes when she sees the display. She must have a bunch of calls or texts from Joe. But she clears her throat and opens a map program.

Her hands are shaking, and she has to enter the information twice before she gets it right. "Okay," she says. "It's a factory. Says it's closed, though. Come on, I'll put the address in."

We follow her phone's directions, and as we drive the streets in the daylight, everything comes into focus: this is an old mill town, full of brick factories, some boarded up. Like the town itself is disappearing.

We drive by the address of the old factory, but we don't stop. It's a large rectangular building with small windows, all covered up, and there's too much movement across the street. It appears to be some construction site, with a crane, men in hard hats, several bulldozers. At first I think maybe they're renovating the factory into some new space. But then I see I was mistaken: the wrecking ball, the dumpsters, the garbage trucks. They're taking it down, piece by piece.

"We'll come back after work hours," I say. "She told us to check it out at night anyway."

I think of all the people here, and what will happen to them. If entire sections of the world go like this. Slipping through some crack in time, swallowed back into the earth.

There's a long way to go until night, and Kennedy sends a quick text, then powers down her phone again. "I'm worried Joe's got some tracking app set up, since he grounded me."

"What did you say to him?" I ask.

"'Trust me,'" she says. She's lucky, I think, having someone checking in on her all the time. The way Joe looked at me when we first met, like I was something he needed to protect Kennedy from. As if he's making up for everything he wasn't able to keep her from before.

The sudden interest from my own parents only seems to be because of Liam.

We go to the same fast-food restaurant again, where Kennedy pays for lunch. "You drove," she says, waving me off. "Again."

The worker looks between me and Kennedy. "Weren't y'all just here?"

I nod but then think it's in our best interest to get out of here. The only place I can think to go is the ballfield, in the distance.

"Come on," I tell her. We take our food to go, and I drive down the road, which dead-ends at nothing. There's no reason for this road to exist, really, except for the ballfield, and even that doesn't seem to be serving a purpose anymore.

The fence around the field is only partially standing, warped and disconnected in sections, and I step through a narrow clearing where the metal posts have come loose from the earth. There are two silver benches beside the baseball diamond, and I straddle one, spreading the contents of the fast-food bag between us. "Quite the picnic spread," Kennedy says, taking a seat facing me.

But all I can picture is the family picnic, two years ago. The food we ate before Liam took off. Fried chicken, potato salad—all the little details I had forgotten.

"Did you know Hunter was Elliot's boyfriend?" I ask between bites.

She shakes her head. "I should've realized it. But he was only there the one time, and Elliot didn't even introduce him to me. I didn't think he was someone important to him. I wasn't really paying attention."

"He never mentioned him?"

She looks up at me and stops chewing. "I never asked. We were the new kids, and I was trying to, I don't know, find my own people. I was too preoccupied with myself to notice what was happening in the rest of my house."

She stares out onto the ballfield, picking at her food.

"What are you thinking about?"

She bites the corner of her lip, doesn't look at me when she starts talking. "Marco told me there were rumors . . . about you and . . ." She moves her hands around, like she's begging me to fill in the blanks instead.

"Me and what?" I say.

Her eyes cut to the side. "Some girl." She clears her throat. "Liam's girlfriend?"

My stomach sinks. "Abby," I say. "Are you asking me if it's true?"

I narrow my eyes, trying to understand where she's coming from. Whether she really doesn't trust me, or if she's asking something more. "It was a mistake," I say. "And it was after. Much after. Do you know what it's like? When you're stuck in this world, and you can't see anything past it?"

She looks my way again.

"It was like that. She was missing him, and I was missing him, and I was there." I didn't tell anyone, but apparently Abby did. I'm surprised. Then my stomach twists—if Marco knows, others know, and that means the police probably know. As Abby's friend, Clara must know, and I wonder how many people in our house have heard it, too. My parents, even? I close my eyes from the guilt, just thinking about it. Is this part of my cloud of suspicion? That I was secretly jealous of him, because of *Abby*?

"It was one time," I say. "One time, when I was feeling really bad, and I regretted it right away."

She doesn't answer at first, just leans her head back, face tipped up to the gray overcast sky. The food is done. She closes her eyes. "I know what it's like." Then she looks straight at me. "I regret so much."

I force the last bite down my throat, but my stomach rebels.

I don't want to think about Abby. I don't want to think about the case the police are building against me. I don't want to think about Kennedy hiding out in the shed behind her house while life as she knew it fell apart just steps away.

We have hours to pass, still. Hours to keep thinking of everything we did wrong in the past, everything we might be doing wrong now. I want to blow off some steam, and we're suddenly in the perfect place for it. "Hey, I have an idea."

Inside my trunk, I still have my baseball gear, from spring practices and games. Kennedy shoved it all to the far corner when she loaded my trunk with her brother's things, transporting everything back to her house earlier this week.

"Can you play?" I ask, sliding on the mitt. It's worn and broken in, and it feels like a second skin to me by now.

"Soccer was more my thing," she says. "But I'm a quick learner."

I hand her the bat. "Let's see what you got, then."

She stands in the batter's box, waiting for my pitch. She hits the first few I throw, one angling off to the side, another popping straight up so I have to run almost all the way back to her just to catch it.

"If you want more power," I say, "think more about the step than the swing."

She nods, taking some more practice swings.

After a few more pitches where she lunges for the ball as it heads her way, I jog over to show her what I mean. "You're swinging on the defensive," I say. "Here." I stand behind her, my hands on her hands, gripping the bat. I don't even think about it at first, how close she is, her hands under my own, until I feel her tense up for a second.

"Sorry," I say, pulling back.

She shakes her head. "No, it's fine. Show me."

So I do, my arms folding around hers, stepping and swinging until her body does the same, in synchrony. I step back, watching her as she takes the swing on her own. "Perfect. You got it."

Then I jog back to the pitcher's mound, and on the windup, I tell her one last piece of advice that my coach once gave me. "Don't swing like you're afraid, Kennedy."

She nods and gets into position. Then I toss her a pitch, and the crack of the bat on the ball echoes through the emptiness. It sails over my head, and she raises her hand to her eyes. She laughs then, her face mirroring my own. We're still smiling at each other when the first drop of rain falls from the sky.

"Probably should end on a high note anyway," she says, the bat hanging by her side. "I think that was a fluke."

"No way," I say. "It's my teaching, obviously." She shakes her head as I take off for the outfield to retrieve the ball, and when I turn around to head back, she's still standing there, waiting for me.

The sky opens up just as I reach her, and we race for the car. I drop the baseball gear into the trunk and she ducks into the passenger side, shaking out her hair. It makes me smile.

"Where to?" I ask after I start the car again.

But I can tell she's leveled. There are dark circles under her eyes, and she keeps yawning, which makes me yawn. The soda has zero effect. We're going to need to wait it out.

"I'm thinking a nap would really help right now. You?"

"You know how I feel about naps," she says.

I drive back up the road until I see an empty parking lot of another empty factory, and I pull the car into the alley behind it.

She reclines her seat first, curling onto her left side, her hands folded into a pillow. The sound of rain on metal picks up, and I curl up on my right side, facing her. I'm not sure which of us drifts off first, but sleep comes fast, dark and deep.

When I wake, it's dark. The first thing I hear is the tap of rain against the metal roof of the car. The first thing I see, coming into focus, is Nolan's face, asleep, his lips slightly parted, so at peace. It's like seeing the Nolan that lives underneath, one that might be possible if his life had followed a different path, a different set of circumstances.

The second thing I notice is the colors, faintly flashing against the window beyond his head. Blue, red, alternating in the streaks of rain against the glass. I push myself to sitting. "Nolan," I say, shaking him awake.

He stirs, rubbing his eyes. "What?"

"The police," I say.

Nolan sits upright almost as fast as I did. "What are we doing," he says, but it comes out slow, like his brain hasn't fully caught up to the sequence of events.

What's our story. Why are we here. We're parked in an alley behind an abandoned factory, in the middle of the night, in some town where we don't belong. What _are_ we doing? We're two teenagers, trespassing. Sleeping. We look like runaways. There's no way the police won't take Nolan's ID, run his name, contact his parents.

"Trust me?" I ask.

"Yes," he says immediately, but he's staring out the window, immobile as the bright light gets closer.

I slide over the console to his seat so I'm facing him, a knee on either side of his legs.

"What—"

He's two steps behind, his arms out and to the side like he doesn't know what to do with them.

"Seriously, Nolan, at least *pretend*." I grab his wrists and hook them around my waist so his hands press to my lower back.

I don't think, I just lean down and kiss him. His entire body tenses, and then his fingers press deeper into my waist, and his other hand trails up my back, and it occurs to me he knows *exactly* how to pretend, when the rap of a flashlight against the window jars us apart.

My heart beats quickly, and his hands still grip my waist. I have to squint from the light, and Nolan raises a hand to his eyes. He lets go of me to lower the window more, and the officer leans into the car, the rain dripping from his black hood, the smell of summer rain filling the car, the humidity surrounding us.

He frowns, and his face, so close, smells of rain and aftershave. "This is private property," he says, though he backs away, seeing the position we're in. He looks away, like he doesn't want to look too closely at the disheveled clothing, the fact that we're young enough to need to be in a car, for privacy.

I duck my head into Nolan's shoulder, then slide from his lap, back to my side of the car.

"Sorry," Nolan says. "We didn't know. It just looked like a"—he winces—"an empty road."

The officer sighs, panning the light back and forth between us. He shakes his head. "Go home," he says firmly.

Nolan nods and raises the window as the cop walks back to his car. We sit in silence, both of us breathing heavily, until the red and blue lights turn off. Then Nolan clears his throat and turns the car around, looping us back onto the main road, where we pull into the parking lot of the gas station, which has a twenty-four-hour convenience store attached.

The whole time, it's painfully silent. He doesn't look my way or try to make a joke to lighten the mood. Nothing.

Not even a *Thanks for the quick thinking, Kennedy.*

I finally look over at him, and he looks decidedly uncomfortable. I thought he felt the same as I did—like Joe had noticed, too. But then I think, *Maybe he's just a great pretender. Maybe I always only see what I want to see: in Nolan, in Elliot, in myself.*

"I need a soda," he says, his voice scratchy, as he exits the car.

"I'll get it," I say. I slam the door, and he jumps, frowning at me. "It didn't have to be that hard, Nolan." I take a step back, toward the store. "But thank you for your sacrifice, either way."

And then I step out from the overhang of the station, thankful for the rain.

38

NOLAN

I watch her walk through the rain under the glow of the gas station lights until she disappears into the brightly lit store. I count the cash in my pocket, taken from the emergency envelope in our kitchen drawer. I hope it's enough to get us all the way back. I hope I don't have to ask her to pay for this, too.

This . . . wouldn't be the best time to ask her for a favor.

She looked so angry, but I don't know how to tell her these things. I'm not good at saying what I'm thinking. The times when I've been fully honest, laying everything out there, have been twisted around on me instead. The police, eyeing me with suspicion. My parents, even, disbelieving.

So I don't know how to tell her that instead of dreaming of my brother, his image flickering in the corner, I now dream of her hair, the sound of her laugh.

That when she talks I am both listening to the words and watching her mouth, imagining kissing her. The rain comes down heavier now, and it's like there's a wall growing between us, the more time that passes.

Shit. I leave the pump and follow her across the lot, and within five seconds, I'm soaking wet. I push open the door to the store, the bell ringing overhead, with the sharp cold of the air conditioning on my skin, and the glare of fluorescent lights. "Kennedy, wait."

I weave through the aisles to find her. She turns around, the cool air from the soda fridge trailing goose bumps over her wet skin. I don't know how to say it, so I just do. Fast, before I can second-guess myself. "I think about you all the time, and not just because of all this." I wave my hands around, and I hope she knows what I mean. "I wanted to, Kennedy. I've *been* wanting to. I didn't want it to be a joke, the first time I kissed you. Or, like, a way out of jail."

She regards me slowly, then pulls two sodas from the fridge, letting the door swing closed behind her. I realize then how close we are, and how she's leaning against the glass, the clothes clinging to our skin, and exactly how little space there is between us.

"I also didn't want it to be in a car," I say, thinking of Abby, then try to shake her from my mind. "*And* I don't want it to be in a convenience store, while I'm making a list."

I get the ghost of a smile then. "You've given this a lot of thought, I see."

"It was a long car ride down here."

She laughs, and it sounds like music. She brushes by me, and I can feel the air move around her, imagining that moment in the car again. Replaying it, and imagining it was real. She pays and exits the store without looking back.

I purchase the gas from the guy behind the counter, and

when I leave, she's standing underneath the overhang, leaning against the car. Like she's waiting for me.

I keep walking until I'm definitely inside her personal space, one hand on the car behind her so her head tips up, just to look at me. "We're sort of close to the car, though," she says. "And a gas pump. And this lighting, I mean, it's not ideal."

"Ha ha."

"And there's a convenience store within sight. Also, there might be animals out there. Are you sure this is okay?"

"Kennedy . . ."

She opens her mouth to speak, but I've closed the distance already.

I'm not sure how to balance this moment with the bigger ones. This connection between us, with a message from somewhere beyond our world. This need right here, with the need for answers. This tiny truth, with the ones that might be waiting farther out, in the universe, on the other side of what we can understand.

I pull back first, because it's night, because I convinced her to come here with me, under the guise of answers, and this is all I've given her. "Are you ready?" I say.

She shakes her head, kisses me one last time, lingering there. Then she opens the car door and slips inside. And I know she understands, too.

• • •

The construction site across from the old Rollins factory is empty. We park the car in the lot, and I take the flashlight from the glove compartment.

"Maps *and* a flashlight," she says. "Nolan, I think I like you." She nudges my shoulder.

"If I knew this was all it would take," I say, and she smiles. We're procrastinating. We're frayed nerves. Misplaced energy. Getting ready to leave a car in the rain in the middle of the night at an empty factory, walking around back to some alleged building, a location given to us by a girl neither of us knows, other than the fact that she caught us trespassing.

This is stupid.

At least it's not raining as hard, but let's be honest, rain is rain, once you're out in it for more than a few minutes. I feel it in my socks, between my toes. My sneakers are a lost cause.

Kennedy walks forward, and I follow her, shining the light in her path. The rain hits the puddles in the dirt on a poorly marked path, overgrown with weeds, as we circle the main building.

Behind it, the trees stretch out in the distance. Until the dark building comes into focus. It seems like just another abandoned building out here, with the windows boarded up, the wooden steps half broken off. It looks like it was once part of the factory but has since been left to disrepair, same as the others. We duck under one of the large oak trees, which shelters us from most of the falling rain.

"Do you see that?" Kennedy says, and it takes me a second to notice what she's pointing out.

The soft glow of a light, from the corner of one of the plywood boards covering the window. A corner forgotten. A sign that not everything is dark and abandoned out here. At least, as Hunter Long's sister implied, not at night.

We sneak around toward the back, where there's a door, boarded up. I'm not sure how they get inside, but there's something happening here. Kennedy stands on a rotted bench under a window, where there's another sliver of light peeking through.

She peers inside, then quickly backs away. She points at the gap and whispers, "There are people inside."

I step up beside her, but it's hard to share the tiny gap in the window boards. We have to take turns, and even then, we can only see random streaks of fabric moving in the distance.

I pry my fingers into the gap—one of the boards is just barely hanging on; one nail in the corner, balanced on the piece of wood below. I pull it out and let it swing quietly down, and then we're staring into the open expanse of what looks like an abandoned shipment center.

There are crates in the corners, broken down and emptied. And in the center of the space, three guys sit in a circle of metal chairs around a lantern. Other than those crates and the wrappers and trash littering the floor, the room is barren. There are sleeping bags behind the guys, making it seem like they're planning to stay here for the night.

Kennedy presses her face up against mine at the window. The kid facing us has white-blond hair, and he laughs at something another one says. Her hand comes down on my wrist. "That's him."

She pulls back from the window, looking at me. "We should talk to him," she says.

"I don't know," I say. I get this feeling, this premonition, standing in the rain, peering into the abandoned factory. He's here because he doesn't want to be found. What happens, then, if we find him?

Kennedy takes a step to the side and stumbles off the bench. She reaches a hand out and grabs a piece of the wood from the window as she falls. The sound echoes through the night.

The guys inside go silent. I crouch down lower, still peering through the window. The three guys all stare back, but I don't think they can see me. And then on instinct, Hunter dives for his bag. I brace myself, thinking he's going to grab a weapon, but he doesn't. He grabs his bag, and he runs in the other direction, for the door.

Before I can reach for Kennedy's arm, she takes off around the building.

Everything clarifies: the night, the rain, this moment. I take off after her, on instinct. She's a blur in the night that I'm following through the trees. My God, she's fast. "Kennedy, wait!" I shout, but she doesn't listen.

I hear her shout in the distance. "Please. I'm Elliot's sister!"

And then I almost collide with her back. She's standing still between the trees, and across from her, Hunter stares back.

He looks her over closely. "I remember you," he says.

She nods. "Kennedy. I saw you once, at the house."

He frowns at me. "Who the hell are you?"

"My friend," she answers for me. "We've been looking for you."

His hair drips with rainwater, and he shakes it out. His T-shirt clings to his skinny frame, and his worn jeans and tan boots are also rain- and mud-covered. "I don't know what happened," he says.

She steps closer. "But you *do* know. You know something happened. You know Elliot's in trouble."

He looks over our heads, as if he's expecting someone else to appear from the trees. "I couldn't stay," he says. "Not for that. Not for the police."

Then he brushes by both of us, and I guess that's a sign that it's okay to follow him back to the old building. He leans his hip into a side door where the lock has worn through the rotted wood.

It's cold and impersonal inside, but at least it's dry, and there's still that lantern set up in the middle of the room. The other two kids who were here are gone—apparently spooked by our presence. Why would anyone want to stay here, I think, unless they don't want to be found?

Hunter kicks an empty can out of the way and settles into one of the metal chairs.

"I saw, on the news," he says, shaking his head. "I'm sorry."

"That's it? You're *sorry*? You think Elliot did . . . that?" Kennedy asks, standing over him. She looks like she's conducting an interrogation.

He runs a hand through his hair. "I didn't. I don't. Not really. Except I saw on the news, the evidence was pretty clear. And I know how he felt about Will."

She frowns. "What do you mean? How did he feel about Will?"

He laughs. "He hated him. Obviously. Which was something I could definitely relate to. Me and my stepdad don't exactly see eye to eye, either," he says, looking around the room. Which I assume is why he's here. He focuses back on Kennedy. "Elliot said he was controlling, manipulative. He kept fighting with his mom about it. Your mom, sorry." I can see his throat move as he swallows. "Said Will wasn't good for her, but she thought his attitude was just because he was failing Will's class." He shakes his head. "It wasn't that. He said there was something off with him. Something no one else seemed to notice . . . I guess Elliot confronted him. I guess he . . . well. I have a hard time believing it, but what do I know? I'd only met him a couple months before."

"So . . . what? You hear what happened, and you take off, and now you're hiding out here?"

He shakes his head. "I'm not hiding. I don't want to go home. I'd been staying near the college up there—no one looks too close, and it's easy to use the dorms, and student services. It's how we met." He bites his lower lip, looking at the dirty concrete beneath our feet. "I had to leave. I don't want to be dragged into the case up there. I'm sorry, Kennedy. I wasn't there, and I didn't see. Last time I got involved with something that wasn't my business, it ended badly. So, yeah, I got as far away as I could."

Kennedy leans over him so his back is pressed into the seat—but there's nowhere else for him to go. "You just left him there." She shudders, like there's a ghost in the room.

And I can feel them, all of them—Liam, her mother—watching us now, thinking about all the things we didn't do, and couldn't stop. She steps back. "Your sister is looking for you," she says. "Go home."

Hunter looks at me instead, like I'm about to absolve him of something. But I am not that person.

Kennedy stays silent on the drive home, twisting around in the seat, staring back into the darkness. "What are you looking for?" I ask.

She doesn't answer. I'm not sure if she knows, either. I drive for ten minutes before she faces forward again, but she's shaking.

I can't tell if it's the nerves, or the fact that we're soaking wet, in day-old clothes, but I just keep driving. I want to go home. I want to get her back.

"I didn't know Elliot hated Will," she says. "He didn't seem warm to him when he was around, but I thought that was just because, you know, he was our mom's boyfriend. We didn't spend a lot of time together other than at my mom's work conference over the summer and the occasional weekend dinner. Most of the time, they would go out, or spend time at Will's, just the two of them." She sits upright in her seat. "I heard them arguing once, Elliot and my mom. About how she didn't see what he was really like—I didn't realize he was talking about Will." She shakes her head, squeezing her eyes shut. "I didn't see. But Elliot did. He saw something that no one else did," she says. "I need to talk to Joe. You know, Will's prints were on the gun, too, right? The police said . . .

they said Will tried to wrestle the gun away from him. But what if that's not what happened at all?"

I try to see both possibilities—Elliot with the gun; Will with the gun. The images switch. Her brother, holding the weapon. An older man, graying beard, holding it instead.

Eventually, the rain lets up, but I keep driving until we're at a rest area on the highway, heading back to Virginia, where we wordlessly take turns standing guard outside the restrooms while the other changes.

It's 2 a.m. and the adrenaline is wearing off. There's a truck stop behind the rest area, lights on in the parking lot, full of people, despite the hour. In contrast to sneaking around an abandoned factory in the middle of the night, this feels decidedly safe.

I try to sleep, but I can't. There are too many thoughts swirling in my head. An hour later, I look over, and she's staring straight up at the ceiling. Wordlessly, I reach a hand out for hers. She laces her fingers around mine, then shifts to the side.

"I need to tell Joe," she says. "If Elliot doesn't remember what happened, then maybe it wasn't him. He can't stand the sight of blood. It makes him sick, always has. And there was so much blood . . ." She drifts off, then continues. "It's possible Elliot took my mom's gun out to protect himself. Or my *mom* took it out to protect herself. Maybe it was Will who did it."

I try to see it, to believe, to make it so. I shake my head. "But then who shot Will?" I ask.

She doesn't answer. And then, quietly, "Elliot," she says. And it's like everything finally clicks together: why he hasn't denied it, why he isn't sure. If the night is a blur, and he pulled the trigger . . . He did do something. It's terrible.

But then I think of what I would do if I saw someone hurting someone I loved.

"Are you ready to go back?" I ask.

"Not really. But I have to. Are you awake enough to drive?"

"Yeah, just, maybe you can talk to me on the way home, to make sure?"

She smiles then. "Pretty sure I can manage."

I look over at her, half in shadow, her eyes reflecting the streetlights, and reach a hand to brush her hair back instead. She closes her eyes for a minute, and I reconsider leaving for an entirely different reason.

She sighs, opening her eyes. "I have to tell the police." Her gaze shifts to the row of trucks beside us. "Will you come with me? I'm scared they won't believe me, on my own."

"Yeah, Kennedy. I'll come with you."

And then we head back onto the highway. I'm not really sure what's waiting for me there. I don't know if I want to face it, what the police think I've done. What they think I know.

I'm starting to believe that this whole search was not about my brother at all, but about helping Kennedy. And maybe it wasn't Liam speaking to me after all that night, but her.

I reach out and take her hand. Because at least it's something I can do.

39

KENNEDY

On a scale of one to ten, Joe is hovering around a sixteen when I come back home. Nolan walked me to the front door, saying we were going to face it down together. I think he's regretting his decision right about now.

The look on Joe's face is half anger, half anguish. No, scratch that: three-quarters anger, one-quarter anguish. "I left a note," I say, wincing. "And a text."

"I've been worried sick," he says. Then he looks at Nolan, like this is his fault.

"It was important, Joe." And then I tell him. How I recognized the photo on Nolan's wall—the missing person. How we drove down to North Carolina through the night (here Joe rubs his temples, like he's fighting off a migraine) and visited his house (I decided *visited* was the best term to use there). How his sister told us that her brother isn't really gone, just choosing to disappear, and her mother doesn't want to admit it. She gave us an address, to prove it.

"We went to the address," I say. "A little while ago."

265

Nolan clears his throat. I can see Joe's face, like he's trying to process, and also trying not to explode, and to somehow hold all these things in balance—the big and the little—and I just need to tell him.

"We saw him, Joe. His name is Hunter Long, and he was in this abandoned factory building, with these two other guys. We talked to him, and he knew Elliot, but he's scared—"

Joe stands then. "Wait a minute, back up, back up. You went to this abandoned factory, and . . . what? Just walked right in?"

"Well, they must have heard us outside, and they stood up, and Hunter ran because he was scared, but I followed him—"

"Oh my *God*, Kennedy!" Joe is yelling again. Well, the scales tipped, and not in our favor. "Are you two out of your *minds*? First, driving through the night, and keeping your phone off so I had no idea where you were. Yes, I noticed that part. Then, tracking down some kid who may or may not be missing, just because you think you saw him with Elliot once—"

"I *did* see him, Joe. He *told* me—"

But Joe keeps going like he doesn't even hear me. "Then," he continues, pacing back and forth so Nolan and I have to turn our heads side to side just to keep up with him. "Wait, let me see if I've got this next part straight. *Then*, you wait until night, and you sneak around some abandoned factory, where who knows *what* is going on inside—obviously, nothing good. I mean, it's an abandoned factory in the middle of the night, and you should be smarter than this. Kennedy, I

266

trusted you. I did. But this is ridiculous. And then you followed him through the woods?"

Nolan's head has dropped lower, like he's ashamed.

"Joe," I say. "He was Elliot's boyfriend."

He stops pacing then, narrowing his eyes. "What?"

I swallow nothing. "He was Elliot's boyfriend. He was a
runaway, staying at the college, which is how he met Elliot.
And apparently Elliot confided in him, his thoughts about
Will. . . . Elliot didn't want them together, you're right. But
it was because he thought there was something off with
Will. Something she wouldn't see. Joe, I think it was Will
who shot Mom."

Joe is speechless. His gaze shifts to Nolan, as if asking
for confirmation that he's hearing this correctly. Nolan nods
once. He hands Joe the file, the one Nolan got from his
house—all the details about Hunter Long. Who he is, where
he lives. And a few notes written over the top, now in Nolan's
handwriting: the name of the factory, the date and time we
saw him.

"Elliot's trial starts *this week*. Don't you think the police
have been through this? It was your mother's gun, and Elliot's prints were on it. There was gunshot residue all over
his clothes, and you *told* me what you saw. . . ." Joe trails off,
shaking his head. "Kennedy, this is wishful thinking."

"It is, Joe. It is. You're right. But I believe Elliot wouldn't
do that. I think you believe it, too. And if you believe that,
it opens you up to seeing something more." I take a deep
breath. "I think Mom took the gun out, to protect herself,
but Will took it from her. I think they were fighting, and
Elliot didn't hear it." I remember what Elliot was like, when

he was in the zone. How I could sneak up on him, with his headphones on, and he wouldn't hear it until it was too late. I saw his headphones on the desk that night, when I peered in the window.

"I think he heard the gunshot," I explain, "and that's when he left the room. I think he tried to wrestle it away, to protect himself, and that's when he shot Will."

Joe just stares at me; I can't figure out what's going on in his head. It's closed off, a mystery to me.

"He says he doesn't know what happened."

"Maybe he doesn't," I say. "You know how he is with blood. He gets sick at the sight of his *own*." Or maybe Elliot does remember bits and pieces, and none of it changes anything. He did pull a trigger. He did do something terrible.

"Joe, I want to tell the police. Not just about that. I want to tell them what I saw. What really happened. All of it."

He pauses, looking me over slowly. Picking his next words carefully. "It's going to look even worse for him, if you say it," he says gently. Elliot, with a gun, pointed in my direction.

I know this. And yet. "If I want them to believe me, I have to tell them everything."

Joe sits down at the kitchen table, head in his hands.

"I'll call them tomorrow," he says. "We'll try to get an appointment for the same day."

"I want to do it now." Before the trial gets any closer, and before I lose my nerve.

"What? It's Sunday. I'm not even sure anyone will get back to us until tomorrow."

"Tell them we're coming. Tell them I have something important to say. The trial starts this week. They'll show up."

Nolan looks at Joe. "I'm sorry," he says. "I knew it wasn't smart. I did it anyway. The whole thing was my idea."

"Oh no," I say, turning on him. "You don't apologize. Not for this."

While Joe is on the phone, I wait with Nolan in the doorway. "Thank you," I say, resting my head on his chest for a moment. His hand comes to the side of my face, holding me there. I can hear the beat of his heart, the sound of his breath. "I guess this is almost done," he says, and he seems wistful. Sad, maybe.

I nod, pulling back, but what I really think is that it's just getting started.

Joe comes out with his keys and the file from Nolan. He's changed out of his athletic shorts, now wearing jeans. "Okay," he says. "We're ready."

He stands there between us and I blink several times, frozen in place. "They said yes?"

The key trembles faintly in his hands. "Is this what you truly want to do, Kennedy? Because if so, they're ready for us. If not, I'll deal with it. But this, right here, is your decision, and it's time."

Now that I'm facing it, I start to picture saying it. But Joe keeps his eyes on mine, like he's keeping me grounded.

"Okay. I'm ready," I say.

He nods, then as an afterthought, "We could use you as a witness, too, Nolan."

Nolan mumbles something that might be a *Yes, sir,* but we're already moving. I trail after Joe, trying to keep the momentum. Trying to just keep moving before something stops me.

As we back out of the driveway, Joe glances in the rear-view mirror, waiting for Nolan to start his car so he can follow.

Joe clears his throat. "You were gone for two nights. Where did you sleep?"

My cheeks heat, and I keep my gaze down, my voice quick. "In the car," I say, and his grip tightens on the wheel.

"This will be a talk for another time. But, Kennedy, it *will* be a talk."

"Okay, Joe," I say, my head leaning against the window. I stare at the sky, looking for that crack—the one I can always find, that runs through everything. But the sky is so blue, and the sunrise is so bright, it makes my eyes tear just to look at it.

Nolan's car pulls in beside ours, and Joe exits first, staring up at the building. He walks up the front steps, but Nolan lingers by his car.

"It's not too late to make a run for it," he says. I smile, which I guess was the intended reaction. Now that I'm here, standing in front of the police station, I'm terrified. He reaches for me, and I rest my forehead on his shoulder, with his hand on my back.

"I don't want to tell it to everyone," I say.

"So just tell it to me," he says.

Inside, there's no one working at the front desk, and we walk by the same vending machine with the crack I saw last week, the same lacquered walls I ran my fingers across.

The three of us walk into the same conference room, but that's the end of the similarities. Now there are two men at the table, along with a woman, and a video camera set up between them. "Oh," I say, freezing at the entrance.

Joe puts his hand on my shoulder and squeezes.

"I've asked my colleagues to be here today, to help make sure we have all the facts. And to make sure there's no . . . confusion," the man in the wire-rim glasses says.

I'm not sure whether he's talking about my confusion or his, but I walk to the seat across from the camera.

I notice that his tie, today, is straight. "So, Kennedy," he says, "I hear you've remembered something important. Something that will shed some light on this case."

I nod. I've always remembered. But I wait until Joe and Nolan take their seats, and then think how to begin.

"I panicked," I say, feeling my throat close, even now, with the thought of it. "When you questioned me in the hospital. There are things I didn't want to say."

His eyes gleam, and he presses Record. They're all watching me, waiting. But instead I focus on Nolan, sitting at the other end of the table. Just one person. One person, who will listen. One person, who will believe me.

I will have to tell them about Elliot, standing and pointing the gun at me. And about hiding in the shed, the call I made for help, which no one received. I will have to tell them I never looked at the shadow house.

I pretend it's just me and Joe, in the car on the side of the road; or me and Nolan, sending messages to each other, back and forth—a connection before we'd even met. And then I start talking. It comes out in a rush, like I've been holding it in forever and it's been trying to escape all this time.

I repeat the things Hunter told me about Will and my mom, what Elliot believed. I tell them about Hunter Long, how he could be a witness, maybe, if they can find him, and convince him. Though I worry he's unlikely to agree—he said he didn't want to be involved. And then I tell them what I think must have happened.

They all look at one another, and I know what they're remembering. The police traced Elliot back to the woods, that night, but couldn't find him. Like he was hiding, ashamed of something he had done. But I try to look beyond that. "Elliot can't handle the sight of blood," I say. "When he was younger, he used to pass out, just looking at a cut. That much blood . . . it could've sent him into shock."

He must've stayed in one spot for hours, just standing there. I imagine him in the circle, where Liam disappeared. The police searched that area over and over, and they didn't find him. Sometimes I wonder if the earth swallowed him up. That crack in the universe. If he slipped right through, for a moment, to be safe. If he escaped for a little bit, too.

When daylight came, he walked back home; up the road, to the driveway, through the front door. Blood-soaked, shaking, fingertips near frostbitten. He came back, and nothing would ever be the same.

When I finish my story, the woman is watching me closely, and the man in the glasses stares at Joe, like he expects him to talk some sense into me. Or like he expects Joe to ask me to leave the room, like last time, so he can explain.

But he doesn't. He sits there, staring back, and then the man asks if he can speak with Joe alone.

Joe shakes his head. "That's what Kennedy knows, and we wanted you to know it, too. I think it's fair to assume that if you call her up to the stand, that's the same truth she will tell you then. We will be sharing this with Elliot's lawyer as well."

Joe hands them the file that Nolan gave him, with all the information on Hunter Long. I have no idea if they'll follow up—maybe not if it's messing up their case. I have to hope that their goal is not just a tally in the win column, but uncovering the truth. And I do. I believe it.

I think there's something tying us all together here. Everyone in this room. The type of people who search for answers, who want to know, who want the proof. I think it's maybe true of all of us, outside this room, too, stretching across the globe, on and on and on.

The man in the glasses looks through the file before frowning. "Kennedy, you've told us Elliot had the gun. He *pulled the trigger*—"

"I know he did. But I don't think he started it. I think he was protecting himself."

He sighs.

"Were my mother's prints on the gun, too?"

He frowns. "They would be there, from any time she touched it. Even if it was a different day."

My eyes widen. "So the answer is yes," I say. I see her, then, racing for the linen closet, opening the compartment, for the safe where she kept the gun. I see her punch in the code, taking it out. I hear them arguing. I see her backing down the hall as Will steps closer, even as she holds the gun. And then Will telling her to stop, reaching for her, taking it from her as she backs into the stairs . . .

I can see that the people across the table are thinking it through, too. That there's something here, that we're reaching for, just beyond the places we can see.

"The evidence supports Elliot as the shooter," he says, but more softly.

"His prints were on the safe?"

Three heads shoot up, and they look at one another. "What safe?" the woman says.

I don't understand and look to Joe. "The safe where the gun was kept."

But the man in the glasses is already shaking his head, just as the others are shuffling papers around. "When we asked you at the hospital, you said the gun was kept in the linen closet. Elliot said the same thing."

"Right. It was hidden in the linen closet. Inside the safe."

"There was no safe," he says.

My heart beats faster, until I can hear it, echoing inside my head. "Inside the wall panel. It's disguised to look like an electrical box. The safe is inside the wall panel." It was just another quirk of the house that she loved, a hidden compartment the previous owners must've installed. One more secret she uncovered after we'd already moved in.

Silence. And then: "Will you go through that night, one more time, Kennedy? Every second of it, to the best of your recollection."

"Yes," I say.

40

NOLAN

I sit in that room, listening to every painful thing Kennedy has to say.

Imagining myself there.

Her voice lulls, haunting in the barren room, and it's like I'm there.

I can feel the rain. I can hear the thunder. The house lights up in the distance, under a crack of lightning.

"I was waiting at the fence," she says. "At the edge of the property. There was a light on, in Elliot's room. That's all I could really make out, in the dark. The lightning felt so close, and I didn't want to get struck while I was running across the fields, but I figured at that point, I could also get struck just standing there, too, while I was waiting at the fence. So I talked myself into it. After the next bolt of lightning, I would go. But then I heard a boom. And it sounded so much closer . . . like something else. . . ." She shakes her head. "So I counted down from three, and then I ran."

I open my eyes, and she's looking straight at me. *I*

counted down from three, she says, and I feel something stir inside.

Three, two, one, I hear, and I can't breathe.

The timing of the signal. We were wrong—it wasn't pi, nothing about the geometry of a circle, or trying to communicate through math. But the count of three. *Three, two, one.*

It was the message.

She keeps talking, telling her story, but I'm somewhere else. I'm no longer in the room at all.

The trees come into focus first, and they blur by as I race through them. I'm running through the woods after Liam, both of us younger, shirtless, in bathing suits. The branches catch at my skin, and he's laughing. *Come on, Nolan*, he calls over his shoulder.

We emerge in a clearing, and he points over the ledge, to a still body of water. We're standing on top of a granite formation, slick gray walls jutting out in geometrical patterns, a pool of impossible blue down below, in the middle. Our parents are somewhere out there on a picnic blanket, looking up—but I can't pick them out from all the others. And there's a lifeguard on a stand waiting at the base. Some people have jumped. Other people are swimming.

There's another lifeguard in the clearing, and he gestures to the pile of flotation devices beside us. Liam hands me an orange life jacket from the pile, but my fingers aren't strong enough to work the straps.

I'm maybe eight or nine, and I'm scared, but I don't want him to know it. But still, he can tell. He fastens it for me, tugging on the straps. *Look, you have a life jacket*, he says, same as his. I remember not stepping any closer to the edge, the feeling that my feet were too heavy to move, connected to the earth.

And then Liam reaches out and grabs on to my hand. He's ten or eleven and had long stopped holding my hand. But he does it then, and says, *Turn around.*

I stand beside him, our hands interlocked, my feet at the edge, but looking off into the trees instead. *Three,* he says, and I join him for the rest. *Two,* in perfect unison. *One,* and we're flying. No, we're falling.

I remember now: We fell together, children who could still hold hands. I saw the sky falling away from us, and it felt like I was sinking into a black hole.

He didn't let go the whole way down, until the cold water welcomed us and my life jacket pushed me back up to the surface.

Liam popped up beside me, smiling, shaking his hair out. "Again?" he asked.

I scrambled up the bank after him, took the dirt path up and up, to the top of the quarry. Over and over we jumped. Counting down together every time.

Three. Two. One.

I open my eyes.

The room is emptying out. Kennedy stands, alongside Joe. I try to smile at her, but I feel nauseated. Disoriented, like I'm both here and somewhere else at the same time.

"Thanks for staying," she says, and I nod, heading toward my car. "Nolan?" she calls after me. "Is everything okay?"

I shake my head, and she stares at me, then pivots in the

other direction, at something Joe says instead. I can't hear him through the buzzing in my ears. I keep hearing Liam's voice in my head; I keep picturing that scene. The trees. The path.

And suddenly Joe is beside us, repeating something. "Is that okay with you, Nolan?"

"Hmm?"

"He's going to see Elliot, and the lawyers. To ask Elliot about Hunter, and to find out if there's something he remembers that he's not telling us. Can I go back with you instead?" she asks.

I nod. "Yeah, of course."

"Be back by eight tonight, Kennedy," he says. "And bring your phone. Leave it on, and please, Kennedy, answer it. I'm trusting you here. Both of you."

She pulls me by the arm to the car, then says, "What happened?"

I shake my head, thinking it's impossible. I can't explain it—who would believe it? But then I think: *She* would. It's possible. All of this is possible.

"I don't know," I say. "You were talking, about the count of three, and . . . I remembered something."

"What did you remember?"

I close my eyes. "I remember being somewhere. Some quarry, like a family park? Somewhere my family used to go together, when we were kids. I remember jumping with Liam. I remember him counting down, from three. Just like you said. And . . . I keep thinking of that picture. The picture in the email."

Her eyes widen.

"I think I know where the picture was taken," I say. "I think I know where he wants me to go."

She takes out her phone, starts searching for things like *quarry* and *park*, but we're coming up empty.

"Come on," I say. I want to see that picture again, enlarged on the living room table. I'm not sure if my parents are there, if the police are there, if they're all looking for me, waiting to bring me in for questioning—but I have to try. It feels like Liam is right there, right on the other side of something, like the memory of his fingers linking through my own—like I can just about reach out and touch him.

There are no cars out front when I pull up to the house. Still, we sit in the car alone for a bit, making sure no one is just waiting around the corner, watching for this moment. I step outside, and nothing. Kennedy follows me to the front door—more nothing.

I start to wonder if maybe I've been cleared. If anyone has noticed that, once again, I've disappeared. If they've forgotten about me. Or whether I'll go inside and find my photo already up on the wall of the missing.

"Hello?" I call, once we're inside. The house is deserted; it *feels* deserted, like no one's been here all day. No leftover scent of food, or dishes in the sink; no mess from Clara or Dave or the other volunteers; no papers left out on the table. It's like stepping into another dimension.

The only thing with presence here is Liam.

His picture is still sitting on the table, enlarged, so you

can't miss it when you walk through the room. He's everywhere. He always has been.

Leaning over it, I look closely at the trees, at the trail beyond him. I run my hand over the edges, as if that will tell me something. It seems familiar, in that way of a dream, a premonition. But I'm not sure if I'm projecting here. If I just want to believe, if I want it to be real.

I need to see images from the same location, to compare. The only computer remaining in this house is a new laptop on the dining room table. All the other electronic equipment has been cleared away, as potential evidence, to see whether I was storing the photo elsewhere—if they can trace it back to the source.

I hope the password is the same from when I've had to help out my parents, and it is.

Kennedy leans over me as I type. I search for *granite quarries plus swimming plus Virginia*, and eventually find a link to a place that was shut down several years ago, after a drought. It's called Old Granite Quarry, and it used to be an open park with a registration hut and a lifeguard station, with a shed for equipment. The article says that the water seeped out over time, drying it out. When I search for *Old Granite Quarry*, there's a relatively new article about the land surrounding it recently being purchased by a developer.

The article shows the map overview, from above. Under the image tab on the main search page, there are a few old family pictures of kids jumping into the water or swimming. It's definitely the place I remember; I just don't know if it's the place in the photo.

But I have this feeling. I need to know before the police come back. Before they start prying at my story once more.

I hear a car out front, and I shut the laptop.

"Go. Through the back," I tell Kennedy.

She heads toward the kitchen, then stops. "Aren't you coming?"

"They've already seen my car. If it's my parents or the police, I can't just run, Kennedy. But you don't have to get sucked into it."

"I don't—"

"Go," I say, and I suddenly understand why she said the same to me, outside the college. There are things you want to protect from each other. Pieces of you that you'd rather not let them see.

I hold my breath when the key in the lock turns, but it's Mike who pushes open the door. "Nolan?" he calls.

I exhale slowly. "Hey, Mike. Sorry. You scared me."

He enters the house slowly, closing the door behind him, looking confused. "Uh, your parents have been looking for you." He looks away, then back. "*Everyone's* been looking for you."

Meaning: the police. Meaning: I'm in trouble, even if I don't understand why or how.

"I've been worried about you, Nolan."

"Mike, I have to go. I'll be back. Just, please don't tell them I was here?"

He shakes his head, then stops. I wonder if he's remembering his own sister, how she disappeared. If he remembers how it feels to lose someone; if he remembers the desperation to find them.

He walks to the dining room, sits in front of the sole computer, and pretends not to notice me. "The others will be pulling up within the next five minutes," he says.

"Thank you." And with that, I'm gone.

It takes an hour and a half to make it to the quarry parking lot, as navigated by the familiar tone of Kennedy's cell phone.

"Is this it?" she asks, leaning around me.

There's no sign at the turnoff, and the road is blocked by an old, rusty metal gate.

"I think so."

She gets out of the car and pushes the gate, which swings open slowly. It looks stiff and heavy, from the way she digs her heels in, leaning her weight into the metal. I inch the car forward and she hops back in.

The road from here is dirt, and it all comes back to me. Bouncing in the backseat with Liam as the car drove over the uneven ground, littered with bumps and potholes. Up ahead is a parking lot, now abandoned. Just a circle of dirt now, surrounded by trees.

The dirt settles when we exit the car, the path ahead leading the way through the trees. I think there used to be a sign here for the quarry ahead, but it's been replaced with one that instead says: WARNING. NO TRESPASSING.

We take the path, which is only wide enough for one of us at a time, and eventually it opens up at the old ticket counter. The open window area is surrounded by rotted wood from being left uncovered, and it breaks off at the corner when I lean my hand on it. Around back, there's a storage area, with a locked door.

I push my hip into it, and the door gives with a gust of stale air, like it's been holding its breath all this time.

Inside is dark and dust-streaked, but there's a pile of old forgotten furniture—some chairs I can remember my family renting—and there's a desk with a mini-television on it.

No one has been here for ages. Maybe I was wrong.

I step outside and Kennedy's looking up, at the corner of the building. She's frowning. "What?" I ask.

She points up, and I see it: a narrow camera, angled off to the side, like it was meant to keep track of the people coming and going. She turns around, and I do the same, as if we are the camera, seeing the same perspective.

It focuses on the path heading back into the trees. Where, I remember now, the quarry is located.

I see the photo in my head, of Liam, the dog, heading into the woods, surrounded by trees.

Maybe the leaves are a little different, the angle slightly off, because we're lower, and it's a different time of year. But I think I was right.

The photo came from that camera. From this shed.

Liam was here.

41

KENNEDY

"This is the path," Nolan says, taking off.

"Wait," I call, but he doesn't seem to hear me.

He weaves through the trees, his hand slightly in front of him, like he's following a ghost, or a memory.

The path diverges up ahead—to the right, it slopes downward, and to the left, it angles up. Another broken sign, with an arrow pointing downhill for a picnic area. But we go the other way. Nolan doesn't even pause, just veers left, on instinct. It's like he doesn't even notice me.

His hand grabs a branch as he passes, and his steps pick up speed, until we're almost running, and I can suddenly envision it myself: the scene he told me about on the drive up.

Two young boys, in bathing suits, racing through the trees, for the clearing. Running, the older one laughing, the younger one struggling to keep up.

And then we're there. We're at the top, at the circular clearing between the trees, overlooking the quarry. Nolan stands in the middle of the open area, panting. He paces, then steps closer to the trees. The wind blows, and you can hear it coming through the trees, like a warning.

Up here, the sun does something odd to the granite, turning it gray-white, and it looks unnatural, like blocks of stone placed down one by one, balancing precariously. The dust blows over them like chalk in the wind.

Nolan runs his hand through his hair, staring off into the woods.

"Liam?" he calls into the trees.

The word is heart-stuttering. It freezes everything; me, and him, and time. It's like he's crossing some barrier, giving voice to what he believes might be true, and possible. And then, louder, "Liam!" The name echoes, fading into the distance.

We listen, but only the wind calls back. He steps closer to the trees, and I start to feel sick. The kind of sick I don't want to think about too deeply, to examine the source. The sort of sick that says it knows something, in the sinking pit of my stomach.

My hands start to shake.

He's yelling off into the trees, and I can picture it again: the brothers together. Two young boys, in bathing suits and life jackets, the sun cutting through the trees, cutting across them. They counted down together. *Three. Two. One.*

It's the reason we're here. It's the reason he knew to come here.

"Liam!" he calls again, just inside the tree line now, and it makes me jump.

I press my knuckles to my mouth. He's not looking in the

right place. I step away from him, turning around, though I don't want to. Instead of walking toward Nolan, I approach the edge.

One step closer, and my mind goes somewhere else: to the shadow house. The horrors I can only imagine. I kept my eyes closed then, because I couldn't bear it. I couldn't.

But if I look now, he won't have to.

My foot breaks a branch in the clearing, shattering the silence of the woods. I look back over my shoulder just as Nolan turns around, his brow furrowed, like he doesn't understand.

I look away. I can't bear to see this, either, the moment when he understands what I'm doing.

And then I lean forward, peering over the edge. . . . It's a long way down. The distance is disorienting, and it makes my stomach drop. The earth below is brown and green between slabs of granite. It's an empty crater, dry and thirsty, but it's not barren, the green pushing back up, like it's beginning anew.

My eyes skim the surface quickly, only with the edge of my vision. But then something catches, and I have to look again. Really look this time. In a circle of green and brown is a different color, not of this landscape. But it's a color I've seen before, in a picture enlarged on Nolan's living room table. The deep maroon of the fabric of a shirt.

I stumble back, squeezing my eyes, trying to undo it.

"Kennedy?" he asks as I backpedal farther from the edge.

I breathe heavily, trying to quell the twisting in my stomach, spreading everywhere. But Nolan's across the clearing, asking.

Here's the thing about the shadow house: In my mind, everything is blurred, and so when I think of my mother, I still see her laughing, sliding a plate of pancakes in front of me. Or holding my chin in her hands years earlier and telling me to keep very still as she dabs the ointment on a cut under my eye. I can still feel the press of her lips on my forehead after, her breath as she says, *Be careful, my wild one.* When I see her now, her eyes crinkle in joy.

And at this moment, Nolan still sees a boy holding his hand, counting down and jumping. And that will be gone, I know it will be gone, five seconds from now, as soon as he walks my way.

I walk toward him instead and put a hand on his chest. Firmly. Until he looks me in the eye, asking. He's been asking all along. But this is not the answer he was searching for.

"Nolan," I say, trying to hold my voice stable, not to cry, not right now, because it's not about me right now. My other arm wraps around his side, to hold him this way. "Don't look."

I feel his muscles give, everything just exhale, like some great hope has left him. And I hold on tighter, though he doesn't fall. He lists slowly to one side, and I guide him to a tree stump, farther from the edge. He sits with his head in his hands, and I think: *He's in shock; he's only part here; he's going to fall apart, but not yet.*

Not yet.

I don't know what to do. Everything feels urgent, and yet it's also not. What am I racing for? It's already happened. Like the shadow house.

It exists, and so do we, and now so does this, and nothing will change that.

It isn't fair.

That's all I can think: It isn't *fair*. This isn't how his story ends. It can't be.

I take out my cell phone and place the call. Someone picks up, but it seems like dead air. No, it's static. It sort of connects, but I can't hear the voice on the other side. "It's only static," I tell him. Static, cutting in and out. Like the voice is too far away, unreachable.

Out here in the quarry, there must be no signal. Not this deep in the woods. But I know we had a signal out on the road. My GPS on the phone got us here, after all.

"We have to go," I say, but he doesn't budge, and I have no idea if he's heard me. I crouch down in front of him. "Nolan, all I get is static. We have to—"

"No," he says, and he looks up then, this haunted, hollow look that I don't think I will ever forget. "I can't. I can't leave—" He shakes his head, and I nod, understanding.

"Okay. Okay, stay here," I say, standing up. "I'll be right back."

I look behind me once, to see him still sitting in the exact same position, before the trees close in around him as I move farther away. And then I start running. I'm only half-paying attention as I race back down the trail, looking at my phone to see when the signal comes back, so I almost trip on a root before steadying myself on a trunk nearby. I shake out my leg and try again, but all I get is static once more. I keep going, veering at the cutoff, back past the shed. I'm almost all the way to the parking lot, and I try again, begging the phone to connect.

I pace beside the shed as the phone in my hands rings.

And then the phone connects, and I grip the phone tighter. "Hello? Can anyone hear me?"—a memory of a call I made months ago. The same greeting. The same response.

"I hear you," she responds. "Miss? Are you okay?"

Something's happening. Something terrible.

"Help us. Please," I say. Because Nolan needs something that no one can give him anymore. I don't know how to help him. I think this must be how Joe felt, standing in the doorway of my hospital room, watching me sit there, staring off at the white curtains.

I give the woman our location and tell her it's an emergency.

I tell her what we've found.

I've just hung up and am about to turn around and run back to Nolan when I catch another glimpse of color through the trees, in the parking lot. This time, a flash of blue.

I step closer, until I can make it out: the light reflecting off the blue of a car.

Someone else is here.

I turn in a circle, confused. I'm not sure whether this car belongs to the developer—someone who can help us. Or whether it belongs to someone who knew Liam was here and sent that picture. "Hello?" I call. I didn't see anyone on the path on the way back, but they could've veered to the right at the cutoff, heading to the base of the quarry.

The car looks familiar, in a vague sort of way. It's parked beside Nolan's, and it reminds me of earlier today.

I walk closer until I'm out in the dirt lot and quietly step around it—until I see, on the back, the decal for the foundation Nolan's family runs, and I know this belongs to that guy who works at his house, though I've never seen him before. Mike, I think he said.

I wonder if he knew what we were doing and followed us here. Nolan trusts him, and it's possible he's here to help. Though I don't recall seeing another car behind us on the back roads, or when we arrived.

I stare back into the woods, remembering what Nolan said—that the picture of Liam was sent from the library. It could've been anyone. And yet, it could've been sent from the library to make it *seem* like Nolan. He used to pretend he had a job tutoring there. Mike would think he worked there. Nobody knew it was a lie.

In the pit of my stomach, there's the feeling of *wrong*.

I try to open Nolan's car door, but it's locked. Thankfully he's left the windows half down, because his air conditioning is always broken, so I reach my arm in until I can disengage the lock, stretching down until it clicks.

Then I open the door and pop the trunk. The noise cuts through the empty parking lot, and I pause, looking around— with the feeling that someone is watching me.

His baseball gear is still tucked in the corner of the trunk, the mitt beside the bat. I can feel his hands on my hands, his body pressed behind mine, his words, explaining how to get more power.

Don't swing like you're afraid, he said.

One more look over the lid of the trunk, into the trees.

I'm not afraid, I tell myself. My hands shake anyway.

I pick up the bat.

42

NOLAN

Everything sounds so far away: across an ocean, a void of empty space. When I look up, the branches move, and the sky shrinks, and it's like I'm falling into a black hole.

This cannot be what had me coming out here—to find this? This nothingness?

What was the point? Of the signal, and the signs, leading me here?

All this, to find he's been dead, all this time?

There are footsteps, slowly trudging up the path—the sound cutting its way through the fog, back to me. It must be Kennedy, but I don't want to look at her. All I'll see is her face when she told me not to look. Her expression, which said everything.

"Nolan?"

It's a man's voice. The footsteps pause for a moment and then continue.

"Nolan? Is that you? Is everything okay?"

I look up, and I'm disoriented. In the middle of the woods,

in the middle of nowhere—it's Mike. I shake my head. *No, everything is not okay.*

Did Kennedy call him somehow? Did he know how to find us? Did time slip from me just like Liam did, here and gone? I look beyond Mike, for Kennedy. For someone to make sense of things.

"Hey," he says, coming into the clearing. "It's okay." He reaches a hand down for my shoulder, where I'm sitting on the stump of the tree.

"Mike? What are you doing here?" There are no police behind him. My parents aren't here. *No one* is here.

His shadow falls over me, his feet braced apart, and my shoulders tense.

"Mike?" I ask again, except this time, I'm asking something else. Something tingling in the back of my mind. "Mike, did you know . . ." But what? *What* did he know? That there was a picture of my brother, taken from this location? That my brother had been here once? That my brother was dead?

"Oh, Nolan," he says, crouching down. "I want you to know how sorry I am." His hands are shaking on his knees, and I can see that he is. Sorry. Except I'm face-to-face with the thing that is wrong, that makes no sense.

It's his hands. They're covered. He's wearing thin leather gloves, in June, in the middle of Virginia.

"What are you doing?" I ask, leaning away. And then I look around frantically—for the police, for my parents, for *anyone.*

Who is this person, who's been in my house since the earliest days of my parents' organization? This man who gave us his condolences, told us what a gift Liam had been to the shelter they worked at together. Did he ever really lose his sister? Or was it Liam, all along, that brought him to us?

"Did you do this?" I ask, fueled by anger instead of grief. I stand abruptly and my head spins. But my body is full of rage, and adrenaline, and everything's on edge. I can't tell which person is in front of me—the Mike I thought I knew, or the Mike I'm seeing now. I don't know which instinct to trust.

He holds his hands up, palm out, and on instinct I step back, losing my balance over the stump, scrambling to stand again as Mike walks closer. I can tell now, this is not the expression of someone here to help me. His face has shifted, set and determined.

"Stand up, Nolan," he says. He reaches a hand down for me, but I push myself upright on my own. He steps closer, and I move back again, into the center of the clearing.

"You sent that picture," I say, pointing my finger at his chest. "You knew he was here all along. You—"

He raises an eyebrow, not denying it.

The pieces start clicking together. "Is this why you work for my parents? You've known all along? Were you in my house to protect yourself?" After the first press conference, the police scanned those images from the television stations for potential suspects. They told my parents that suspects often like to insert themselves into the cases directly.

We didn't look close enough, though. We didn't check our own home. Mike gave us a story, and we believed it, because Liam knew him and my parents wanted answers.

Now I'm here, finally getting answers, only they're not the ones I want. I've been racing toward the thing that would devastate us all, and for what? For this? One more betrayal?

"What did you *do* to him?" I ask, my thumb jutting over my shoulder, pointing to the edge of the quarry behind us. Needing to know, and needing desperately to be wrong about all of it.

Mike shakes his head. "He did it to himself. I'm so sorry. Your brother was good at a lot of things, but he didn't know how to keep his mouth shut."

I picture Liam over the sink, the razor clattering, the drop of blood—his hand shaking. Something had been on his mind. Somehow, I knew, even then—something was wrong. But I said nothing. The thought was fleeting, barely registering. And in the chaos that followed, I'd all but forgotten it.

"I thought you . . ." Everything twists. I thought Mike was on our side. I thought Liam trusted him. And now I see that he did; I finally understand how Liam would disappear from the park, with a dog, without putting up a fight: only if it was someone he knew. Only if he trusted that he would make it back unharmed. I remember, then, how Mike told my parents Liam probably ran away. Because it was unlikely someone would take and harm both Liam *and* the dog. Mike planted that seed, and it grew.

"Someone was spreading rumors," Mike explains. "About me. It's all so unimportant, such a small thing. All of this about people who *don't even matter*. Who no one even *misses*. But someone confided in your brother. And he couldn't let it go." He shakes his head, like it's all some big regrettable thing. Instead of something he had control over all along.

"But this, Nolan. I *am* truly sorry. I want you to believe that."

I shake my head, not understanding. A step behind, as I've always been.

"Thing is, Nolan, this body is going to be found, one way or another now. The land was purchased. It's unfortunate, really, but that's the truth of it. Your brother's case was going to be reopened, with or without that email. And I'm tired of trying to hide it. It's time he was found, don't you think?"

Yes, I do, except I also realize exactly how Mike wants Liam's body to be uncovered. An email, with a photo, sent from *me*.

"So, what, you decided to blame it on me?" I say. It's ridiculous. He couldn't imagine this would work.

But he smiles, his lips pulling back, baring his teeth. It's a look I've never seen on him before. "I didn't realize you'd know the location, Nolan. Didn't know it meant anything to you at all. But it was obvious you figured it out. Left it up on the computer screen right before you took off on this little excursion." He shrugs. "You make do with what you get." Then he smiles again. "Maybe it was a sign."

I'm confused. I don't see what he has at all. "The body will still be discovered," I say.

"Yes. And the person who sent the picture, who obviously knew more about what happened to Liam Chandler all this time but tried to hide it, has been overcome with guilt. He came out to the spot where he was responsible for his brother's death."

We've been shifting, slowly, as he leans closer and I lean back. Inch by inch. And then it dawns on me. The edge is behind us, and there's nothing to stop his momentum—it's just the granite below my feet, and then a cliff. "You're going to frame me and then make it look like I killed myself?" He's out of his mind. There's no way I'm going down without a fight. I look all around me for something I can use.

I'm almost his size. I could strike first. But then I run the risk of being tossed over the edge, with or without him. There's one way out, and he's standing in front of it.

Oh God, Kennedy's out here somewhere.

Either he found her and I'm too late, or he doesn't know she's here. And I don't want him to figure it out.

"It's a sad story, either way," he continues. "One brother, missing for years. Another, suffering alone, overwhelmed with his grief and regret. It's a story people will believe. This moment was inevitable, Nolan."

I take a deep breath in, because I think I finally understand.

This moment *was* inevitable; he's right. My brother was going to be found. That picture would be recognized by me. I would be out here, looking for him. Mike would find me.

All of this, I can see, a fall of dominoes set in motion—leading us to this moment, right here, right now.

I shake my head at him, but he doesn't understand. He thinks I'm giving in. But I feel surrounded suddenly.

I look beyond him, into the trees, and everything is perfectly clear. Why the universe sent me to her, and her to me. It wasn't to prove anything. It wasn't for a picture, or a clue, or a sign.

It was for us.

Maybe it *was* my brother talking to me all along. Because this moment I'm facing was *almost* inevitable. Almost. But Mike has one part wrong. He doesn't know I'm not out here alone.

Her shadow hovers just beyond Mike's shoulder. She's so quiet, moving like a ghost—easy to overlook if you're not paying attention.

She's got my bat in her hands. For a moment, everything is too bright. The sunlight escaping from between a gap of clouds. I close my eyes. She knows what to do. *Don't be afraid*, I think.

She swings.

43

KENNEDY

The man before me stumbles for a second, and I start to panic, thinking I'm going to have to hit him again, but my hands are already reverberating from the impact—and then he sinks to his knees before collapsing onto the ground, face-first. I swung just the way Nolan showed me—for power. My hands are still throbbing, my fingers trembling.

Nolan stands over him, his expression blank. This must be Mike, though I've never met him. All I know is he was trying to hurt Nolan. I heard him, everything he said—about Nolan, about Liam. This man was working for their parents. How often the danger lurks inside our own homes. How often we let it inside without realizing it.

Mike covers his head with one hand, then pushes himself onto his knees, but Nolan grabs his arm out from under him, sending him back to the dirt. Nolan's got his arm in his grip still, and they're inches from the edge.

"Nolan," I say. He looks up, surprised, like I'm calling him back from some darker place. Like he's forgotten himself, and then finds whatever he lost once more, as he places a knee on Mike's back, holding his arm behind him.

Nolan looks up at me, like he's asking me what to do. And I just stand with the bat in my hands, seeing every possibility play out before us. "The police are on their way," I finally say.

Mike struggles against the ground, but Nolan's stronger, and I still have the bat, just in case. I hope I don't have to use it again. But I will if I have to.

Nolan digs his knee into Mike's back until he winces and coughs.

Mike's one blue eye, visible against the ground, is staring straight at me.

I wonder what he sees. I shake off the chill. The evil you think you can see behind the walls, through the window. So much closer than that.

Mike seems to lose all strength then, and his eyes keep drifting shut, and part of me feels sick, even in the relief—wondering what I have just done. Whether this will be something I can never come back from; some crack in the universe. A line that divides my life anew. Before. After.

And once again, all I can do is wait. I count in my head, like I did that night. Until it's safe.

It feels like forever before we hear the voices down below. The crackle of static from a walkie-talkie.

"Up here!" I shout. "We're here!" I call again, over and over, until finally, finally two officers come into view.

But they don't bring relief. Instead, they have weapons drawn, and one of those weapons is pointing at me. Just like Elliot, that night, his eyes unseeing.

For protection, I realize, imagining Elliot as well. In case they need protection.

"Put down the bat!" one of the officers yells.

"Oh." It drops from my grip, my hands rising over my head.

It makes sense, I guess, that they're not sure about the scene in front of them—whether Nolan is the suspect here, or whether I am. There's a man on the ground, Nolan is on top of him, and I still had that bat in my hands.

Nolan releases Mike and raises his hands over his head, but the two officers are still assessing the scene, moving slowly, yelling at us to back away, then to get on the ground.

"I called you," I say, nearly breathless, as my knees hit the earth. "That man tried to push Nolan off the edge," I explain, gesturing to Mike on the ground.

But it's Nolan who finally says it, the reason we are all here: "He killed my brother."

The finality of it. The answer. The truth.

Nolan gestures toward the edge, and I'm afraid he's going to look. But it's the first police officer who does it instead. He peers over the ledge and jerks back, making some hand signal to his partner.

He takes control of Mike on the ground, and several other officers emerge from the woods below, the scene filling with chaos. Nolan and I are quickly separated while the police assess the scene, setting up a perimeter, barking out orders. I can only watch from the distance.

Meanwhile, the officer in front of me keeps asking me questions, but they're not the right ones.

Who are you—

What were you doing out here—

How did you know—

I give my name, and my statement, and he makes me wait some more. I'm to stay put beside the entrance ticket counter until Joe arrives.

They must be questioning Nolan somewhere else, because I haven't seen him since.

By now, there's some makeshift center of operations set up in the clearing behind the old ticket booth, a white tent with sheets for walls. I stand at the sound of several cars pulling into the lot, followed by the approaching footsteps. A police officer leads Nolan into view, but he doesn't even look at me. He's looking at the group of people heading from the parking lot. A man in a suit, and a man and a woman who must be Nolan's parents.

I keep waiting for someone to speak, to make some noise, to start running. But the only thing I hear, carried across the expanse, is Nolan saying, "Mom," before she reaches him. I watch the three of them, leaning into one another, his father with an arm around each. No one cries out. No one says a word. It ends like this, with silence.

• • •

Joe is the last person they're waiting on.

Nolan and his parents were led inside the white tent, along with the man accompanying them. At times, I can see their shadows moving against the light, but the woods have gone silent, other than the occasional crackle of a walkie-talkie somewhere just out of sight.

"Kennedy?"

I turn to see Joe jogging from the parking lot. When he reaches me, he pulls me toward him in a panic.

"I'm so sorry," he says. "My phone was off when I was at the jail. I didn't get the message."

I throw my arms around his back, and he doesn't let go.

He holds my face between his hands, like my mother might do; his fingers are rougher, and strong. I close my eyes then, no longer trying to hold back the emotion.

"Did you see Elliot?" I ask when I pull back.

"Yeah. I'm sorry, Kennedy." He shakes his head. "His memory, it's in fragments. He remembers the sound of the gun. The feel of the recoil. When we asked him more about that night, he shut down." Joe closes his eyes, like he wants to block it out as well. "But he confirmed the details about where the gun was kept. Hearing what you believe happened, he's agreed, at least, to try hypnosis, or other therapy. To try to get the pieces back. We'll have to wait to see what the forensics team pulls from the house. It's been a long time, Kennedy."

I had been hoping for a big miracle. For Elliot to suddenly remember. For everyone to automatically believe. But at least it's something. At least it's a start.

Joe puts a hand on my back, leading me away. "Come on, let's get you home."

I stare at the white sheets of the makeshift tent, moving in the breeze. Joe starts to walk toward the parking lot, where there's a single officer stationed.

I stop moving, and Joe turns around. "Wait. I need to check on Nolan before we leave," I tell him.

Joe pauses, his hands in his pockets, looking toward the tent, where they all must be waiting. "He'll want some time, Kennedy."

But I think about that, about the time I was in the hospital, when no one came for hours. And then when I was alone in Joe's house, and still, no one came. All I had was time and space, stretching forever, an endless echo.

"No, Joe," I say. "You're wrong."

Inside that tent is a shadow house, a place of horrors Nolan can only imagine. He's coming face-to-face with it now; I know he is. All the things that might've been. The way his brother might've fallen, the way he could've twisted. What he might've called out as he fell. What Nolan believes he could've done to prevent it. The what-ifs will run through his mind, over and over. He will close his eyes, and he will see it.

He won't notice the rest. The things I shut out for months. The people I didn't see, right there, on the other side.

"I need to stay," I tell him. Even if he doesn't see me yet. "Will you wait for me?"

"Of course, Kennedy."

As I turn away, Joe calls after me, leans in close so he's

speaking into my ear. "How did you find him? Just between you and me. How did you know where to look?"

I pull back, looking him in the eye. "There were clues in the signal. I told you. It was meant for us."

I can see it in him, how he wants to believe me. I think he's trying. I hope it lets him see.

44

NOLAN

There isn't enough room at the service. Every seat is taken, and there are people standing around the walls, in a sea of gray and black. So that after, even though people are trying to speak quietly, I still can't escape the constant buzzing, and I can't pick any one face from the masses of people here to pay their respects, even two years later.

All these people who missed him. Who miss him.

A shadow has fallen over the house during the last three days, since we found Liam. Since the end.

People have been in and out—police officers, detectives, Agent Lowell—trying to make a case against Mike, all while the news vans have lined the street outside. A new type of chaos. I've been asked, over and over, to explain, with my parents sitting beside me. To remember exactly what Mike said to me, what we might be able to use for proof. But their words seem to come through glass, like they're on the other side of some great divide.

Instead, my mind keeps drifting to that day, over and

over. That morning at the sink, with the cut, the drop of blood, the razor clattering.

Why didn't he tell me? I was *right here*. If something was on his mind, why didn't he just say it?

It was Agent Lowell who finally explained, his words cutting through the haze.

"Nolan, I need you to understand, it's all circumstantial," he told me yesterday, after my parents left to handle some last-minute arrangements. "We're holding Mike on an attempted murder charge against you, given your witness statement, alongside Kennedy's. But is there anything else you can tell us? Something else he said to you about Liam?"

They have no proof. That's what he was trying to tell me. That all we really have is a statement from me and Kennedy. Everything else is a connection we can see but not prove. The only one who knows for certain what happened that day is Mike.

Mike said Liam didn't know how to keep his mouth shut, but that's not true. Whatever was bothering Liam—his hand trembling over the sink—he kept it to himself. He came to the picnic. He must've run into Mike there.

We only have what we believe happened after: that Mike took Liam and Colby from the park, brought them to Old Granite Quarry, and pushed Liam over the edge. Then, noticing the video camera, he took the feed from it. And he kept it, for years, until he got word that a developer had bought the land. And then, to save himself, he sent that still-frame photo of Liam to his old girlfriend, Abby, in the hopes of nudging the investigation open again.

If he was trying to pin Liam's death on me, the photo

would have to be sent to someone else. He knew Abby from two years earlier—she had been a big part of the search the first time around.

Mike had worked with my parents in order to keep an eye on any information about Liam that came through. He always knew exactly what was happening in the case.

But they can't try a case against him on belief alone. They need something solid. Something real.

"Something happened at the shelter," I told Agent Lowell, but I was sure I'd already said it. We'd been at this for two days, in one form or another, but it all blurred together.

"I know," he said. "And we're interviewing everyone we can, taking statements. But there's been a lot of turnover, and people aren't always willing to talk."

Or able to.

I closed my eyes and pictured Kennedy, peering into the bedroom window that night. Or Elliot, jarred from his desk, walking out into the hallway. The way some details stick and others fade; how time slips.

My phone buzzed beside me on the couch. Kennedy, I was sure. Each morning for the last three days, there's been a message waiting for me. Throughout the day, too. I never know what to reply, how to balance both things: the grief overwhelming everything, alongside the rest. Even though I never respond, the notes keep coming. Little things, just to let me know she's there. And that one, the one I read with Agent Lowell sitting across from me, said she would be here today. At the service.

• • •

Every time I think I catch a glimpse of her, the crowd shifts and I lose sight. Every few steps someone else stops me to see how I am, to offer their support, or a memory. It's the memories, each time, that pull me back. Like they're giving me something. Something new. Two years later, and a piece of Liam still catches me off guard.

I'm in the middle of a circle of his friends, home from college, when someone steps aside, making space for Abby. Her eyes lock with mine, then drift to the side.

My throat tightens. I remember the last words she spoke to me as well. *You are so cruel.* I wanted her to be lying. I wanted her to be wrong.

"Abby," I say, stepping closer, even though it's crowded. With the number of people around us, talking, it's almost the same as being alone.

She waves a hand in front of her face. "It's okay," she says, like she can tell exactly what I'm trying to say.

I shake my head. "It's not."

She looks over her shoulder, to the pictures of Liam up at the front of the room. "No, you're right," she says. I can see her throat moving. "I just missed him so much," she whispers, and it's like she's talking about something else. That day in the car, the one we've both tried desperately to forget.

"I know. Me too."

A guy I've never seen before places a hand on her shoulder, and she looks up at him. "I'll just be one moment," she says, and then the pink rises up her neck.

I watch him go, but he doesn't make it far. Just waits beside the wall, eyes scanning the crowd. Someone here not for me, or for Liam, but for her. "You have a boyfriend?" I ask. I can't keep the surprise from my voice. But I don't know what I expected—for life to just freeze for the rest of us?

She fidgets with her hair. "Yeah, yes. Five months now."

I nod slowly, and she presses her lips together. "Oh. I mean, that's good. He looks . . ." But I don't know what to say. I don't know anything about him, other than the fact that he's not Liam. "I'm glad he came with you."

"I'm sorry," she adds, her eyes turning glassy. I want to tell her she doesn't need to be sorry, that it's a stupid thing to say to me. But then I think that maybe it's not meant for me.

"He'd want you to be happy," I say.

After Abby leaves, the crowd thins, and I've missed Kennedy. I drive home with my parents, feeling too cramped in the backseat, none of us sure what to say to one another.

The silence, when we walk through the front door, feels permanent. This is the way it will be from now on. Until tomorrow, at least, when the volunteers return, at my mother's request. I didn't understand. *They all deserve to be found*, she told me. I thought finding Liam would mark the end of something. A line that divided before and after. But I was wrong. Tomorrow, they'll keep going.

But today, there's just the silence. Just the three of us, in this quiet, empty house.

Mom drops her bag on the couch and steps out of her shoes. Dad takes off his suit jacket and stands facing that wall—all those eyes, looking back.

The phone rings, shattering the silence, and my mom

jumps. For a while, they had the ringer turned off, letting the calls from reporters and friends alike fill up the voice mail.

It rings again, and my mom just stares at it, and it reminds me of when Liam first went missing, how they had been waiting for a call, any call, that would tell them their son would be coming home soon—and now that call will never come.

I answer the phone, just to get it to stop.

"Hello? Hello? Is anyone there?" The voice on the other end belongs to a woman who sounds about my mother's age, maybe older.

"Yeah, I'm here," I say. Last thing I want is for them to call right back if I hang up.

"I've been trying to get through for days. I saw on the news . . ." Her voice wavers with emotion.

I close my eyes, willing this call to go faster, to get this over with. A well-meaning stranger. Or worse.

"I live in Collins County," she continues, which doesn't mean much to me. "And my house, it backs up to Northridge Forest." Still nothing. "I think I have something that belongs to you."

45

KENNEDY

In the end, it's a lawyer I've never met who convinces Elliot to see me. To talk to all of us, to try to piece together his fragmented mind.

I've taken this drive before, and I'm just about to direct Joe when he swerves over to the exit ramp. I check my phone one last time before sliding it into my bag. My nerves are frazzled. The initial excitement about seeing my brother again has turned to fear, and the only person I thought could read between the lines of my message—Going to see my brother today—still hasn't responded to any of my texts. It's been two days since I saw Nolan at the service, and still nothing.

Joe eases the car into a parking spot, and suddenly I don't know what I'm doing here. I don't know what to say, how to act. Joe opens his car door; then, seeing I'm still sitting there, he closes it again.

"I don't know what to say," I explain, shaking my head.

Joe sighs. "He's your brother. You'll know what to say."

But it's been six months, and I've been out here, and he's been in there, and it suddenly seems like an impossible distance to bridge.

Joe shifts in his seat so he's facing me. "Okay, so, a few things. He's lost some weight. His hair is ridiculous again, always half in his eyes; it's driving me crazy."

I raise my head and crack a grin, picturing the Elliot he used to be. Remembering the look on my mother's face when he cut his own hair. The laughter I could barely contain.

"And," Joe continues, "he's scared."

"But I thought you said the lawyer was optimistic—"

"He's scared of what you think of him. That's why he didn't want to see you, all this time. What he remembers . . ." Joe looks out the window, like he's seeing it, too, then shakes it off. "What he remembers is seeing you through the glass, with the gun in his hand. *You* are the one thing he remembers." The one thing that breached the divide that night. That cut straight through to him.

I stare out the glass, remembering his expression. The line that divides his life as well.

"I'm ready," I say.

When we finally make it through—leaving our things, all connections to the outside world—the first thing I see is the lawyer's back, leaning across the table as he speaks.

But then there's the sound of metal on metal as his chair pushes back and Elliot stands, looking over the lawyer. He is exactly like Joe said: skinny, in desperate need of a haircut. I can see the toll of six months in here. Six months alone. But none of it matters right then; I only see my brother.

His eyes, shadowed underneath, jump from Joe to me,

and he holds my gaze, his expression softening. Whatever he was looking for, he must already see it.

"Hi," he says, and the word makes me smile, despite where we are, and everything that's happened. It's the sound of his voice—a thing I didn't even realize I'd been missing these last six months.

And then I hug him, even though I know we're not supposed to, but that's okay, because Joe was right—he's my brother, and I don't even have to think about it. I hear him mumble "I'm sorry," over and over, until he takes a seat at the table.

"No," I say, sitting next to Joe, across from Elliot. "*I'm* sorry. I'm sorry I left you there." I look up at him, across the table, through my blurred vision, and he's shaking his head, like he doesn't understand. "I'm sorry I left you *in here*." That's what I've been thinking, all this time. If only I had called his name that night, called him back to me. Let him know that I believed him right then—that he hadn't done this. If maybe that would've brought him back, right away.

"I should've done so many things differently," he says. "Before. After." He shakes his head. "I missed you a lot, Kennedy."

My eyes lock with his across the table, and it's then I believe it: he will come back to me.

The lawyer walks us through the case, but Elliot keeps his eyes down on the table the whole time, his hands folded together, like he can't bear to hear it. How many times, I wonder, has he had to endure this? The horrors he's seen, which I can only imagine.

"Elliot was sitting at his desk, working on a project, and

didn't hear his mother and Will come home. The first thing he remembers is the sound of a shot," the lawyer says.

Joe puts a hand on Elliot's arm, as if to steady him. Just as he did for me.

The lawyer lays out the things Elliot must have told him, about the Will none of us ever saw. The controlling, manipulative version, who used Elliot's grades and his status at school to undermine his concerns, who isolated our mother from her colleagues—and us.

"The night of the crime," the lawyer continues, "Elliot noted a bruise on his mother's collarbone before she left the house, which she covered up with a scarf. He confronted her about it, asking if she had been hurt."

I close my eyes, picturing it. Watching her in the mirror as she readjusted the fabric, examining her own reflection. I wonder if it was Elliot's comment that finally tipped things; if my mother broke it off that night. If that's what had Will so enraged, and had my mother running for her gun, for protection.

Elliot was the only one who could see the type of person Will was. He always saw more than the rest of us. He was always looking for signs.

"I remember the scarf," I say, my voice scratching against my throat. "I didn't know," I say to Elliot.

The lawyer pauses, making a note. "Good," he says. "Your statement will help."

Elliot runs a hand through his too-long hair. "I pushed her to it. I set it in motion, that night, whatever happened."

I shake my head. "*He* set it in motion."

The lawyer looks between the two of us and continues. "The police have spoken with Hunter Long, confirming

Elliot's accounts," he says. "Hunter can at least corroborate that Elliot confided in him his concerns about Will. Though Hunter has a history of running away, and he's something of a flight risk as it is."

But Elliot shakes his head. "He won't testify. Don't make him. Something happened to him the first time he ran away, when he was staying at some shelter nearby. He won't want his name in the public. . . ."

Something rattles in my chest, but the lawyer continues. "The hope is it won't get to that point, anyway," he explains. "The evidence supports Will firing the first shot. Forensics has confirmed: the only fingerprints on the gun safe behind the wall were your mother's."

They go over the evidence in support of their case—that Elliot was surprised by the sound of the first shot and ran out of his room straight into a horrific scene. Overwhelmed as he was by the blood, and the reality in front of him, his memory fractured. He acted on instinct, facing a man holding a gun.

But Elliot will have to live with what he's done. It's all still terrible. That feeling, he said, was what made him believe that he was guilty of something. Was why he couldn't look me in the eye.

The trial has been postponed, with the gun safe as new evidence; they found it, untouched, behind the wall panel. The lawyer says he expects some sort of deal to be offered, at the very least. They are presenting Elliot's shooting of Will as self-defense, and are waiting to hear back from the DA's office.

I expect Elliot to look relieved, but he doesn't.

And then I understand. Mom is still gone. None of this changes the past, or the present—though I hope it will help him move on.

It must be impossible, I think, to imagine a future when you can't see beyond the walls that contain you.

"Elliot," I say as we're saying our goodbyes. "I'll see you soon."

He nods, but I stand there waiting until I hear his echoing *See you soon.*

On the walk back to the parking lot, I turn on my phone, but there's still no reply.

"Joe," I say, "I have to call Nolan." Something about what Elliot mentioned, about Hunter and a shelter . . . I wonder if maybe Hunter can act not as a witness for Elliot, but against Mike.

"I don't think that's necessary," Joe says, nudging my shoulder. I look up, and Nolan's car is parked beside ours. He sits on the trunk, his feet resting on the faded bumper, and waves when he sees me looking.

I start walking faster, and when I'm close enough to see him clearly, he grins. "Sorry I'm late," he says, and I smile.

He looks over my shoulder at Joe, strolling across the lot. "Should we introduce your uncle to the world's best pizza?"

46

NOLAN

Agent Lowell sits across from me and my parents, on that same couch where Abby and her parents once sat, setting everything in motion again. He's told us there have been new developments. *Some questions, some answers,* he said.

"Did he talk?" my dad asks.

It was Elliot who provided the missing link. Who let us know that Hunter Long had been in that shelter at the same time as Liam. That he might've known something about what happened two years ago.

Agent Lowell spreads his hands apart. "His mother brought him back in yesterday, and we were able to fill in a few more holes."

Kennedy told me the police found Hunter, managed to convince him to talk after promising not to bring any charges, but he was still afraid.

"The timing adds up," Agent Lowell says. "His mother says Hunter first ran off right after she remarried. He'd gotten into a fight with his new stepfather and disappeared for months. Hunter told us that soon after he arrived at the shelter, he noticed that one of the volunteers was taking money from the younger people who were living there. Money they should not have had. He realized they were working for him, most likely distributing drugs."

"Liam found out?" I ask. Mike had told me, leaning over me in the middle of the clearing above the quarry, that Liam didn't know how to keep his mouth shut.

Agent Lowell sighs. "Hunter says he confided in another volunteer—one who looked about his age. When he didn't see that volunteer again, he took off, afraid."

Liam. It had to be Liam. Liam must've asked Mike about it, maybe not realizing it was him. Or maybe he did realize, but he wanted to believe the best of Mike, that there was some mistake. Liam must've debated going to the police, turning Mike in. His hand shaking that morning, the razor falling, the drop of blood. When he saw Mike at the picnic, Liam must've agreed to hear him out. If you take not only a person but also a dog, it seems like a runaway. Mike knew this. He knew this, and he used it.

"Is it enough?" It's the first time I've heard my mother ask Agent Lowell a question.

"It will be," he says. "We know what questions to ask now about Mike's work at the shelter. We've heard that he worked closely with the teen runaways. And now we think he must've operated by threatening to turn them in to authorities, or turn them in back home, unless they did what he asked—distributing for him, collecting the money. Problem was, there was so much turnover there anyway.

Sometimes they came back to the shelter, sometimes they didn't. I guess, if things didn't go Mike's way, he thought no one would look too closely when they didn't turn up again."

Until Liam.

There are witnesses this time. Me, and Kennedy, and now Hunter Long. Hopefully, with the support of the police, we will have more.

We don't have proof, but we have enough.

Agent Lowell looks up at the ceiling, at the scratching I also hear, coming from my brother's room. It's becoming a habit. "Is that who I think it is?" he asks.

"We keep finding him in there," my mom says, almost smiling.

Turned out, all the press was good for something. The phone call we received after the service—the woman on the other end who'd been trying to reach us for days. "I think I have something that belongs to you," she said.

Then she described Colby—the brown-and-white coat, the tail that was a solid brown. "One day, two years back," she explained, "I saw this scrawny thing digging in my garden. He looked too skinny, and he seemed frightened."

My back straightened; even my parents noticed.

"Well, he had no collar, you see. I thought he was a stray. I put up signs, just in case. But, you know, it's not really near you. And I think . . ."

"Nolan?" my dad said, stepping closer to the table. "What is it?"

I shook my head, dropping the phone to my side, barely able to believe it. "Colby," I said. "Someone found Colby."

And now he's back, half ours, half belonging to someone else. And he keeps gravitating to that empty room. He spent the first day pawing at the door until I let him in, and then he sat in the middle of the room, staring at something no one else could see.

He's in there again now.

Sometimes I think he can sense something we don't.

And sometimes I think how things can still come back, even after we stop looking for them.

47

KENNEDY

In the hallway of the shadow house, everything is too new. The paint, the lightbulb, the handrail. A terrible history we've been trying to ignore. So that when I look at it, I can only imagine the horrors and the dark.

The first picture that goes up is the hardest, my hands trembling as I hold the nail. But the second goes up quicker, and then the next, and the next. Until the stairway is lined with them—images of my mother, and me, and Elliot, smiling back. All the photos the Realtor took down and left in storage.

I think there's something to it, in Nolan's house—the faces of the missing lining the walls. A reminder, or a hope, that keeps you going.

There's a knock at the front door, but I didn't hear a car pull in. It's officially summer break for me, but Joe still has to be on campus, and Nolan was meeting with the detectives on his brother's case, going through the latest developments.

I peer through the living room window first, but I can

only see a sliver of a body, fidgeting back and forth on the front porch. When I open the door, Marco seems surprised to see me standing there. He's half turned away already, though he was the one who just knocked on the door, so.

"Hey," he says, "I saw your bike." He points to the side of the house.

I open the door wider, and though he hesitates, he eventually steps across the threshold, looking around.

"The For Sale sign is gone," he says. "Does that mean you're coming back?"

"We're not sure yet," I say. But it's possible. We're all in one big holding pattern, waiting to see what happens with Elliot; waiting to decide where we'll all be comfortable living, if he comes home soon, like the lawyer believes will happen.

But if he comes back, and he steps inside this house, I want him to see beyond the shadow house, to what else might be possible.

Marco looks around once more, running his hand through his hair, in the way I once used to love. "Lydia told me what you guys are doing tomorrow."

I nod, putting my hand on my hip, not sure whether I should be on the defensive.

I don't know what he's doing here, only that he's here.

"Will you be there, too?" I ask.

He looks at me then before putting a hand on the door-frame. "Probably. I mean, I'm usually there anyway."

I smile then, and he grins back, and he's both the Marco I met last summer and the Marco who's been changed by all that came after, just like the rest of us.

"Guess I'll be seeing you, then," I say.

48

NOLAN

Sometimes, when I first wake up in the morning, I close my eyes and try to go back. To find the crack in the universe, where time is malleable and I can change things.

I wish he had talked to me.

I would beg him: *Tell me. I'm right here.*

My parents say I have to accept that we may never know for sure. To be okay with the things we know but cannot prove.

Which is ironic, since no one seems interested in the things *I* know but cannot prove. No, it's all too much for them. Something they try to explain away as a series of coincidences orchestrated by two kids looking for something, and falling for each other.

Never mind that we both found it.

They'd rather brush it all aside, the things we've told them. There are too many leaps for our families to accept.

We cannot explain why I received Kennedy's words that night, in the form of my brother speaking the same words. *Help us. Please.* Her message, coming through.

Well, I *can*. It's just not something my parents, or the police, are interested in hearing.

Nothing is provable.

So they would rather explain our connection by location, through a circle of friends who overlapped. They would rather explain my feeling about Liam disappearing as subconscious intuition, instead of premonition. And it's the same with everything that followed. The static I kept hearing, like a warning of what would happen that day. The baseball field, calling to me. Kennedy with my bat.

They want to chalk it all up to coincidence, and fever dreams. Pieces we want to connect; a pattern we want to believe in.

But sometimes, late at night, I play that video I took—the one of the signal coming from Liam's room. And when it stops, I can still feel it. The memory of a pulse that I can sense in the palm of my hand. Like it was his, holding on. Counting down. Calling after me, *Come on, Nolan*—

My phone lights up with a new message: **Are you ready?**

On my way, I reply, shutting down my laptop. I think I've got it all together now, the things I want to say.

Sometimes I'm not sure what brought us together, or why. Whether it was for Elliot, or for her; whether it was for my brother, or for me.

It all feels so close, too difficult to untangle. Maybe that's the point, though. I think that's what we're trying to explain with all of this.

• • •

I'm meeting Kennedy at the house first. I find her around back, cleaning out the shed, taking pictures of the equipment with her phone—I'm assuming in case we figure out a way to include them.

I walk inside, and instead of just the shed I remember from last time, now I see the place where Kennedy hid, all alone, in the dark of night, as a storm raged past. And today she stands in front of me as someone who stepped outside again. She pulls me closer, leaning into my side, and my arm slides around her back, like second nature.

And then we walk across the field together, the same one I know she sprinted across in the storm, all alone, the night her life was split in two.

Lydia leads us down the steps to the basement, where Marco sits on a couch across from her computer setup. He waves at us as we walk by, and Kennedy nods hello.

"So," Lydia says, holding out a small microphone positioned on the table, "right, you just . . . press this button and speak."

"That's it?"

"That's it."

Kennedy hands me the microphone. "Want to go first?"

I shake my head. "No, you."

We've made a promise to tell what happened. All of it. The bad and the good, the devastating, the hopeful. The things we know, and the things we believe. To send it out into the world for anyone to find. Lydia has promised to upload it, make sure it's searchable, findable.

In case someone's out there, listening, wondering. Searching, like we had been. Sitting at a computer all alone at night, sending questions into the void, waiting for something to make sense. The hope is that, whatever it is they're searching for, something will inevitably lead them here, to us.

To let them know that this all happened, and it's still happening, and it's not over yet. We're still here.

On and on it goes.

I nod at her, and she begins.

ACKNOWLEDGMENTS

Thank you, as always, to the friends and colleagues who have helped bring this story to life:

My agent, Sarah Davies, for the guidance, support, and enthusiasm for this book since it was just an idea in my head. I am so grateful for your feedback at every step along the way, for each and every project.

At Crown Books for Young Readers, I am so fortunate to get to work with my fantastic editor, Emily Easton, on our seventh book together! Thank you also to Sam Gentry, Phoebe Yeh, and the entire team at Random House Children's Books. It's such a pleasure working with you all.

I am so incredibly thankful to my friends and critique partners, Megan Shepherd, Elle Cosimano, Ashley Elston, and Romily Bernard, who are always willing to offer their feedback and advice. Also a huge thanks to everyone at Bat Cave 2015 and 2016, who helped give shape to this story early on, when it was that idea I kept coming back to.

Lastly, thank you to my family, for all of your support, and for taking this journey beside me.

SOMETIMES THE PIECES WE LEAVE
BEHIND TELL A DIFFERENT STORY....

WHAT IF EVERYTHING
YOU THOUGHT YOU KNEW
ABOUT SOMEONE
WAS A LIE?

FRAGMENTS
OF THE
LOST

MEGAN MIRANDA
NEW YORK TIMES BESTSELLING AUTHOR

A Blue Door

There's no light in the narrow stairway to the third floor. There's no handrail, either. Just wooden steps and plaster walls that were probably added in an attic renovation long ago. The door above remains shut, but there's a sliver of light that escapes through the bottom, coming from inside. He must've left the window uncovered.

The door looks darker than the walls of the stairway, but it's hard to tell from this angle, without light, that it's blue. We painted it during the summer from a half-empty can he'd found in the garage, a color called Rustic Sea.

"A complicated color for a complicated door," he joked. But it turned out to look more like denim than anything else.

He stepped back after applying the first stroke, wrinkled his nose, wiped the back of his hand against his forehead. "My feelings on this color are also very complicated."

There was a smudge of Rustic Sea over his left eye. "I love it," I said.

I reach for the door now, and I can almost smell the fresh paint, feel the summer breeze coming in from the open window to help air it out. We painted it all the way around—

front and back and sides—and sometimes, the door still sticks when you pull it open. Like the paint dried too thick, too slowly.

There's a speck of paint on the silver doorknob that I've never noticed before, and it makes me pause. I run my thumb over the roughness of the spot, wondering how I missed this.

I take a slow breath, trying to remember the room before I see it, to prepare.

It's got four walls, a closet, slanting ceilings before they meet at a flat strip overtop. There's a fan hanging from the middle of that strip, the kind that rattles when it's set to the highest speed. Shelves built into the walls on both sides, giving way to a sliding closet door on my left. A single window, on the far wall.

There's a bed, with a green comforter.

A desk to my right, with a computer monitor on the surface, the tower hidden below.

The walls are gray and the carpet is . . . the carpet is brown. I think. I'm no longer sure. The color blurs and shifts in my mind.

It's just a room. Any room. Four walls and a ceiling and a fan.

This is what I tell myself before I step inside. This is the whisper I hear in my head as I stand with my hand on the knob, waiting on the top step.

For a moment, I think I hear his footsteps on the other side of the door, but I know this isn't possible. I picture us sitting across from each other on the floor. My legs, angled between his.

He leans closer. He's smiling.

Then I remember: the carpet is beige. The door will squeak as I push it open. The air will be hotter or colder than the rest of the house, depending on the time of year.

All these things I know by heart.

None of this prepares me.

SATURDAY MORNING

▶ ◀ ▲

His mother asked me to do this, because she said it wasn't something a mother should ever have to do. I don't think it's really something an ex-girlfriend should have to do either, but mother trumps ex any day of the week.

"The room is full of you, Jessa," she explained, by which she means the pictures. They're taped around the room, directly to the gray slanting walls, and in all of them I have my arms looped around his neck, or his arms draped over my shoulders from behind me. I can't even look directly at the photos, but his mother is right. I'm everywhere.

Sometimes I wonder if his mother knows about the ex part. If he told her, if she overheard, if she could tell all on her own. Though something about the way she stands at the base of the stairway watching me linger at the entrance to the attic room, something about the way she asked me to do this in the first place, makes me think that she does.

There's a chill up here, but I know it's nothing more than the poor insulation of a converted attic, heat escaping through the cracks of the window frame, the November air seeping in from the outside.

His clothes are still on the floor, however they fell when he last kicked them off, on that rainy day in mid-September. His bed is unmade. His computer monitor sits black on the desk, my distorted reflection looking back. His desk is stuffed full with ticket stubs and old homework, and more, I know, and so is the closet. Caleb wouldn't want his mother doing this, either. Under the bed, between the mattresses, there are things a mother shouldn't see. My stomach rebels, but I can feel her still watching, so I step inside.

I don't know where to start.

I don't know how to start.

If Caleb were here, he'd say, *Just start.*

I hated that, the way he'd brush aside everything else, forcing the point, or the issue, or this moment.

Just forget about it—

Just leave it—

Just say it—

Just pick up the shirt at the foot of the bed, the one he wore the last time you touched him.

Just start.

Dragonfly Necklace

The shirt still smells of him. Dove soap. The cologne that always let me know when he was behind me, a smile starting even before he'd place his hand on my waist, his lips on my cheek. I don't bring it to my face. I don't dare bring it any closer. I throw it into the corner—the beginning of a pile.

See, Caleb? I'm starting. I've started.

Underneath the shirt, there's also the jeans. Knees worn thin, hem slightly fraying, soft and familiar. I'm holding my breath by the time I get to the pockets, except I already know what's there, so it should prepare me. But it doesn't. The chain crackles, cold on my fingers. And then I feel something else: the memory of his warm skin as I placed it into his open palm.

I said: *Please hold this for me.*

I said: *Please be careful.*

He put it in his pocket, no big thing. He did it like that because of everyone watching. To show me he didn't have to be careful anymore. Not with me.

The clasp of the necklace in my hand is broken, had already broken when I gave it to him, but the gold chain is now kinked and knotted too, from sitting buried in his pocket. I wore it every race, even though we weren't supposed to, taping the dragonfly charm to the inside of my jersey to keep it in place while I ran. I wore it because it was good luck, because it was a ritual, because I had a hard time doing things any other way than how I'd always done them.

It broke on the starting line as I raised my hands over my head in a stretch. The pop against my skin, sickening. My body already wound tight, waiting for the gun. I scanned the crowd, and there he was—familiar. It didn't occur to me right then that he had no reason to be there anymore. It didn't even register. There was no mystery, just the momentary panic of a broken necklace and a race about to start.

Wait, I begged, leaving my place on the field. I jogged over to him, standing near the starting line, as everyone else took their places.

Please hold this for me.

Please be careful.

He frowned at the dragonfly in the crease of his palm, closed his fist, slid his hand into the right front pocket of his favorite jeans. Shrugged.

I wish I had known that this would be it—the last time I saw him. I would've made sure the last image I had of him was not like this: this apathy; his blue eyes skimming over me, settling to the side; and then the breeze, blowing his light brown hair across his eyes, shuttering everything. The image I see constantly, now burned into memory.

He left before the race was over, probably remembering he didn't have to be there for me anymore. Or maybe it was something else. The rain. A word spoken. A thing remembered. Either way, he left. Came back home. Tossed his jeans on the floor of his room, my necklace still inside. Left them there. Changed.

Changed everything.

Caleb. Be careful.

The attic is too quiet without him, and the angled walls too narrowed, and I want to be *out of this room*, but then I hear his mother arguing below. She's arguing with someone very particular. She's arguing with Max. Sometimes his voice reminds me of Caleb's. Sometimes, when I hear him, it takes me a second to remember Caleb's gone.

"She shouldn't be here," he's saying. "I told you I'd do it."

"She will do it," his mother says.

And this is how I'm sure that this is my penance.

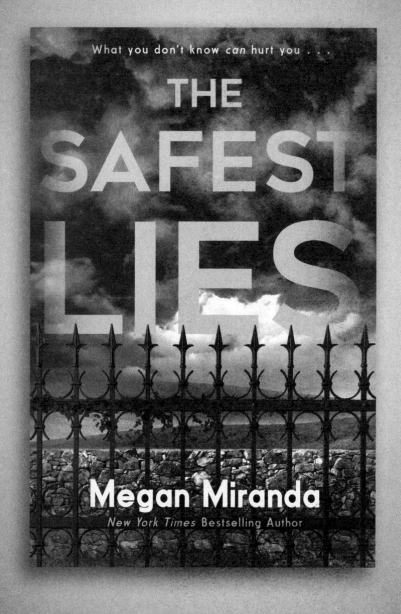

YOU'RE NOT PARANOID
IF THEY'RE REALLY AFTER YOU.

What you don't know *can* hurt you . . .

THE SAFEST LIES

Megan Miranda

New York Times Bestselling Author

CHAPTER 1

The black iron gates used to be my favorite thing about the house.

Back when I was younger, they reminded me of secret gardens and hidden treasures, all the great mysteries I had read about in children's books.

This was the setting of fairy tales. The vegetation creeping upward in places, ivy and weeds tangling with the bars, and the way they'd light up in a storm, encircling the house—a stark surprise against the darkness.

And we were on the inside.

It was better to see it from this direction, on the way out. It looked different as I grew older. From the other side, through a different filter. A glance over my shoulder as I walked away, and all I could see were the cameras over the entrances. The sterile, boxed walls of the house beyond. The shadow behind the tinted window.

I didn't realize, for a long time, that *this* was the secret.

Still, there was a familiarity to the iron gates, and I couldn't help tapping them as I passed each morning, a routine goodbye as I left for the day. In the summer, the bars would be hot from the sun. And in the winter, when I was bundled up in wool, sometimes I'd feel a spark underneath the cold, like I could sense the current of electricity that was running through the top.

Mostly, though, they felt like home.

Today, my palm came away damp, coated with morning dew. Everything glistened in the mountain sunrise.

Now that I was beyond the gates, and because I saw my mother's shadow, there was a routine I was supposed to stick to:

Check the backseat through the windows before unlocking the car door.

Start the car and count to twenty so the engine had time to settle.

Wave to my mother, watching from the front window.

Two hands on the wheel as I navigated the unpaved driveway made of gravel, and then the winding mountain roads on the way to school.

The rest of the day was a tally of hours, a routine I knew by heart. Swap this Wednesday for any other Wednesday and nobody would notice. My mother said there's a safety to routine, but I didn't exactly agree. Routines could be learned. Routines could be *predicted*. But it would be a mistake to say that. Honestly, it was a mistake to even *think* that.

Here was the rest of my Wednesday routine:

Arrive at school early enough to get a parking spot near a streetlight, since I'd be leaving late. Avoid the crowded hallway, hope Mr. Graham opened his classroom early. Claim my seat in the back of math class, and coast through the day, mostly unnoticed.

Mostly.

My books were already out and I'd just about finished the morning problems when Ryan Baker swept into class.

"Hey, Kelsey," he said as he slid into his seat, just as the bell rang.

"Hi, Ryan," I said. This was also part of the routine. Ryan looked the way Ryan always looked, which was: brown hair that never fell the same way twice; legs too long for the desk beneath him, so they stretched under the seat in front or to the aisle between us (today: aisle); jeans, brown lace-up boots, T-shirt. Autumn in Vermont meant a sweatshirt for me, but apparently Ryan hadn't gotten there yet.

Today he was wearing a dark blue shirt that said VOLUNTEER, and he caught me staring. I didn't know if it was supposed to be ironic or not.

His fingers drummed on the desk. His knee bounced in the aisle.

I almost asked him, on impulse, but then Mr. Graham called me up to the board for a problem, and Ryan started drawing on his wrist with blue ink, and by the time I returned to my seat, the moment had passed.

First period was mostly quiet and mostly still. People yawned, people stretched, occasionally someone rested their head on their desk and hoped Mr. Graham didn't notice. Everyone slowly came to life over the span of ninety minutes.

But Ryan always seemed the opposite—all coiled energy, even at eight a.m. Rushing into class, his leg bouncing under his desk, his hands continually drawing patterns. His energy was contagious. So by the time the bell rang, I was the one coiled to jump. I'd spring from my seat, wave goodbye, head down the hall toward English, and pretend we hadn't once shared the most embarrassing conversation of my life.

The rest of the daily routine: English, lunch, science, history. Faces I'd grown accustomed to seeing over the last two years. Names I knew well, people I knew casually. The day passing by in a comfortable string of sameness. Blink too long and you might miss it.

Wednesday also meant tutoring after school to meet the volunteer component for graduation. Since I was a year ahead of most everyone in my grade, taking mostly senior classes, this was the easiest way to fulfill it.

Today I was scheduled to start with Leo Johnson, a senior taking sophomore science who I kind of knew from the Lodge. *Kind of knew* because (a) Leo was the type of person that everyone kind of knew, and (b) Ryan and I shared a shift at the Lodge twice a week over the summer, and they were friends. Which meant when Leo came in, he would occasionally nod at me, and even less occasionally mention me by name.

He dropped his notebook on the table across from me. "Hi, my name is Leo, and I'm failing." He flashed me a smile.

"Yeah, hi, we know each other already."

He slouched, narrowing his eyes. "Yes, but did you also know I was failing?"

"Seeing as you're assigned to be here after school on a Wednesday, I kind of assumed. Even more telling that you didn't bring any books."

He tipped his head to the side and scrunched up his mouth like he was thinking something through.

I looked at the clock. Only two minutes had passed. He didn't even have a pencil. "Look, I get credit whether I help you or we just sit here staring at each other. Just let me know which you prefer."

He stifled a laugh. "Okay, Kelsey Thomas," he said. "I get it now." He gestured to my stack of textbooks. "Let's do this. I'm told I do need to pass this class for graduation."

Leo turned out not to be the worst student in the world, though he was possibly the most easily distracted. He paused to talk to any person walking by the library entrance, and he checked the clock every five minutes or so.

His head shot up again an hour into our session when he heard footsteps in the hall, and he called, "Hey, Baker!" even though it was the library and he echoed. Leo was the type who didn't mind the attention—good or bad.

Ryan slowed at the library entrance but didn't quite stop. "Gotta run. Later, man." Then his eye caught mine, and he lifted his hand in a half wave. "Bye, Kelsey."

I half raised my hand in response.

Leo laughed under his breath. When I looked back at him, he was still grinning.

"What?"

"Nothing."

I felt my face heating up. I gripped the pencil harder and jabbed it at the paper, waiting for Leo to refocus on the problem.

Thanks to my mother, I was way ahead in terms of school material. But I was too far behind in everything else. I assumed this was how Leo must've felt, staring at these problems like they were written in a code he'd never seen before.

This was the code of high school. I had yet to crack it.

* * *

Leo and I both got our credit forms signed by the librarian, who took off just as fast as we did, locking up behind us.

"Been a pleasure, Kelsey," Leo said as he flew by, a gust of wind as I rifled through my purse for my phone.

The evening routine: call my mom, grab a soda, drive straight home.

"On my way," I said when she picked up.

"See you soon," she said. Her voice was like music. A homing device. I heard dishes in the background and knew she had already started dinner. This was her routine, too.

I hung up, and Leo was gone. The librarian was gone. The halls were silent and empty, except for the hum of the vending machines tucked into the corner. I slid a crisp dollar from my wallet, fed it to the machine. The gears churned, and in the emptiness, I started imagining all the things I could not see.

I felt myself taking note of the exits, an old habit: the front double doors through the lobby, the fire exits at the end of each hall, the windows off any classroom that had been left unlocked. . . .

I shook the thought, grabbed the soda, and jogged out the double front doors, my steps echoing, my keys jangling in my purse. I kept jogging until I made it to the ring of light around my car in the nearly empty lot.

It was twilight, and there was a breeze kicking in

through the mountains, and the shadows of the surrounding trees within the overhead lights looked a lot like the shadows of the black metal gates at home, when they were lit up in a thunderstorm.

I ran through the morning routine again, in reverse: check the backseat, start the engine, let it warm up. My phone in my bag, my bag beside me, nothing but gnats and mist caught in the headlights.

This was a good day. This was a normal day. A blur in a string of others, passing in typical fashion.

The reflectors on the double yellow line caught my headlights on the drive with a predictable regularity, almost hypnotic.

October came with a chill at night, and I wished I'd brought my coat. I leaned forward, turned the dial to hot, pressed the on button, and listened to the rush of air surging toward the vents as I leaned back in my seat.

A burst of heat.
A flash of light.
The world in motion.

I didn't know the air could scream.

Want more psychological suspense from MEGAN MIRANDA?

A *NEW YORK TIMES* BESTSELLER!

Available now wherever books are sold
or at SimonandSchuster.com